FREEDOM TRIALS

WITHDRAWN

FREEDOM TRIALS

MEREDITH TATE

PAGE STREET
PUBLISHING CO.

//

To my husband, Vincent
To my dad, Paul

And, especially, to my mom, Jessica Ross Tate—
Thanks for all those years you spent reading my stories.
I wish you could've read this one.
I hope I've made you proud.

//

Margot swiped my Tuesday jumpsuit again. She'll never admit it, but I know it was her. She smirks at me from across our block, perched at the end of her tightly made bed. Her grin widens as I tear through our cell.

I sigh. "Margot, have you seen my Tuesday peels?"

She ignores me, running a finger along the edge of her shiny metal collar.

5:59 a.m.

Shit.

I rip off my night suit and throw on my white Wednesday clothes, kicking my navy blue nights to the side as the steel door clanks open. Margot and I snap to our feet.

"Morning inspection!" booms the stiff-legged guard, banging his AK-47 against the barred door.

Don't check the day label. Please don't check the day label.

Two nurses in seafoam scrubs and the armed jack bustle inside our cramped cell. The shorter nurse approaches me and shines a dome-like light into my pupils. She deposits a blue pill into one hand and shoves a paper cup of water into the other. I down it in one gulp and thrust out my tongue to show her my empty mouth. She holds up her silvery device and presses it to my neck above my collar; it pierces my skin with a sharp stab, drawing a few droplets of blood.

The jack narrows his eyes and steps toward me. I raise my right hand in a stiff salute. He scrunches a fistful of my uniform in his meaty hand and yanks out the label.

"Prisoner E.S.-124." His smooth, acidic voice sinks into my bones.

"Sir, yes, sir."

"These are your Wednesday clothes."

"Sir, yes, sir."

"And do you know what day it is?"

"Tuesday, sir."

He flings his hand back and slaps me across the face. Tears prickle in my eyes, but I don't let myself wobble.

"Get going." He spits a wad of saliva at my feet. "State your manifesto."

Clenching my teeth, I watch the shiny silver button on his gray uniform. "I don't know what I have done; I just know that I am bad. I am here because I deserve to be here, and I am here because I must be fixed. I seek to reform under your guidance."

He moves down to Margot, who repeats the words. My cellmate and I stand two feet apart and salute as our guests proceed to the door. The two nurses chatter between themselves as the suffocating white hall light drowns the dimly lit cage that is our cell.

The guard pivots back around mid-step. "Prisoner E.S.-124?"

I startle. "Yes, sir?"

"Block Director Levine requires your presence in her office immediately. Make it quick. Then down to breakfast without delay."

He struts into the hall without another word, unclicking the dead bolt. I swallow.

Why does Director Levine want to see me?

Margot smirks and kicks a wad of white fabric out from under her bed—my now dust-covered, crinkled Tuesday jumpsuit. She slams her shoulder into mine as she brushes past me into the hall. I close my eyes.

Day 741 in this hellhole.

///

Director Levine's office reeks of egg salad and mildew, as if rotting garbage festers in the cement walls. I wrinkle my nose. Did something shrivel up and die in her drop ceiling?

She stretches out a hand with well-manicured finger-nails, inviting me to plop down on a cold metal chair. I take a seat, hands jittering in my lap. An oscillating fan whirs softly on the block director's desk, creating a light breeze that frees a few dirty-blond hairs from my bun.

Levine shifts in her chair and it squeaks. "E.S.-124. Evelyn Summers." She sucks the butt of a pen. "How long have you been with us?"

"Seven-hundred-forty-one days, ma'am. A little over two years."

Her lavender-walled office mocks me; they probably painted it to signify a step above the gray concrete rooms of the lowly inmates of Block Four.

"You've done remarkably well with your rehabilitation, Evelyn."

"Thank you, ma'am."

"You've been a Level Three for what, nine months now?"

"Yes, ma'am."

"And don't think I've forgotten your record-breaking seventy-four days in Level One when you arrived. Shortest I've ever seen someone wear Level-One orange." She winks. "You've progressed quickly through your reformation."

My lip twitches. "Thank you, ma'am."

"You have not come to me once asking to have your collar loosened."

"I have pain because I deserve it, ma'am."

"Indeed." A half smile spreads across her face, so gaunt it could belong to a corpse. "I think you're ready to begin your Freedom Trials."

My heart jolts.

I force the balloon of joy inside me to deflate, for fear of bursting and exploding forbidden happiness all over the room.

"Thank you, ma'am."

Director Levine brushes a strand of copper hair behind her ear and slumps back in her chair. It's the most laid-back I've ever seen her. I tighten my spine and keep my eyes straight ahead, fighting back the giddy somersaults in my stomach.

"And you know what it means," she says, "if you complete your trials?"

"It means . . . I'll be free."

Home. I can go home. I can see my mom. See my friends. Finish school.

"Indeed." She grins, folding her fingers beneath her bony chin. "Collar off, back out in the world. But you'll need to prove to everyone—to me, to the other directors, and to yourself—how bad you want your freedom."

I nod.

"Personally, I believe you're ready," she continues. "But before you officially qualify to begin your trials, you'll be given one prerequisite task volunteering with the lower levels. To ensure that you are, in fact, ready to proceed and fight for your freedom. That you truly reject the reprehensible nature of the crime you committed. Can I count on you to do that, Evelyn?"

The smile bursts across my face before I can stop it. "You can, ma'am."

"Good. So tell me." She clasps her hands over the desk. "What was your life like before you came to us?"

I'm taken aback. "What information would you like to know, ma'am?"

"I would like to know about the Evelyn before rehabilitation. What brought you to us."

It's an odd request. She could easily look this up in my file. I stroke my slick white collar with my forefinger, pressing it farther into my neck.

"I lived with my mother, ma'am. I was a student—an honor student. I played JV basketball, the only freshman on the team. I was finishing ninth grade when . . . the crime happened."

Whatever it was.

"When the crime *happened*?" She raises her brows in an unspoken challenge.

Shit. "I mean, when *I* committed the crime," I correct, my face heating. Taking responsibility for one's actions is the first lesson they drill into our heads. If I can't do that, they'll never approve me for the trials.

But Director Levine doesn't comment on my mistake. She purses her lips in a display of fake sympathy. "Can you see yourself returning to that old life, Evelyn?"

"Yes, ma'am." My hands fidget in my lap.

"And can you see yourself committing another crime?"

"No, ma'am."

"Why not?"

"Because I have reformed, ma'am."

"Good. That's all." She pulls herself up with a curt nod. "Report to the cafeteria for breakfast. You'll receive further instructions shortly."

///

I scratch my plastic fork across the Styrofoam tray, creating indented crop circles around my breakfast. A prong from the utensil snaps off and flies across the table. I guess in prison, flimsy forks are better than metal ones—or as the jacks say, potential weapons. The over-dulled blade of my plastic knife barely makes a mark when I scrape it around the edge of the cardboard masquerading as toast on my tray. A nearby jack glares daggers at me with each *scritch scritch.*

What tasks do they want me to do with the lower levels? So close. I'm so close.

Margot and another Level Three sneer as they pass my empty table, crowding into a full one several places away. A few girls at their table whip their heads around and catch my eye, then whisper feverishly to one another and burst into giggles. I slink lower in my seat.

Across the cafeteria, two bulky jacks lead a string of cuffed, orange-clad slug boys to their tables. They shuffle through the room like a herd of sheep, eyes on the ground. Two Level Three guy hacks in white peels jump to their feet, hollering something like "fresh meat," to a slew of jeers from their comrades. A jack roughly grabs one of the taunters by his shoulders and forces him back into his seat. They make sure the guys stay on the other side at all times. Genders aren't supposed to mix in the Center, but some people still find ways.

The dining hall has the same charm of my old high school cafeteria, aside from all the guards. And the guns. Okay, maybe they're not that similar. But if I close my eyes, I can almost pretend I'm back home, eating lunch with my friends after geometry. That day, a month before the end of freshman year, I almost had the guts to ask Matt Houston to grab coffee after class. He was a senior, but we'd become friends over the year and awkwardly hooked up on New Year's Eve. Maybe he would have become my boyfriend. If I hadn't gotten shipped here.

I wonder what happened to him.

Ronnie slams her breakfast tray down beside me, and I snap out of my daydream.

"I swear to God, if Chloe leaves her shit on the floor for one more inspection, I'm gonna strangle that bitch."

I raise my brows. "Cellmate problems?"

"You have no idea."

"Sorry!" The word comes out higher and happier than planned. I morph my toothy grin into my best empathetic pout.

She scoffs, sliding into her seat. "The happy fairy crap in your OJ this morning?"

"Ronnie." I force myself not to blurt out the words bubbling up inside me. "Guess what Director Levine told me."

"What?"

"You're not going to beli—"

"Just tell me."

I lower my voice to a whisper. "I'm going to start my trials."

She doesn't look surprised at the news. "What, you're gonna leave me here by myself?"

"Sorry." I bite my lip. "You'll get there too. Soon, I bet."

"Yeah, three years later, I've heard that before." Ronnie rolls her eyes. "I'm never getting out of here." She tugs at the neck of her gray peels, a constant reminder that she still hasn't progressed past Level Two.

"You haven't gotten busted for making your bed sloppily in a while, right? That's a start."

"Shut the pity party, Evelyn. Go on, start your trials. See if I give a—"

The five-minute-warning bell cuts her off. We nibble our toast in silence, and the cardboardy chunks wedge themselves in my throat like sandpaper.

"Amber got the four-piece suit yesterday," Ronnie says, mouth bulging with scrambled eggs.

I shake my head. "What'd she do now?"

"Tried to clock a jack."

"Why?"

"I dunno." She shrugs. "Bet he deserved it."

"Is Amber okay?"

"Yeah. They hopped her up on bug juice, though; she's sedated and looks like a vegetable. Least that means she'll shut her yap tonight and not talk to me in the bathroom when I'm trying to take a dump." She snorts. "It's kinda funny, actually. Amber's usually such a perfect little prude. I'd thought she was, like, a Center spy or something. A plant."

"Wow, paranoid much?"

"Not paranoid, just vigilant." She gulps down her orange juice. "But they wouldn't have made one of their own take the bug juice. You ever get your hands on that stuff? Knocks you on your ass."

"Nope. Jacks never had to sedate me."

"Well, let's hope they never do. Happened to me twice. You can't feel your own legs."

Sometimes I picture Ronnie as a wise old lady from folktales. Some sort of curmudgeonly mentor warning me of all the stuff she's done that I probably shouldn't do: screwing around till they drug you and cuff both your arms and legs at once in the four-piece suit is one of those things.

"So, when do you start the trials?"

"I dunno."

"They didn't tell you?"

"No."

"This girl Abby on my floor went to the trials last month. Real badass kid she was. She didn't pass."

My breakfast settles in my stomach like a brick. "Can

you, like, not go there right now? Jeez."

"Please." Ronnie swats it off like it's nothing. "Don't even worry. You'll pass. I know it. And then I'll be stuck here all alone."

"You'll still have Chloe."

She shoots me a deadpan. "Thank you for that. Well, I'll see you on the outside, kiddo, I guess." Ronnie raises her empty juice glass to me. "Cheers."

//

EVELYN SUMMERS: PRISONER E.S.–124
REHABILITATION DIARY
DAY 1

I don't know what I'm supposed to do with this journal. They told me to write in it: my feelings and what's happening. It's the only thing I'm allowed to keep private now that I'm a criminal.

I'm scared. I don't know how else to say it. They said some people wet the bed on the first night, but I didn't. Reaction to the memory wipe or something. I woke up dressed in orange on a bed in this cement room, a hulking woman with a gun hovering over me. I screamed bloody murder. I thought I was in some weird dream.

The first thing I noticed was that I couldn't breathe right. I grabbed at my neck, and my fingers caught this metal collar I can't take off.

They're calling me a criminal. I don't know what I did. I don't remember committing any crime. The woman said they erased my memory of the crime, so I remember everything else in my life EXCEPT this one little hour, two days ago. I don't know what the hell happened. I'm straining to think, THINK. But nothing comes. I guess they did a good job erasing it.

I asked the ponytail woman if my mom knew where I was, and she said she did, but I can't talk to her until I leave. I asked how long I have to stay here, and she said until I reform. What the hell does that even mean?

This morning they made me take this little blue pill called Memoria. They say it keeps the bad memories erased; otherwise, they come back. I had to show them my mouth after I swallowed it. So embarrassing.

I have a roommate, or I guess I should say a cellmate. Sharing a cell with me is this girl Ronnie Hartman. She freaked out on me this morning for screaming in my sleep and has ignored me ever since. She mentioned something to some other girl about "peels." I think "peels" are our prison uniforms. But she called me a "slug" and told me to go F myself when I asked her. Real charmer. I shouldn't be here. It's a mistake. It has to be. I'm an honor student. I'm not a criminal.

I want to go home.

A mustached jack with steel-toed boots leads me and the other Level Three girl hacks to morning chores. We clink down the gray cement corridor single file, linked together by heavy ankle chains that dig into my skin. The girl behind me kicks my heel, and I trip into the next hack.

"Slinger," she whispers snidely as I collect myself.

I grimace.

I'm almost out of here. Just gotta do my trials . . . whenever that will be.

We reach a line of armed jacks at the end of the hall. One of them unlocks our ankle cuffs, and I stretch my legs.

"Prisoners K.S.-498 and N.P.-192, you're on dusting duty. I want these ledges spotless," he says with a grunt. "Prisoner E.S.-124, you're on—"

"Ahem." A blond-haired jack with a mean glint in his eyes steps forward. "I'm looking for Level Three E.S.-124 too."

I raise a shaky hand.

"Come with me," he grumbles.

The other hacks don't hide their scoffs and eye rolls as I allow the jack to cuff my wrists. There's always a nasty little spark of jealousy when someone gets promoted a level or sent to the trials, but it must piss them off extra that it's me.

My breath quickens. The burly jack and I traipse in silence down the corridor, him a half step behind. With each turn, he roughly shoves my shoulder in the direction he wants me to walk, as if I'm a dog and his arm is the leash. My white Level Three sneakers skate along the tiles, probably freshly waxed by a Level One. We turn a corner into a dimly lit stairwell.

"Three floors up. Let's go." He pokes me in the back with his rifle.

This is it. Whatever's waiting at the top is my first step to freedom.

I clomp up three flights, calves burning by the time I reach the landing. A green metal door swings open, revealing whitewashed walls and a hallway of closed doors. A red-haired twentysomething woman peers around the door.

"E.S.-124?" she says.

The guard shoves me toward the woman as if disposing some vile piece of garbage. I can almost hear his unspoken words as he stomps back downstairs: "She's your problem now."

I stare straight ahead to greet the woman.

She unlocks my cuffs. "State your name."

"My name is Evelyn Summers—Level Three, E.S.-124. I don't know what I have done, I just know that I am bad. I am here because I deserve to be here, and I am here because I must be fixed. I seek to reform under your guidance." The robotic words fly out of my mouth without thought. I snap my hand up in salute.

"Very good." A smug smile blooms across the woman's mousy face. "Come with me."

My chest tightens. I follow her into a smaller room, where Director Levine sits at a beat-up wooden desk surrounded by filing cabinets.

She points to a seat opposite her. I slide into the chair, back straight, palms up on the tabletop, just like they taught me. Her jack bodyguard keeps his eyes locked on me and his fingers wrapped around his rifle.

"That will be all." Director Levine dismisses Red Hair and the guard with a wave.

The jack nods. "I'll be outside when—"

"That won't be necessary. We'll be leaving shortly." The block director speaks with an air of superiority. "And, Casey," she says to Red Hair, "go find the others and bring them to the intake room." The jack and the red-haired woman slink out without another word. It's strange seeing Levine give orders to someone who isn't wearing peels.

The moment we're alone, Levine clasps her fingers over her desk. "Hello, E.S.-124. Are you ready to complete your prerequisite task?"

"Yes, ma'am."

Director Levine opens a rickety drawer and pulls out a thick yellow file crammed with documents. Humming to herself, she thumbs through the pages before unveiling a crisp sheet with tiny print and my signature scribbled across the bottom. She slides it toward me.

"What can you tell me about this paper, Evelyn?"

That I haven't seen it since I got here.

"It's my oath of commitment to rehabilitation, ma'am."

She rests her elbows on the table and perches her chin on her hands. "And what does that mean to you?"

"It says I commit to changing. That I know I'm bad, but that I'm committed to reforming my behavior, ma'am."

"I know what the oath says, Evelyn." Her cherry lipstick–painted mouth stretches into a wide grin. "I want to know what it means to you."

I open my mouth to speak, but the words stick in my throat like molasses. What does it mean to me? I don't know. The whole thing always seemed a little superficial. Like reciting lines on a cue card because someone told me to.

"This document, this oath"—Director Levine strokes the paper like it's a cat—"is your saving grace. Do you remember when you first arrived? The choice you were given?"

"Yes, ma'am. They said I was deemed savable and could choose my fate; either attend the rehabilitation program, or . . . be executed." Not much of a choice, actually.

She leans back in her chair. "And why did you choose rehabilitation?"

Is that even a valid question? "Because I want to reform, ma'am."

"When you came to us as a mere fifteen-year-old, you were so young. So young to commit such a crime." She shakes her head. "Such a thoughtless, unthinkable crime."

My ears perk.

"And," she continues, "if you had been a legal adult and committed such a crime, do you know what would have happened?"

"I would have been executed instantly, ma'am. Without a chance at rehabilitation."

"So you realize you were given an enormous gift, with the chance to reform with us?"

"I do realize that, ma'am."

"And you've done remarkably well. You've stuck to all the rules, followed all your orders"—she counts on her fingers—"and completed most of your rehabilitation in almost record time."

Why would I break a rule? I just want to get out of this place.

"And you proved almost instantly upon arriving at the Stephens' Center that you were committed to reforming. Do you remember that?"

I swallow hard. How could I forget? My horrible deed. The unspeakable thing I did to move up to Level Two.

"Yes, ma'am."

"Well then, I believe you're ready. Come with me." She rises from her chair. "It's time for your prerequisite task."

Heart pounding, I follow her back into the hallway.

An armed jack emerges from the shadows, startling me. His mustache twitches with a hint of satisfaction when I jump.

I trail after Director Levine, sandwiched between her and the hairy jack, up two flights of stairs into the unknown.

We arrive at a padlocked steel door. The block director presses her hand to a keypad, which flashes an iridescent green light before releasing a metallic groan. The door unbolts itself, and the jack yanks it open.

I force my feet into the dingy room. Brown and red blotches stain the gray cement walls. The stench of mold and bodily fluids stings my nose. I step backward, smacking into the jack's belly. Goose bumps prickle down my neck.

A padded table sits in the center, surrounded by metal stands holding medical instruments. Over the table hangs a large circular light with skinny rubber tubes dangling down the sides. It looks like a big spider.

My heels turn up on instinct, drawing me back to the door in vain. It slams shut, flanked by two hulking jacks. Their eyes dare me to try anything.

I stand for an eternity, wringing my hands, until the door clanks open once again. Five adults in button-downs and ties stroll inside, as if heading to a company picnic. I recognize Director Zepp from the Level One girls' block, followed by Director Hannon from Level Two. Three men saunter in after them, whispering among themselves; they're the directors from the guys' blocks. The red-haired woman trails faithfully behind, clipboard in hand. I see Director Zepp hasn't bothered to update her beehive bun hairstlye that was already horribly outdated two years ago, when we first met. Hannon, likewise, hasn't changed—same pigeon's beak nose and permanent scowl.

"Evelyn, come here," Director Levine says, as if commanding a dog.

I cautiously tiptoe toward the group like a rabbit approaching a fox den. I force my shaking hand into a half-hearted salute, but my eyes keep darting to the medical table.

"E.S.-124, I believe you know Block Directors Zepp and Hannon?" Director Levine indicates the two women behind her, who each nod in turn. "And these gentlemen are Director Zane"—an older Black man with bulging biceps gives a curt nod—"Director Agarwal"—a brown-skinned younger man with black glasses smiles kindly—"and Director Marewood" —a muscular white man with a cropped beard grunts, barely acknowledging me. "They run Levels One through Three of the male blocks." I shake each of the men's hands, my fingers going limp in their tight grips.

"You're the Level Three I've heard so much about?" Director Agarwal grins. "I'm still fairly new here, so I wasn't here when you . . . uh . . ."

I focus on the cement floor.

"Yes, she's the one." Director Levine rests her hand on my shoulder. "One of our top young women, almost ready to begin her Freedom Trials. This is her pre-req."

"Ironic," Director Zane says under his breath.

Before I can ask why it's ironic, clomping footsteps behind us jolt my attention. Six jacks enter the room and encircle the padded table, as if ready to pin me to it. A nurse fiddles with a bag of liquid hanging off one of the metal poles while a second nurse drapes a white cloth over the table. My mind races to all sorts of grotesque things they could do to me with that stuff.

Director Hannon laughs coolly. "Look at her, she's shaking like a leaf." The others share amused glances among themselves. I clench my teeth, laughter the furthest thing from my mind.

A white-suited woman with jet-black hair strides into the room and heads straight for the table. She wipes down the instruments, dropping one to the floor with a sharp clang that makes me jump again.

"That's Doctor Wang," Director Levine says. "And don't worry, that table isn't for you. You've done your wipe already."

I keep my eyes on the doctor and her torture tools.

"My what?"

"This is our intake room. After their arrests, new prisoners are brought here to sign their oaths and get memory wiped and tattooed."

I slide my finger up the back of my damp neck, squeezing it under my collar to touch my mysterious tattoo.

"What is my task, ma'am?"

Director Marewood steps forward. "Tonight we will enroll, mark, wipe, and collar seven new inmates—'slugs,' as your type would say." He chuckles. "Your task is to assist with this process."

I release a trembling breath. Enroll some new slugs? Easy. Freedom Trials, here I come.

"Yes, sir. What do I do?"

"We'll give you further instructions as needed. You'll be assisting with the memory-erase and tattooing processes."

"Yes, sir."

I got this. No problem.

Agarwal holds a small radio device to his mouth. "We're ready. Send in the first one."

A side door flings open. Two jacks drag a handcuffed, freckle-faced girl by her armpits and shove her to the floor. She collapses in a sobbing heap, arms wrapped around her knees. I sway awkwardly on the balls of my feet.

Director Zepp's heels click against the cement as she approaches. "Ashley Pr—"

The girl's wail drowns out the block director's voice. The nearest jack sets his jaw. I press my hands over my ears.

Well, I hope I demonstrated a little more dignity than this slug when I got enrolled. Maybe it's a good thing enrollment is wiped from your memory with your crime. Who wants to remember blubbering like an idiot?

"I didn't mean to do it! I didn't mean to!" she cries.

Director Zepp approaches her. "Prisoner Ashley Preston? You have been found guilty of six felony counts of shoplifting in amounts totaling two thousand dollars, one felony count of illegal possession of firearms, and one count of attempted felony grand theft auto."

Ashley whimpers, wiping her runny nose on her sleeve.

"Fortunately for you," Director Zepp continues, "you have been deemed savable by the Center Board. Therefore, if you choose, you may come to the Stephens' Rehabilitation Center to serve your time until you have been rehabilitated. Should you choose not to be rehabilitated, you will face instant execution by firing squad."

"Re-rehabilitation," the girl stammers, steadying herself.

"Excellent choice."

Marewood and Zane lift the girl off the floor and pull her into a standing position. Red Hair thrusts her clipboard toward the girl, which I'm guessing contains the oath.

"Read it carefully and sign at the bottom," Director Zepp says. "You'll be shown a copy again when you recover from the procedure."

Ashley, shuddering and wobbling, drags a shaky pen across the unread contract, which is then ripped from her hands.

"From here forward," Director Zepp says, as the guard cuffs the prisoner's wrists, "your number is A.P.-492. You won't remember it when you wake, but you will be given this information again upon arrival to your cell. That is your name, and you will respond to that name."

The girl nods furiously, tears clinging to her eyelashes.

"We're going to wipe your memory now. Once the process is complete, you will have no memory of your crime. Knowledge of past indiscretions only hinders your ability to reform."

Ashley's lip trembles, but she nods.

"Our nurses will ensure you follow up this procedure with daily Memoria pills. Failure to consume the medication or tampering with your required dose is prohibited, and will result in immediate dismissal from the program by means of execution. This will all be explained further when you wake."

The director circles the girl, sizing up her wounded prey. "You'll be collared. The collar will not be removed until completion of your sentence. We will first, however, tattoo the nature of your crime onto the back of your neck, under your collar. You will not be permitted to see this tattoo until you earn your freedom. While you will never regain specific memory of the details of your crime, you will see the title of your crime upon release. That tattoo is a permanent reminder to you and everyone you meet, from here on out, that you are a criminal, and crime doesn't pay."

The girl looks like she's going to puke. I covertly step back to remove myself from projectile-vomit range. The jacks direct her to the padded table. My fingers fidget with the shirt hem of my peels.

"E.S.-124!" Director Zepp snaps. I whip my hand up to salute. "Come here."

Inhaling the deepest breath I can muster, I approach the group. The nurse starts the IV to sedate the new slug, her cheeks still glistening with tears. Ashley's eyes flutter shut, entering a deep, medically-induced sleep. I'm struck with a pang of pity. If this isn't bad enough, now she'll be a slug for everyone to torment.

Why'd you do it? I stroke her palm with my thumb. *Why'd you have to steal all that stuff?*

Why did any of us do the awful things we did?

The process is quick. Doctor Wang shouts out orders; I pass medical instruments to her. That's my whole job.

Three minutes in, Director Agarwal lowers the spidery fluorescent lamp until it rests two inches from Ashley's still face. The rubber tubes suction onto her forehead like tentacles.

"Here we go." He presses buttons on a keypad. "Lauren, can you double-check these dates for me?"

Zepp squints at the tiny screen. "Yeah, that's correct. Should erase the whole crime and the past hour completely."

"Can you believe this one?" Hannon mutters under her breath. "Stole an AK-47 and tried to hot-wire a Mercedes. Unbelievable." The other directors shake their heads. Looking at the frail girl before me, it's hard to picture her doing anything wrong.

Wang snaps a bulbous white machine over Ashley's skull like a helmet. It beeps and whirs, flashing tiny blue lights. I run my fingers over my tight bun, caressing the curves of my skull.

They did this to me, two years ago. That weird thing sat on my head.

When an airy whoosh fills the room, the helmet unclasps itself. Doctor Wang removes it from Ashley's head and rests it gently on the floor. The guards hoist the prisoner up and quickly flip her over so she's lying face down on the table.

"Almost done." Doctor Wang slides her glasses onto the top of her head with her forefinger. "Hand me that black tube."

I search the rickety metal table beside me and find the small, narrow tube that looks like a ballpoint pen. Wang clicks it open, and a needle pops out.

She pierces it into the back of the prisoner's neck, hastily branding a single word in sloppy handwriting: Theft. I guess they're going for simple; there's no mention of the assault rifle.

I press my hand to my own collar. Soon as this thing is off, I'll know my tattoo. Finally. Only the trials stand in my way.

I hold the unconscious slug's head while the technician secures a brand-new white metal collar to her neck. It clicks shut, the mechanism locking with a sucking *thwiss.*

I help the jacks lift the girl onto a gurney to wheel her to her new block.

"Good work, E.S.-124," Agarwal says. "One down, six more hacks to go."

We enroll two more girls, then three boys, each one in varying degrees of shock and tears. Not surprisingly, they all choose rehabilitation over execution. The directors nod their approval each time, as if the whole thing is actually a legitimate choice.

I disinfect the table with an antiseptic wipe after each intake.

"Last one," a jack says.

Fighting back a yawn, I brush a strand of dirty-blond hair, escaped from its elastic, behind my ear.

Good. Let's get this done with, I'm starving.

Director Levine tenses beside me. Maybe I imagine it, but her eyes seem to flit between me and the door. Two jacks perch beside the entrance, weapons at the ready—just in case.

"I've heard this one's a handful," Agarwal whispers to the other directors.

The door flings open and two jacks march inside, flanking a tall boy with golden brown skin and chin-length black hair, about seventeen. The slug lumbers into the room, eyes fixed on the floor, hands cuffed behind him. His green T-shirt exposes toned biceps. If he weren't scowling and a criminal, I'd probably say he's hot. A jack grabs the boy's shoulder, but the prisoner roughly shrugs the man's hand away. At least this one's not thrashing around or sobbing uncontrollably—that's a first.

Director Zepp strolls toward the boy. Brows lowered, back hunched, he doesn't meet her eyes.

"Alex Martinez." Zepp clicks her tongue. The boy slowly raises his head as the director continues. "You are here because—"

"Stop."

Well, that's bold.

I expect Zepp to slap him, but she looks too shocked at being interrupted by a slug. The boy's eyes lock onto mine, and my blood runs ice-cold. My breath hitches in my throat.

He leans forward and squints. "Eva?"

I freeze.

No one calls me Eva. Just my mom. No one else.

"Eva Summers, is that you?"

I step back. No. What?

"That's enough," Director Levine says, wild-eyed. "Sedate him."

The jacks lunge at the boy, but he bucks forward, slamming his head into a jack's chin with an earsplitting crack.

"Eva! Eva Summers!"

"Restrain him!" Zepp thunders.

Blazing with fury, the prisoner ducks Agarwal's sloppy punch, kicking the director in the shin. The man collapses to the floor with a wince.

With one swift movement, the boy rips his arms out from behind him, sending the metal cuffs flying through the air. My heart stops. He broke them clean off his wrists like they were paper. Who the hell *is* this kid?

Alex sprints toward me. I stumble backward until my fingers scrape the wall. He grabs my upper arms, holding me captive in his vice-like grip.

"No . . . please . . ."

Two jacks charge toward us.

"Eva. Eva, it's me. It's Alex. Please remember. Please remember me, Eva! This is all my fault. What did they do to you?" He shakes my shoulders. "Come on! Eva!"

A jack yanks Alex back. The prisoner whirls around, and in a series of kicks and punches, he disarms both guards and throws them to the ground. One jack twitches on the floor. The other lies unconscious beside him. Directors Hannon, Marewood, and Zane sprint out the door, abandoning us. Doctor Wang runs after them, her shouts for backup echoing down the hall. Director Zepp reaches for Alex's arm, but the slug backhands her across the face, sending her sailing five feet in the air.

He's a monster.

I bolt to the side, but the prisoner latches on to my waist, tackling me to the ground. He pins me into the cement, his elbow digging into my chest. I thrust my knee into his groin. He doubles over, and I slither out from under him.

"Stay away from me." I scramble backward on my palms until I hit the opposite wall. "Guards! Help!"

Alex shakes off the blow and lunges at me. I try to smack him, but he pins my squirming arms behind my head.

"Let go!"

"Eva." He pants, his face inches from mine. I can feel the heat emanating off his body. "Listen to me. There's not much time. Please remember. You have to remember. It's me. Alex." His eyes crinkle at the sides. "You're not safe here. Not after what happened. They're gonna make you do it again. You don't know what's going on outside this place. I'm going to get us out.

They're coming for us. Please remember, Eva. You—"

"*Facultas.*" Director Levine's clear voice rings over the scuffle.

My elbows snap up without warning. In one swift movement, I fling my head forward, smashing into Alex's skull with a sharp crack. I don't even feel it. He flinches, and I ram my knee into his stomach, knocking him to his side. What's happening to me?

"*Desine.*"

Four jacks swarm the flailing boy, ripping him to his feet. Alex yells as a guard jabs him in the neck with a needle. He stops bucking and collapses unconscious into the jack's waiting arms. Alex's chest rises and falls in a peaceful, sedated slumber.

Shaking, I pull myself to my feet, wrapping my arms around my torso. Levine runs to my side and props me up on her shoulder.

"Are you all right?" she asks.

Words won't come, so I force a nod. He attacked me. Why did he attack me?

"Evelyn, I'm so sorry. That boy is a hardened criminal and a master manipulator. We should have brought more guards from the beginning; it's our fault. I don't know what happened."

"What . . . what were those words you said? Desine. Fac—"

"Andrea, let's get this guy collared. I don't want him waking up and freaking out again." Director Hannon saunters by, arms folded across her chest. "And for God's sake, send that poor girl back to her block."

Levine's mouth thins into a terse line. "Yes, yes. Director Hannon's right, Evelyn. You passed your task. You may begin your Freedom Trials orientation in the morning."

"But I—"

"The guards will escort you upstairs. It's dinnertime anyway. You must be starving from missing lunch. But first . . ." Levine searches the medical table beside her and grabs a clear plastic vial. "Hold out your hand."

I hesitate but do as she says. The director pours two white pills into my palm and passes me a plastic cup of water.

"You know the drill, E.S.-124."

These aren't Memoria. "What is it?"

"You've had a stressful day. These will help you relax and get some sleep tonight."

I don't know why, but I don't argue. I knock back the pills in one gulp.

Levine smiles. "There you go."

I open my mouth to ask about those strange words, but she's too quick. She snaps her fingers at the nearest jack before speed-walking to join her colleagues, who huddle in a hushed circle. I wish I could hear what they're saying.

A jack slips cuffs over my wrists and ushers me from the room. She's young, barely older than me.

It strikes me as we walk toward the cafeteria that I can't remember what I wanted to ask Levine in the first place.

Something about what happened at the pre-req. But it's suddenly growing blurry around the edges, like I dreamed even speaking to Levine at all. I remember that scary prisoner attacking me but . . . nothing else. Five minutes are just . . . gone.

I'm straining to remember, but all I can recall is that prisoner's face. His words. His body, throwing me to the ground. A shiver ripples through me.

Alex Martinez. He knew my name. He knew . . . me.

But I've never seen him before in my life.

//

EVELYN SUMMERS: PRISONER E.S.–124
REHABILITATION DIARY
DAY 9

This place gives me the creeps. My cell isn't like ones in the movies. There aren't metal bars on the walls, only in the tiny window on the door. The door itself even creeps me out. It's six inches thick of pure steel. I feel like they're sealing me in a bank vault when they lock it at night. Gray concrete walls and two beds make up the rest of my cell. That's it. No windows, no sunlight. If I have to pee after they lock our door there's a little pot for a toilet. I try not to use it, though, because then there's a bucket of piss festering in the room until morning.

The collar still hurts, and the more I play with it, the tighter it seems to get. It sucks. I'm getting used to the schedule, though, I guess.

6:00 a.m.: The nurse takes my pulse, gives me my memory pills, and pricks my neck. Why does she stab me with a needle every day? I don't even know.

6:15 a.m.: Breakfast—usually porridge that tastes like cement and toast you could easily mistake for cardboard. The cafeteria is one of the only places you can see the boy prisoners. They sit on the other side of the room, but we can't talk to them.

6:45 a.m.: Chores—HOURS of chores. They make us wash the nasty bathrooms and stuff. We aren't allowed to talk during chores either—unless you want to get slapped.

12:00 p.m.: Lunch—I'd like to say it's an improvement from breakfast, but I'd be telling a horrible, horrible lie.

12:30 p.m.: Exercise time aka "MINDFULNESS" aka push-ups and jogging in the courtyard. The courtyard isn't even outside. It's a big square room with some rusty basketball hoops and a track surrounded by more cement walls. The guards blow their whistles and make us jog. If anyone complains, we have to run longer. Someone passed out today. The guard waited until she recovered and then made her do the workout again from the beginning. I'm super out of shape, but I do it because I want them to SEE ME TRYING and know that I've REFORMED so I can go HOME.

2:00 p.m.: Group. They call it "group," but it's not a support group. It's not like we sit in a circle, and I stand up and say, "Hello, my name is Evelyn Summers, and I'm a criminal." Hell, everyone here could probably use some actual therapy, but that's not happening. Groups are done standing. Usually after the first twenty minutes I'm stuck with a dull ache in my calves. We stand straight as boards and chant the oath repeatedly for three hours: "I don't know what I have done, I just know that I am bad. I am here because I deserve to be here, and I am here because I must be fixed. I seek to reform under your guidance." I had it memorized after the first dozen repetitions.

Director Zepp and a few guards patrol the ranks, stopping in front of every person to make sure they're chanting correctly.

5:00 p.m.: Dinner. I'm pretty sure they disguise the leftover breakfast and re-feed it to us.

5:30 p.m.: Back to the cell.

6:00 p.m.: Behavior modification therapy. Every day of the week, we work on a different principle of rehabilitation. Again, not actual therapy. More like school, but where they teach us the same things over and over. There are seven fun-filled principles, and when the week is done, guess what? We get to do it all over again!

8:00 p.m.: Showers

9:00 p.m.: Lights out

I toss and turn for hours until I finally fall asleep. The morning alarm always rings too soon. And when I do fall asleep, I get nightmares. Actually, the same nightmare.

Whenever I had nightmares when I was little, I'd walk that long, creepy hallway to get from my bedroom to my mom's room. The bottom of our house is spacious, but the top floor only has two rooms connected by a hall: my mom's room, and my room. I always felt a little jolt of fear making my way down that long path between our bedrooms, like the monsters could get me as I sped by. I'd hold my breath and make that sprint as quickly as I could to my mom's doorway. I wouldn't say anything, wouldn't wake her up. I'd just stand there and let her presence put me at ease. I'd count her sleeping breaths for a moment. Then I'd go right back to bed. That first walk scared the living crap out of me, because the dark hallway was so damn long. But going back to my room I walked with confidence, as if overcome with a sudden sense of calm.

In my nightmares now, I'm walking that long hallway by myself, only it keeps stretching. It's dark and scary, and I never make it to my mom's room. And then I wake up in a cold sweat shouting and shaking until my cellmate, Ronnie, yells at me.

I don't think Ronnie likes me much. If we're together, she's either screaming at me for doing something wrong or ignoring me completely. She keeps calling me a slug, so I just don't talk to her.

The girls in the next cell over, Ariadne and Sarah, talk to me at breakfast every day. Honestly, I wish one was my cellmate instead of Ronnie. Actually, ALL the other girls are nice, so I'd take ANYONE over Ronnie.

I guess Sarah and Ariadne have been Level Ones for a couple of months now. They said "slug" means "new person." It's slang—not some sort of slur, which is what I thought Ronnie had been calling me. The guards are called "jacks"—I don't know why. Oh, and any prisoner here, newbie or not, is called a "hack." I really don't get that one.

At meals I sit with Sarah, Ariadne, and their other friend Courtney from down the hall. Courtney has a twin sister back home. I think it'd be so weird to have a twin, but then again they all think it's weird that I'm an only child. Go figure.

Sarah says that if you screw up around here, they make your collar shock you. And if you REALLY screw up, they put you in solitary confinement in this place called "the Hole." Sarah only got put in the Hole once, but apparently Ronnie gets in trouble all the time. I'm not surprised—she's a HUGE BITCH.

"So what'd they make you do for your pre-req?" Ronnie rolls her eyes as if speaking the question aloud physically pains her. She slurps a spoonful of this morning's brown gruel disguised as oatmeal. "You passed, right?"

I swallow a gloppy mouthful without tasting a thing.

I got attacked by some violent prisoner who thought he knew me. That's what.

"Yeah. I passed."

She leans in closer. "So, what'd you have to do?"

"Nothing. Just help with intakes." I stir my spoon through the gluey mess.

"You know"—Ronnie points her spoon at me—"the pre-req is the easy part . . ."

Easy?

"... It's the trials where they really get you."

Shut up, shut up, shut up!

She wrinkles her nose at the oatmeal. "If you suck it down real fast, it doesn't taste like glue."

I prop my cheek against my hand, sifting oatmeal with my plastic spoon and pouring it back into the Styrofoam bowl.

Ronnie lowers her brows at my untouched food. "Come on, eat your glop. You usually guzzle that shit down."

"I'm not hungry."

A jack in the corner watches me, never once looking away. *Don't come over here. Don't tell me it's time for my trials.*

"I'm on scrub duty today," Ronnie says. "Again." Bits of porridge fly from her mouth, showering the table.

"Sorry." I pour another spoonful into the bowl with a *plop*.

"What's with you today? You're acting weird."

I don't respond. My eyes drift toward the boys at the other end of the room, but Alex Martinez isn't among them. I never want to see that guy again. Ever.

"Whatever, if you aren't gonna eat it, I'm taking this. I'm starving." She snags the toast off my plate and stuffs it into her mouth.

Alex probably heard a jack mention my name and then repeated it to freak me out. Typical criminal, I guess.

Several tables down, a cluster of Level Threes whisper together, peering up at me every few seconds and bursting into giggles. I concentrate on my bowl. I'd think they would've found something else to talk about by now.

"So, what's the first thing you'll do on the outside? Get some really greasy fast food?" Ronnie flicks her bowl, causing the thick liquid inside to splatter around. "That's what I'm gonna do someday. Not have to eat this shit anymore."

"Um . . . I don't know." I snap out of my trance. "I'd really like to see my mom."

I can't believe I haven't heard her voice in over two years.

Ronnie's forehead crinkles. "Not your dad?"

"Never met him." I shrug. "He left when I was born."

"Oh. Well, you can share my dad. He'd love you."

I smile. "What's he like?"

"Big dude. Makes the best mac and cheese. Between his mac and cheese and my mom's pierogies from our Polish side, oh my God." She groans. "I could stuff my face for days."

"I would kill to eat any of that right about now."

"Right? Seriously, you'd love my family. My dad tells really corny-ass jokes to everyone. I never thought I'd miss those damn jokes, you know?" She slams her hand on the table, and the nearby jack narrows his eyes. "Only good thing about this place is I don't have to babysit. Ha, bet my parents are having fun raising the two mutants without me."

"When we get out"—I emphasize the *we*—"I wanna meet your twin brothers."

"Why? You can have them. I'll trade—I'd love to be an only child. Have a quiet house for once. Not have relatives stopping by every five seconds. Seriously, you're lucky it's just you and your mom."

"Well, I do have my aunt Lily." I push my tray away with a sigh. "But she only comes over when she's drunk and violent. Last time, I remember she reeked of vodka and broke two of my mom's best dishes before flying into a cursing fit."

Ronnie almost spurts water out of her nose from laughing. "I can totally picture it. And I can totally see your horrified face. Kind of how you look right now."

"Glad my family amuses you."

A pit forms in my belly, harder than a whole bowl of the cafeteria's oatmeal.

Mom's been alone for over two years, all because I committed some pointless crime. I don't even know how she's doing. If my mystery crime doesn't make me the worst person in the world, abandoning her definitely does.

The breakfast-end bell rings. I say goodbye to Ronnie and join the other Level Threes to return to our block for chores. A line of shackled male hacks shuffles past us on the other side of the cafeteria.

"Let's go," hisses a jack, roughly shoving the last hack boy into the next prisoner. "Keep your eyes where I can see them."

I stand at attention waiting for my ankle chains, but a jack grabs my shoulder and tugs me backward.

"Not you," she says. "You're coming with me."

I swallow hard, laboring to hide my panic as she pulls me from the line. Margot smirks from her place in line, elbowing another hack.

"Dead meat," my cellmate mouths at me, running her forefinger across her neck with an evil grin. The hacks snicker, having a grand old time at my expense. I follow the guard out of the cafeteria without meeting their eyes.

My heart flutters with anticipation. I trudge beside the jack, my hands chained behind my back.

The trials are a highly guarded secret, the holy grail of the prison world sparking hushed conversations laced with concurrent admiration and fear. It's a mystery everyone simultaneously longs to solve and fears the day they get the chance to try.

My nerves manifest themselves in gurgling bile in my stomach. We take corner after corner into a wing of the Center I've never seen before. The halls twist and turn like a maze, jutting off into hallway after hallway of closed doors. My head dizzies in a vain attempt to keep track of our direction. The Center is enormous, an underground fortress of mystery made to keep the most dangerous offenders from getting out. I'd say it's effective, given the fact that I already have no idea where the hell we are.

The jack leads me to a red-walled room the size of a large bathroom, with a circle of black chairs in the middle. With a sharp tug, she uncuffs my wrists. I wring my hands around the red indents left in my skin by the metal.

FREEDOM TRIALS ORIENTATION reads a plain white placard at the front of the room. I take a seat and twiddle my thumbs, waiting for something to happen.

Other pairs drift inside, each duo consisting of a jack escorting his or her prisoner like some twisted Noah's Ark. Four other girls and three boys, all in Level Three white peels, claim their chairs, leaving a two-seat buffer between them and me.

I smile at the nearest hack, a Black girl with broad shoulders and cornrows who I think is from Block Six. She frowns in response.

"Slinger," she whispers, nose upturned as if the mere word stinks to pronounce.

I tilt my head down.

My reputation precedes me. Great.

We sit in silence, with varying levels of fidgeting, one jack perched beside each hack. At first, I wonder if we're waiting for more hacks to arrive, but soon it becomes clear: this is it.

A white man with a leathery face like a gorilla's strides into the room, flanked by two jack bodyguards. Dressed head to toe in a pressed black suit with red-framed glasses perched on his nose, he shoots us a broad grin that makes the wrinkles trench deeper around his mouth.

"Congratulations, prisoners," he says. "You have reached the end of your rehabilitation. You are only seven simple challenges away from earning your freedom. Once heartless, amoral criminals, you will now reenter the world as productive citizens. Give yourselves a round of applause."

We break into weak clapping, no one daring to look anyone else in the eyes.

"I would like you to go around and state your names—your real names and your ID numbers—plus an interesting fact or two about yourselves. That's fun, right?" He wiggles his eyebrows. I don't get why they care about interesting facts. No one from the center has ever tried to get to know us lowly prisoners before. "I'll start. I'm Doctor Allard, I've raced in the Boston Marathon three times, and I once climbed Mount Kilimanjaro. See? Easy." The other hacks stare vacantly at him. I force a weak smile. "Let's start with you, the tall one on the left." He winks at me.

I take a deep breath and pull myself up.

"My name is Evelyn Summers, Level Three E.S.-124. Block Four. I don't know what I have done; I just know that I am bad. I am here because I deserve to be here, and I am here because I must be fixed. I seek to reform under your guidance."

Two hacks stare daggers at me; the rest won't meet my eyes.

"And I . . ." My mind races to conjure anything remotely interesting about myself. Does saying I hate awkward icebreakers count? "I'm allergic to mushrooms. And, uh . . . I used to play the clarinet back in school."

"Ah, who doesn't love a woodwind instrument? Very good." A smile curls across the man's wrinkly face. "I've heard the most wonderful things about you, E.S.-124. And of course, how you moved from Level One to Level Two in record time."

My jaw tightens. "Thank you, sir."

The hack closest to me rolls her eyes. I hold my posture firm and steady.

"Okay, you may be seated," Doctor Allard says. "Next?"

The sneering hack with the cornrows introduces herself as Carolyn. "I lived in a foster home for two years when I was little, then I lived with my grandparents. Uh . . . and I love to bake."

One of the guys goes next, a skinny Black kid who introduces himself as Miles. "I draw my own comics. Also, uh, I love old-school martial arts movies." He rushes to return to his seat.

Tiffany follows him, a short white girl with blond hair, thin black glasses, and a stutter. She informs us she used to be a local figure skating champion, then messes up the wording on her oath and has to do ten push-ups.

An Asian girl with a permanent smirk goes next, identifying herself as Desirae, who spent her childhood summers with her grandparents in Tokyo. She is quickly followed by a muscular brunette white boy with piercing green eyes named Andrew, who wants to be an MMA fighter. Rebecca—"but I go by Bex"—is a white girl with curly brown hair who winks at me at her introduction. She tells us she can do a split, then promptly feels the need to show us on the floor. I'm kind of shocked Doctor Allard allows it.

A curly-haired boy with golden brown skin named Tomás—"call me Tom"—wraps up the circle, speaking with a tremor in his voice that gets worse when he explains he's named after his Dominican grandpa. There's no way I'm going to remember all these names. But they probably already know mine.

Eight prisoners collared and almost reformed. All ready for freedom.

Doctor Allard welcomes each inmate, reciting our numbers off a printed sheet. He paces behind our row of chairs. It makes me uneasy when he passes behind me.

"I am the master of the Freedom Trials. Therefore, it's safe to say that I am the master of your freedom." Allard chuckles at his humor, drumming his fingers against the back of Desirae's chair. "These trials were designed to test your rehabilitation, to ensure that you have indeed reformed before releasing you back into society." He slowly circulates the room, meeting each of our eyes in turn.

"The trials are not easy," he continues. "They will test you on the seven principles of rehabilitation. Each trial represents one of the seven principles. If you complete your first trial successfully, you'll move on to the next trial. Complete all seven, and your collar will be removed. You'll be sent straight back home."

I tug at my sleeves, trying to stop my stomach from doing somersaults.

The trials will not be easy. I knew that. Why am I freaking out?

"The seven principles on which you will be tested are as follows: strength, mindfulness, self-control, accountability, reflection, justice, and fear." He pauses between each principle for effect. "The principles reflect qualities necessary for true rehabilitation. By demonstrating these traits, you prove you are capable of reentering society without committing a crime. Own the seven principles, and you will be free."

I squirm, wondering how they can possibly test any of that stuff.

"You will no longer be known as prisoners but as contenders. While competing in the trials, you will share a private block with the other contenders. You will dine with them, and you will bunk with them. As the nature of the trials is protected information, you will have no further contact with the inmates from your old blocks, with a few exceptions."

Sorry, Ronnie. I hope I'll see her again someday, on the outside. But on the bright side, I never have to see that awful Alex Martinez slug again.

"Sir," the hack Tom addresses Allard. "Permission to speak, sir?"

"Permission granted."

"What happens if we fail a trial?"

The silent rustling of eight prisoner bodies comes to an abrupt halt. Eight sets of ears perk at the one question everyone was thinking but no one wanted to ask. There are rumors and there are whispers, but in truth, no one knows for sure what the answer really is. I almost don't want to know.

Doctor Allard's stare grows hard and unyielding. "That question always arises during orientation, contender

T.P.-129." He removes his glasses, folds them, and drops them into his pocket. "If you made it here, to the Freedom Trials, it's because your block directors believe you are reformed. We cannot help rehabilitate you any further than you are now. There's nothing more we can offer you. Therefore, if you fail a trial, we will conclude that your rehabilitation has failed. You will be sent to the Green Room. And you will be executed."

//

EVELYN SUMMERS: PRISONER E.S.–124
REHABILITATION DIARY
DAY 35

Director Zepp made me do fifty push-ups this morning because my bed wasn't made to her liking. Of course, I had to screw up on the one day the director tagged along on morning inspections with the nurses and jacks. A corner of the top sheet poked out, she said. If that wasn't bad enough, she made Ronnie do push-ups too—because apparently Ronnie should have seen the bad corner and made me fix it before morning inspection. As if my cellmate didn't already hate me enough.

As soon as the nurses, jacks, and Director Zepp left, Ronnie was all over me. She shoved me into the wall and started screaming, something about how she was going to get tendonitis from the push-ups. Then she stomped on my foot really hard and stormed off to breakfast. I'd do anything for a new roommate. We can't switch cellmates until one of us moves up to Level Two, and since Ronnie gets in trouble literally every day, I'm guessing she won't be first. Guess it's up to me.

I'm going to be more careful with my bed. But I'm so drained in the mornings because I'm up with nightmares half the night. These damn dreams won't leave me alone, and they're wrecking my ability to focus. Every night is that same hallway. It's like a horror movie or something. Then I wake up screaming or in tears.

Sarah says I'm too stressed, which is why I'm getting the dreams. She told me to stop thinking about it before I go to sleep–but how can I not think about it when I know it's going to terrorize me the moment I doze off?

Sarah, Ariadne, Courtney, and I played this game at dinner last night: We tried to remember as close as we could to our memory wipes, then we made up what one another's crimes could be.

The last thing Ariadne remembers, she was walking into a T.J.Maxx. We all guessed shoplifting, but armed robbery crossed my mind too. Courtney was at a theme park, standing in line for the upside-down roller coaster. We had fun with that one—maybe she tampered with the roller coaster to make it break down during the loop-de-loop, and someone fell out and died. That or some creepy guy grabbed her ass in line, and she beat the shit out of him. They're all plausible—anything's possible, after all.

I've been thinking really hard about my crime, trying to remember every little detail about that day. It was May, and I had a throbbing headache; I used to get them a lot. I'd spent two hours in an algebra exam, but I couldn't concentrate on anything other than overanalyzing a text from Matt Houston. I remember thinking I probably failed the test, but I'll never know, because they hauled my ass here before I got the exam back.

Here's the funny thing: The very last thing I remember, the last possible second before the hour they erased, I was staring at a bulletin board outside the music wing. People always posted fun stuff on there, tryouts for school musicals, babysitters wanted, things like that. Sometimes, people added their own artwork to the board before it got ripped down by a teacher. The last thing I remember was an orange flyer about not smoking pot. That's it. Next thing I remember? Waking up in this shithole.

4

A jack leads Carolyn, Desirae, Bex, Tiffany, and me down a snakelike corridor to our contender quarters. Shackled together at the ankles, we clank into one another, passing endless expanses of gray concrete walls. After an eternity, the guard unlocks a steel door and we make a final turn into a straight, narrow hall. The door slams behind us.

A dim light flickers from the ceiling, creating an eerie glow reminiscent of my mother's sinister upstairs hallway; the similarity sends shivers down my spine. It's like my recurring nightmare came alive and manifested in this damn hallway.

But this hall is different. Another vast display of gray concrete makes up the left wall, but a long glass window stretches across the right. It spans the entire length of the passage, floor to ceiling. I squint, but can't see past the pitch darkness on the other side. A white corded telephone hangs at the edge of the glass, beside a square metal panel in the wall. We march in silence past the window to a steel door with chipping red paint at the end of the hall.

"These are your quarters," the jack says, her voice cold as ice. "The hallway door back there is dead-bolted, but you are free to enter and exit your room, this hallway, and the bathroom as you please." She unlocks our chains, and the metal clanks to the floor in a heap. I do a mental fist pump for not having to use the piss pot in the middle of the night anymore.

"Dinner is served at five, so line up in the hall at that time to retrieve your tray—we won't wait for you." She locks eyes with each of us in turn, progressing down the line. "You eat in your room now. You'll find your new jumpsuits in your closet. Breakfast will be delivered to your room every morning at five thirty. Trials begin tomorrow morning at six sharp. A guard will meet you in the hallway at that time to lead you to your destination. Do not be late." We offer the jack a final group salute before she strides back out, bolting the hall door behind her.

I stand alone with the other four hacks. Carolyn shoves past me, knocking her elbow into my side. She disappears into our new room with Tiffany trailing close behind.

Desirae smiles sweetly at the brunette beside her. "Rebecca, right?"

"Yep." The girl shakes her hand. "But call me Bex. All my friends do." Her eyes coast over to me, and she smirks. "You can call me Rebecca, slinger."

My face gets hot.

"What's up, slinger?" Desirae steps toward me, close enough that I can make out the details of her face. One of her top front teeth is chipped, while another is a shade lighter than the rest—probably a fake. Maybe she got her teeth knocked out in a fight. "You enjoy orientation?"

"Yes. It's nice to meet you." I offer my hand, but she doesn't take it.

"Glad you enjoyed yourself." Desirae smirks. "You watch your back out there at the trials. I've heard slingers have a way of . . . disappearing."

Bex winks at me.

Desirae brushes past me after Carolyn, undoing her bun and flinging her sleek dark hair over her shoulder. Bex shoots me a peace sign that looks anything but peaceful and follows after them.

I take a deep breath, allowing myself a quiet moment alone in the hallway.

Seven trials. That's it. Then I'm out of here.

I push the red door to enter my new shared bedroom. Carolyn, Desirae, Bex, and Tiffany huddle on a bed, whispering and giggling. They've managed to push four beds to one wall, leaving one solitary mattress in a corner by itself. I don't even have to ask. I release a heavy sigh and collapse onto the lonely bed.

The room is only slightly larger than the cell I shared with Margot, but with the added bonus of three additional beds, two silvery metal chairs, and what appears to be a small closet.

Across the room, Bex squeaks open the closet door. "Oooh, check out our new peels. They're intense."

Carolyn, Desirae, and Tiffany rise to join her, speaking in hushed voices as they paw through white jumpsuits dangling from plastic hangers. Bex grabs a suit and begins stripping off her peels, right in the middle of the room, down to her white undies. She kicks her Level Three clothes to the side and pulls on her new slick white jumpsuit and white boots. Tiffany shyly shimmies into hers, turning her back when her bra and panties make an appearance.

I cautiously step toward the group as if approaching a pineapple-sized hornet's nest. Hand shaking, I reach for a hanger.

"Wait your turn, slinger." Carolyn shoves me backward. I stumble to the floor.

"Oh look, here's one for the slinger." Desirae flings a jumpsuit my way. It smacks me in the face. I hold up the uniform; they've so generously given me one with a blotchy brown stain in the crotch. I clench the fabric in my hands until my knuckles turn white. Deep breaths.

"It's perfect for you, slinger." Carolyn chuckles as she slides into her own stain-free peels. "It's full of shit, just like you."

Bex flares out her fingers. "Boom. Shots fired."

I muster my best attempt at a friendly smile and grab the corresponding new set of night peels. "Thanks."

The girls burst into laughter, thrilled with their own joke.

"I'm gonna go change in the bathroom," Desirae says. "Hey, slinger, if you touch my bed, I'll break your face." She grabs her peels and boots and strides into the hall, knocking into me on her way out.

I retreat to my segregated bed and curl up against the wall, not daring to turn my back on my new roommates. I'll wait until the bathroom is clear before changing into my new peels; I don't trust Desirae not to stab me in the back—figuratively or otherwise—when I'm naked.

Two minutes later, the door whips open, and Director Levine saunters inside. We scramble to our feet, mustering a hasty salute.

"As you were." She dismisses us with a lazy wave of her hand. Our arms drop to our sides with a collective clap. "E.S.-124, come with me for a moment, please."

I swallow. What the hell did I do now?

The other hacks smirk as I follow Levine back into the hallway. Desirae makes a face when she passes me in the hall, but quickly morphs it into a stiff salute when she spies Director Levine a step behind. She speed-walks back to our quarters and shuts the door.

That's right, bitch, you better keep walking.

"Evelyn, I wanted to have a word with you," Director Levine says.

"Yes, ma'am."

"If you'll come over here, I want to show you something."

I follow her to the dark window taking up the entire wall. "This is our solitary confinement." She gestures toward the black abyss. "It's okay, you can take a closer look."

I cup my hands around my eyes and press my face to the glass, but overwhelming darkness obscures my vision.

The Hole.

"We keep our solitary prisoners here because we like them to interact with those who are almost reformed, the contenders in the Freedom Trials. Get some good to rub off on them, show them what they could aspire to if they'd only behave and commit themselves to changing."

"Yes, ma'am."

"You can communicate with the prisoner inside with this telephone here, see?" She plucks the white corded phone off its dock and clicks it back down. "The point is for the contenders to be a good influence on the person in the Hole."

"Yes, ma'am." Why is she telling me this?

"I wanted to show you this now so you won't be alarmed later. There's nothing to be afraid of." She pulls back the square panel on the wall and flips a switch. The dark room behind the window illuminates with blinding white light.

I jump back.

Balled up in the fetal position in the corner of the Hole, knees tucked tightly to his chest, is Alex Martinez. He squints, blinking furiously at the burst of fluorescence.

"He's been sedated. After his performance during his intake, we couldn't take another chance. And with what he did to Director Zepp, he's likely to be in solitary for a while."

I replay the memory of him backhanding the director and sending her flying across the room. It was so surreal. So violent. My heart thrums like a bass drum against my ribcage.

I don't want to see that monster. Why is she showing me this? And why is he so close to where I'll be sleeping tonight?

"I thought it would be better if you found out now, instead of later. This window is nearly indestructible." She taps the glass with her long fingernail. "He can't hurt you. And if he becomes aggressive, we'll sedate him again. See that camera up in the corner?" She points. "He's video monitored twenty-four seven."

"Yes, ma'am." I try to convince myself that the tiny camera's blinking red light is enough to deter this criminal from attacking me again.

Alex stirs, pulling his knees up closer to his chin. He rocks back and forth on the cement floor, shivering quietly. His room is bare, nothing but gray concrete and a single steel door sturdy enough to protect the crown jewels. A sandwich sits untouched on a plate beside him, wilted lettuce peeking out from under the bread. My breathing slows to a steady rate.

He doesn't look so scary now.

"He won't even remember attacking you, Evelyn. We had to wipe a lot of this boy's memory. Don't worry; our technology is very advanced. There's a lot he won't remember." She rests a sympathetic hand on my shoulder. "But with the violent ones, sometimes that's the only way."

I nod. I hope it's enough.

///

I lie on my bed in silence for two hours while the other girls giggle and chat. They've gone from deriding me to flat-out ignoring me. I'm not sure which one I prefer.

I stretch my hands behind my head and stare up at the ceiling. Alex is only fifty feet away. One hundred, if I'm lucky. What if he snaps again and shatters that vault door as easily as he broke his handcuffs? Every possible terrifying scenario plays through my mind like a horror movie. What if he gets in here and tries to kill me?

"Hey, slinger," Carolyn calls. "Heads up!" Her old Level Three shoe sails across the room and smashes into my nose with a crack. Tears sting my eyes.

"Five points!" Desirae high-fives Carolyn.

Bex makes her voice low and robotic. "A new high score."

The girls burst into laughter. I suck in a deep breath and clench my teeth, pressing my pillow to my face to catch the stream of blood trickling from my nostrils.

Flat-out ignoring me. I prefer that.

//

EVELYN SUMMERS: PRISONER E.S.-124
REHABILITATION DIARY
DAY 56

Today sucked. It's that time of the month, and when I woke up, cramps were already kicking my ass. But on top of that, I knew something bad was going to happen. I got the same feeling back home when storm clouds hovered outside my bedroom window and I knew I'd have to trek out to the bus stop in a deluge. We don't have windows here, but I got that same feeling—a storm was coming.

I arrived at breakfast still shaken from my nightly creepy-corridor nightmare, and Ariadne was crying into her oatmeal. She couldn't speak, just kept heaving between intermittent sobs. A jack lingered nearby and told her to shut up at least twice. She made no signs of stopping until he physically came over, dragged her up, and smacked her across the face in front of everyone. Then she leaked silent tears. Sarah, Courtney, and I attempted to learn what happened, but she wouldn't talk.

By lunch, we had the news: Ariadne's father was diagnosed with pancreatic cancer, stage four. When she told us, a veil of relief settled over me. That's all it was?

Sarah's face broke into a smile alongside mine. No one's died from cancer in at least a year, not since the invention of Klaurivex. What was she so worried about? That miracle drug was a game changer, and our friend was freaking out for nothing. He'd receive the Klaurivex injection, be groggy for a few days, then poof! No more sickness. But

Ariadne angrily shrugged us off when we tried to comfort her.

She said they weren't going to treat her father with the drug. Our smiles melted into perplexed frowns as we asked her why not, but she didn't have an answer. All she knew was the truth descending on us all: He was going to die.

I guess Director Zepp had called Ariadne into her office and told her the news, but wouldn't let her call her father, visit him, nothing. She's still two levels away from her Freedom Trials, so we all know what that means—she'll never see him again. She probably won't even get to attend the funeral. I've never seen someone so distraught. I thought that would be the worst part of the day.

I was wrong.

Sarah whispered something to me at dinner. Something awful. I don't even know if I should be writing it here, private diary or not.

They want to break out.

I guess the three of them have talked about it for months, concocted elaborate schemes with every possible method of escape, but never followed through. Ariadne's news was the last straw.

They planned the whole thing down to the last detail. A week of hiding their Memoria pills would get them at least a few of their memories back. Then they'd wait until someone assigned them shifts cleaning the fifth-floor tiles—one of the few chores we're allowed to do without cuffs.

I'd seen the big elevator on that floor a few times in passing but never gave it much thought. It looks like a regular elevator, but I guess there's a mystery to it. It's the only exit from the Center. It goes up, out of the ground, and back to the surface.

They only assign one jack to supervise the hacks who clean that hallway. It seems like a lapse in judgment, but they must trust us not to run away. Either that or the elevator isn't as innocuous as it appears.

All it would take is one heavy object to the head to knock the jack out cold. We'd take his ID card, swipe into the elevator, up to the surface, and OUT. Sarah swears there's nothing else—no barbed wire, no fence to jump, nothing—that elevator is somehow the only obstacle. It seems fishy to me that a simple elevator and a single jack are the only things standing between us and the outside. We'd reach the top and be free—on the run, but free.

We. As in, me too. Ariadne could see her dad. And I could see my mom.

This came out of nowhere. It was the last thing I was expecting today. Seriously, I don't know how this plan could ever work. We'll get caught and killed, that's what will happen. If they catch us, that's a one-way ticket to the Green Room. At first I told them no. But now I'm not so sure.

I'm a Level One, years from getting out of here. I'm stuck with the cellmate from hell. What if we could really do it? What if the four of us could actually manage to escape? They've been here way longer than me, and they seem confident in the plan.

I know I'm going to regret this. I know something bad will happen. But I'm going to do it. I'm going to run away.

The alarm buzzes way too early. I drag my heavy feet across the contender quarters and shimmy into my new uniform. The clingy white fabric hugs my hips, showing off all the pudge and bumps in my body that I don't want anyone to see. I've worn nothing but loose, pajama-type peels every day for the past two years. My body feels cramped and constricted in the tight new jumpsuit. I bunch up the fabric in an attempt to hide the crotch stain, but it springs back without holding a wrinkle.

Unlike our old peels, this stretchy material reaches my wrists and ankles. It goes right up to my chin like a turtleneck. I tug the fabric away from my collar, but it snaps back into place, constricting tighter over the metal. My new white boots hug my shins, sealed below my knee with a band of white elastic. I run my hand across the rubbery soles, fingers catching in the various nooks and crevices.

Good traction. Built for running.

Carolyn and Tiffany pull on their peels across the room. For once, they're silent—the only noise is the occasional snap of elastic. Bex starts humming something that sounds oddly like circus music but stops when the others cast irritated glares in her direction. Desirae tiptoes back from the bathroom and dumps her night peels onto her bed with a heavy sigh. A veil of unspoken fear looms over our heads like a shroud as we prepare for our first trial. The nurses and jacks bustle in to give us our daily Memoria pill and neck prick. Breakfast arrives on a tray, but I can hardly force myself to nibble a corner of the dry toast.

I follow Carolyn, Desirae, Bex, and Tiffany into the hall, speeding past the darkened window with my head down. A twisting pain knots in my chest, as if my body caught up to the realization my mind already knew: fail this trial, I'll never walk this corridor again. It's all over.

"Come on, come on." The jack bangs the butt of her rifle against the metal door. She's barely older than us. "Hurry up. Hustle. Let's go."

She chains our ankles and wrists, and we amble out the hall door, back into the mazelike corridors. A door creaks open to the right and another jack emerges, escorting the line of cuffed male contenders. We each offer the boys a nod, and they return the gesture. It's my first interaction ever with the guy hacks.

Well, unless you count the scary one in the Hole.

Tension hovers thick in the air as we march on, shackles clanking together, toward whatever lies ahead in trial one. I can't help feeling like we're cattle, herded together en route to the slaughterhouse.

We reach a large rectangular room with gray walls and a high drop ceiling. Eight evenly spaced steel posts tower over us, sprouting from the floor and stretching upward, reminiscent of fireman's poles on kids' playgrounds. They reach about fifteen feet in the air, five feet from piercing the ceiling. A metal platform no larger than one square foot sits on top of each pole.

The six directors stand poised like statues, hands clasped behind their backs, muttering to one another in low tones. Doctor Allard paces the room, but throws his hands out in an obvious display of feigned enthusiasm as we enter.

"Contenders!" His bleached teeth glimmer through his giddy smile. "Welcome to your first trial."

Director Levine catches my eye, the tiniest flicker of a half smile on her lips. I whip my hand up into a salute, and my seven competitors follow.

"Today"—Doctor Allard strides back and forth down the line of hacks— "you will be tested on the first principle of rehabilitation: strength. This requires two things: strength of body and strength of mind. You'll need both to succeed in the real world without crime—and to complete your first trial."

Carolyn's breaths grow ragged beside me. Her hands

quiver madly at her sides.

So big tough Carolyn gets scared, too, huh?

"So with that said," Doctor Allard continues, "good luck to you all. Let's get on with the trial."

With a mechanical rumble, the ceiling comes alive. Seven ropes drop down, one beside each metal post. Each rope is as thick as a python and hangs about three feet to the side of its corresponding pole. The ropes stretch at least twenty feet down from the ceiling, dangling a foot off the ground. They sway for a moment before stiffening, eerily reminiscent of gallows.

Don't make us climb them. That'd be my worst nightmare. I have zero upper-body strength.

"For your trial, you'll need to climb to the top of your rope."

Shit.

"Once you reach the top, you must ring the bell and get to the platform." He points upward. "See the platforms at the top of those poles? Those will act as elevators, and bring you safely back to the bottom when you complete the trial."

It sounds too simple.

I trace my eyes up the nearest pole, squinting to see the square metal surface at the top, almost scraping the ceiling. Several feet from the rope, it would take the strength of a ninja to make that leap. My mouth runs dry as I mentally calculate the required jump. Climbing and jumping are not my forte.

"Reach the platform, pass your trial."

I guess he doesn't need to reiterate what happens if I don't.

The muscly hack, Andrew, grins. Biceps bulging through his peels, this challenge must be right up his alley.

"But, beware!" Allard flashes out his hands like a game-show host. "It's not that simple."

I tense. Of course it isn't. "Keep your eyes out." He winks. "We may throw in a few surprises."

I close my eyes in a vain attempt to calm my rapid heart rate. My arms hang limp at my sides, suddenly feeling about as strong and capable as hay straws.

Either way, it'll all be over soon.

A jack escorts us to our respective ropes. Thankfully, Desirae is far away, in the corner by herself. Bex's rope is sandwiched between two of the guys. Carolyn, however, gets assigned to the station at my left. Tom takes the rope on my right, rubbing his hands together and bouncing up and down on his toes in some sort of warm-up.

"You ready for this, slinger?" Carolyn whispers. I ignore her. "You know, Doctor Allard said you need brains *and* brawn to complete this trial. Too bad you have neither."

I clench my teeth but don't respond.

"Sucks they don't have a trial on mudslinging abilities," she adds. "'Cause you'd dominate that one."

I focus on the swaying rope, doing my best to tune her out.

"When you fall and splat all over the cement," she

continues, "at least you'll miss the Green Room. I hope that's how you go, because I'd really love to watch the tragic end to your slinging days." She pretends to wipe a fake tear off her cheek.

"I'm sure you would, Carolyn."

"On your mark . . ." Doctor Allard's voice booms over us. "Get set . . ." I suck in a deep breath. "Go!"

I latch on to my rope, channeling every bit of rage toward Carolyn into climbing. The prickly hemp fibers bite into my palms. I wrap my hands around the rope and pull, but go nowhere. Sandwiching the rope between my knees, I push and pull, sweat already beading across my brow.

There has to be an easier way.

Grunts and gasps fill the room. I hang, forcing my muscles not to give as I survey the other contenders. Several places over, Andrew has mastered a technique; he makes a foothold by wrapping the length around his foot and linking his ankle into the rope, inching upward. He breezes up, almost at the top after only a few minutes.

Fingers slipping, I take a deep breath.

I can do this.

Four feet off the ground, I pull my knees up to my chest. I curl my left ankle into the rope, rotating slightly until I'm hooked onto it by my boots. I push my right foot off of my left ankle and use it as a stepping stone, extending my body up the rope like an inchworm. My face scrunches. I blink back the salty sweat seeping into my eyes.

For once, I'm grateful they forced us to do all those damn

push-ups. Still, my arms protest, triceps burning and quivering with each movement.

Curl, rotate, pull. Curl, rotate, pull. Perspiration drips down my face like rain.

Halfway there.

An orange glare catches my eye. Flames scorch six feet high from the bottom of Tom's rope, licking the soles of his boots. He scales the remaining climb in seconds.

My heart slams. They're setting the ropes on fire.

Tiffany screams, frantically stamping at the encroaching blaze beneath her. Gray smoke billows around me; it stings my throat, making me gag. My neck swells against my collar.

Fire engulfs my rope, two feet from swallowing my feet. Heat smothers my face.

Somewhere, a bell chimes. Andrew hollers victoriously in the distance. Then another—Desirae reached her platform too.

I pull, twisting my leg around the rope. It cuts into my thigh, searing my skin, but it's all that's keeping me from falling to my death. Whether I'd die from the impact, or the flames, or just face a serious mauling from the cement floor, screwing this up would mean a one-way ticket to the Green Room.

With a joyful "ye-ah" that echoes around the room, Bex rings her bell.

Ten feet left. Eight feet.

Muscles screaming, I force my body up. The flames race after me, scorching my heels.

Another bell, then a fourth; Tom and Miles reached the

top. I'm watching Tom, perched on his platform like an owl, when my foot misses the curl. I slip, my sweaty hands grasping at the rope. It slides through my grip, burning my palms. I drop five feet, straight into the flames. They smolder against my back, biting and searing my skin. Tears mingle with sweat across my face.

I squeeze my eyes closed, succumbing to the flames baking me alive.

No. It's not over. Not yet.

Propelled by adrenaline, I pry myself upward. My scorched hands throb, but I press on, curling and inching, fighting through the burns blistering up my legs. The fire follows close behind, igniting two feet of rope for every one foot I climb. The platform comes into view. Smoke clouds my stinging eyes.

It's so far away.

A bell chimes, followed by Carolyn's triumphant, "whoop!"

The flames sear my toes, melting away the rubber on my boots. I thrust my body back, forcing my weight to swing the rope as hard as I can. Closer to the platform, then back, like a pendulum. Even closer, then back.

Blood oozes from my palms, staining the rope crimson. My heart thuds in my ears, drowning out the shouts and cries below.

It's now or never.

I fling my body off the rope, throwing myself at the

platform. The metal digs into my ribs at the impact, knocking the air from my lungs. The blaze eats the remaining rope behind me.

Gasping for air, I wobble to my feet, covered head to toe in blistering burns. I yank the string dangling from the bell, filling the room with the tinkling chime of my success. A smile brims across my face.

I did it. I actually did it.

I meet Carolyn's beet red eyes on the next platform. A sweaty film coats her face. Her bare brown ankles stick out beneath frayed white pants. She slides to the edge of her platform, inhaling ragged breaths, pressing her fingers against the burned skin on her legs. Tom coughs on his platform, muttering congratulations to Miles beside him.

A sharp cry rings out.

"No!" Tom shouts.

Thud.

Tiffany lies motionless on the ground, engulfed in flames. A halo of long blond hair fans out on the cement around her head. Neck bent backward at a sharp angle, her right leg folds unnaturally underneath her. A sulfuric odor fills the air. I slap my hand over my mouth, laboring not to puke. Two jacks bustle over with red canisters, blanketing her in fire-extinguisher foam.

Director Zane kneels, pressing his fingers to Tiffany's neck. "She's done."

I swallow a dry lump.

Zane stands back up, kicking the girl lightly with the toe of his boot. "Clean this up." Two more jacks rush over and lift Tiffany's charred body onto a gurney.

Smoke floods my lungs with each inhale. I choke out exhales in sputtering coughs. Dizziness swarms my head. I run my fingers along the back of my scorched leg. Each rattling breath grows more ragged.

I collapse in a heap on my platform, edges of the room blurring in and out of focus. Three jacks with extinguishers spread out between the seven ropes, drowning the flickering orange in puffy white foam. Tom's and Carolyn's hacking echoes around me.

"Congratulations." Doctor Allard's voice bounces between the walls. "You passed your first trial."

With a mechanic rumble, my platform descends like an elevator, carrying me safely to the ground below.

My platform hits the floor with a sharp *slam*. Everything spins around me, faster and blurrier as I wobble to my feet. Blood gushes from my blistering skin. Bile swirls in my stomach, rocketing up my esophagus. Hands on my knees, I spew a heap of vomit onto the floor. I rock in place for a moment, then fall headfirst onto the cement. Everything goes black.

//

EVELYN SUMMERS: PRISONER E.S.–124
REHABILITATION DIARY
DAY 63

I can't concentrate on anything. When they make us write lines, my hand shakes so bad, the words look like gibberish on the page. If my sleep was bad before, it's gotten worse—I'm lucky to get three hours a night after spending hours tossing and sobbing into my pillow. I hardly eat more than a couple nibbles at each meal. I'm so paranoid about the runaway plan, I've started hiding this journal under my mattress, even though no one reads it anyway.

My friends scheme in hushed whispers in the cafeteria—morphing their conversation into chitchat if a jack comes—but I don't hear a word.

I'm terrified.

They want to put our plan into action next week, because that's the next time we'll be on floor-scrubbing duty together. It seems so soon, and I feel so unprepared. Sarah's given me the job of knocking out the jack. Seriously? Clock someone? Me? How the hell am I supposed to do that?

They tell me to visualize it, to really see myself doing the job. "Job." They say it like bashing another human being in the head is part of everyday life. Hitting a guard is an unforgivable offense. What if I hit him, but he doesn't go down? I'm screwed. I'm so screwed. Every time I think about it, I feel like I'm going to puke. This is one crime the Center won't forgive. I won't be savable anymore. If they catch me, they'll drag me to the Green Room and shoot me in the head without question.

I can't go home if I'm dead. I can't. I can't do it.

I'm going to tell them tomorrow—I'm out.

My mom's long hallway stretches beneath my feet. The nightlight flickers in the corner, creating elongated shadows against the wall. I press my back against my bedroom door—the starting line—and squint ahead to my mother's door in the distance—the finish line.

I inhale a shaky breath and take my first step forward, feet walking on cue, as if yanked by invisible puppet strings. My stiff legs stumble with the grace of a rickety newborn calf. The familiar sense of fear creeps down my neck. I close my eyes, fighting the urge to turn and run.

It's just a hallway; stop freaking out.

My feet force my body forward into the smothering darkness. Halfway to my mom's room, something gurgles to my left. I spin around. The wall beside me oozes and parts, creating an empty void the size of my shoe—a swirling black hole in the middle of our home. I step backward until I collide with the opposite wall.

The opening grows, twisting and morphing like ripples in a pond. I open my mouth to scream, but nothing comes out—the black hole sucks my voice into oblivion. The emptiness crawls upward—four feet, five feet, six feet high.

Walls don't open. This is impossible. I've walked past this wall a zillion times; it's solid. What the hell is happening?

I gape, frozen in fear. The black hole widens, threatening to engulf me at any moment.

Up and up the blackness stretches, spreading and widening until . . . it stops. The borders of the hole thicken, forming straight lines with clear, defined edges. The expanse before me is about six feet tall and three feet wide. It isn't a black hole at all.

It's a door.

Words squeak out of my mouth no louder than a whisper.

"It's just a summer job."

I wrench my eyes open and thrust myself up, gasping for air. White light floods my vision. A squishy IV bag dangles from a metal post beside my bed, the machine beeping in rhythm with my heart. I yank my arm up, but it won't budge—chains bind my hands to the bed rails. I startle at the old nurse hovering over me

"It's okay, Evelyn. It's okay. You're safe. You're in the

infirmary." She's got kind eyes and an impressive Afro. "My name's Ellen. I'm a registered nurse."

My frantic eyes dart around the room. "What . . . what happened?"

Nurse Ellen pats my forehead with a damp cloth. "You have minor smoke-inhalation damage, along with several other contenders." She pulls a pink tube from her back pocket, untwists the cap, and squirts a dollop of thick white cream on my exposed leg. "You also had some pretty severe third-degree burns. Luckily, this stuff works like magic."

Sure enough, the harsh blisters from the trial have already faded into slightly pink, smooth skin. "Thank you."

"Just doing my job." Deep wrinkles form trenches across her dark skin as she rubs the ointment on my burns. If I didn't know better, I'd say a hint of empathy lingers behind her eyes.

"How long have I been here?" I ask.

"A little under forty-eight hours. You're scheduled to stay in my care until the end of the day, at which point you'll be escorted back to your quarters to prepare for trial two tomorrow."

A pit drops in my stomach at the mention of another trial.

I lie back, resting my head against the starchy pillow. The nurse bustles through the swinging doors, into the back room. My pulse slows to a normal rate.

I grasp for details of my dream. I can't let it fade away. Something different happened.

Over seven hundred nightmares. All the same until today, when my brain invented a random door in my mom's hallway. It makes no sense.

Someone grunts beside me, and I turn my head.

Eyes half closed, lips parted, Alex Martinez lies in the next bed. He inhales and exhales deep, steady breaths. Someone cuffed his arms and legs to the bedposts in the four-piece suit. I inch myself as far away from him as possible, not daring to blink. His eyelids flutter slightly as he glances at the dripping IV bag hooked in his wrist.

The nurse jostles back into the room, balancing a turkey sandwich, macaroni salad, and an overflowing glass of water on a thin metal tray. She sets it on my bedside table and swivels the table toward me. My stomach grumbles at the sight of a meal that doesn't resemble cardboard.

I point at Alex. "What . . . what's he doing here?" My voice trembles.

"Prisoner A.M.-624?" The nurse scrunches up her face, unlocking the chains binding my hands. "Poor kid wasn't eating at all. Almost starved himself to death." She clicks her tongue. "The directors decided to bring him here for a few days, for observation and to get some fluids into him."

"Is he sedated?"

Please say he's on bug juice. Please say he's on bug juice.

Nurse Ellen shoots me a sympathetic smile. "No, not really."

My face must parade the terror inside me, because the nurse gives my hand a sympathetic squeeze. "But he's chained up pretty good. Don't worry, he's not going anywhere. Eat up." She hands me a plastic fork and shuffles back through the swinging door.

I nibble at my lunch, fixing my unblinking eyes on Alex. Someone chopped his long black hair to a simple fuzzy layer.

His eyes drift open, the slightest hint of sadness shadowing his gaze. An unexpected jolt of pity stabs me in the gut.

"H-hi, Alex."

He twists his neck toward me but doesn't answer.

"How are you feeling?" I ask.

His shoulders rise in a weak shrug. "Been better." He shuts his eyes once more, and I turn my attention back to my food.

I can't stop thinking about my dream. I cling to the fading images, but they slip away like fingers grabbing at smoke.

I spoke in the dream. I said, *It's just a summer job . . .* for some reason.

I don't know why Dream Me said it. I've never had a summer job. I was only fifteen when I came here, not old enough to legally work. Terrible possibilities flash through my mind—maybe my job wasn't legal. Maybe it was my crime, and that's why it was erased. I could have been selling drugs, or guns, or something worse. But that doesn't sound like me. I've never so much as taken a hit off a joint. I wish I knew the truth.

Alex once thought he recognized me. The words bubble up inside me in a sudden burst of curiosity I can't force down.

"Do you know me?" I blurt out, a little louder than intended.

Alex's eyelids sweep open. He crinkles his forehead, deep in concentration studying my face.

"No."

///

Hours pass before they send me back to my room. They feed me painkillers and some other meds to counteract the smoke inhalation before discharging me. A jack escorts me back to my quarters, which now contains only four beds. A thin layer of dust coats a rectangular section of the bare cement floor, where the fifth bed used to be—the only evidence Tiffany ever slept here. They don't waste any time before erasing the dead contenders, apparently.

Carolyn lies on her side, her singed forearm mummified in thick white gauze. Bex sits on her bed brushing her hair, a bandage wrapped around her left foot. Desirae perches on the metal chair, leaning it back on two legs. She got through the trial unscathed.

"It's alive," Carolyn says when I enter the room.

I take a deep breath. Here goes nothing. "Congrats on passing the trial!" I stretch my mouth into the widest fake smile I can muster. "I wanted to say . . . good luck in tomorrow's."

Carolyn snorts and rises from the bed. "Luck? You're wishing us luck?"

"What a beautiful gesture." Sarcasm drips from Bex's words. "The slinger's luck will save us all."

"Look, Carolyn." Desirae smirks, leaping up from the chair. "The slinger wants to be your friend."

"You gonna send us to the Green Room, you mouth-running hack?" Carolyn saunters toward me.

"No! I just—"

"That sounds about right to me," Desirae says. "Mudslinger wants friends so she can spew her mud all over the trials." She takes a step toward me, grinning. "Come on, slinger. I'll be your friend. Why don't you come over here?"

I step back until my fingers brush the concrete wall behind me. The other girls encroach, backing me into a corner. Carolyn may be short, but she's about fifty pounds of muscle ahead of me—and Desirae and Bex are just scary. Desirae flicks my shoulder.

"Not so tough, are you?" she says. "Especially when your buddy Director Levine isn't around."

"I just—"

"Let me tell you how it works in the Center," Desirae says. "It's us versus them. The Center staff, and us. You've already proven your loyalties, and they sure as hell aren't with us."

"Bitches before snitches." Carolyn cracks her knuckles. "Stay the fuck away from us."

"Or I will literally kill you," Bex adds with a wink.

"I don't wanna start anything." I hide my shaking hands behind my back.

Bex crosses her arms. "First smart thing the slinger's said all day."

"That's right," Carolyn says. "Cause if you run your fucking mouth, you're gonna end this thing in a whole world of hurt. Got it?" She thrusts her fist out, two inches from my nose.

"Yes," I whisper.

I retreat to my bed without another word.

When lights out finally comes, I lie awake for hours until roaring snores fill the room. I'm dreading being exhausted for trial two, but no way can I fall asleep first. I don't doubt for a second they'd make good on their threats. My eyelids grow heavy until I can't force them open any longer.

//

The dream jolts me awake with the same urgency as in the infirmary. I catch my breath. Holy shit. What is going on? I flip onto my back and stare at the ceiling.

The random black-hole door cropped up again. My disembodied voice also made a reappearance, whispering those same bizarre words. It makes no sense. Why the sudden change?

Every nerve in my body aches, but at least burns and blisters no longer dapple my legs and back. I pick at the burned skin on my arm, longing to drift back into painless sleep. The last thing I need is to be half asleep for tomorrow's trial.

Light from the hall seeps through the bars in the door, casting a glow across the room. Sheet-covered lumps on the other three beds rise and fall as Carolyn, Bex, and Desirae enjoy the sleep that eludes me.

The lights flash on, and the door whips open.

I lurch upward. Carolyn flails around in her sheets, her startled holler muffled by her pillow. Desirae springs out of bed like a panther, dark hair poofing in all directions. Bex literally rolls off the bed and slams face-first into the floor before shaking herself awake.

A young nurse races into our quarters, followed by a pale-faced female jack and tight-lipped Director Levine.

Levine claps her hands. "Hacks, at attention!" Exhaustion hangs heavy under her stern eyes.

We plant our feet on the ground, drowsy and wobbly, and offer stiff, half-awake salutes. Carolyn blinks furiously, eyes still gummed together by sleep. The green-numbered clock on the wall flashes 3:00 a.m.

What the hell? I've been here two years, and not once has a jack or director entered my block after hours. They've been known to peer through the bars in the door to check on us, but never actually come in. Something's up.

My senses spring to life—this could be our second trial.

"It appears your last dose of Memoria was given in error," Levine says. "Unfortunately, we had a packaging glitch. You were administered expired medication. It is of utmost importance that you retake your dose immediately."

"Will the expired pills hurt us?" Carolyn asks.

Levine shakes her head. "The expired medication will not harm you, but it's ineffective. Missing even a day can have catastrophic effects on your memory wipe. Come now, mouths open. Let's go."

Ineffective. The pill I took yesterday didn't work. If missing a single dose is that crucial, could my memories have already begun to return?

Carolyn downs her dose and opens her empty mouth to show the jack and nurse.

No. I still can't remember a damn thing about my crime. Nothing. Except . . .

Desirae swigs back the water and sticks out her tongue.

The dream. The dream has been different since I missed my pills.

Bex gulps down her own dose.

What if it isn't just a dream?

The young nurse thrusts Memoria and water at me.

What if it's a memory?

If it is, if I take this pill, I'll never dream the black hole again.

There's something about it. It means something.

I drop the pill into my mouth.

I must obey. I must swallow.

I don't know why I can't. In one swift motion, I force the pill under my tongue, chug the water, and show them a seemingly empty mouth. They don't check too closely.

They never do. I'm one of the good ones.

"Dump out those old pills in the trash, no more accidents," Levine snaps at the sheepish nurse. They stomp out, and the lights click back off.

Carolyn, Bex, and Desirae whisper for a minute, then their sleepy voices fade into silence. I pluck the active medication from my mouth and clench my fist around the wet pill.

For the first time in over two years, I disobeyed an order.

.

//

EVELYN SUMMERS: PRISONER E.S. – 124
REHABILITATION DIARY
DAY 73

My heart won't stop pounding. Director Zepp called me into her office right after morning inspection. That's only happened once before, to get my schedule the first day I arrived.

This time was different. I got to her office, and there were a bunch of adults already there: Director Zepp, but also two other women who I think are directors of the upper levels, and then a bunch of men and jacks.

Director Zepp was being super nice. She gave me some chocolate and told me to take a seat. One of the jacks even vacated his chair, so I could have the comfy leather swivel one. Eight sets of hot stares bore down on me, and I felt like a fly in a spiderweb. I didn't know what they wanted from me. Then Zepp spoke.

She knew about Sarah's plan. Well, not really. She knew something was up. I guess we weren't super inconspicuous during our planning meetings in the cafeteria, and a few jacks got suspicious. The moment Zepp mentioned it, my insides turned to jelly.

She knows, she knows, she knows—that's all I could think while she was talking. I thought she was going to punish me for being involved, even though I backed out last week. Tears sprang to my eyes. I wrung my shaking hands in my lap, hating my nerves for presenting my guilt to the room. I thought they were going to do something really bad to me. Punish me. Hurt me. But they didn't.

What Director Zepp said next, I didn't see coming at all.

She told me I could move up to Level Two in record-breaking time. I'd be only one level away from my Freedom Trials. She said I'd get a different cellmate and not have to live with that awful Ronnie Hartman anymore. She said I could take a shower longer than five minutes, and that the jacks would take it easy on me during exercise for a few weeks. Maybe even give me some off-duty alone time in my room, while everyone else does push-ups and laps. I could get a fresh set of peels and double helpings at breakfast.

All I had to do was tattle. Spill the plan.

One of the men spoke next. He said they'd take it easy on my friends. Sarah, Ariadne, and Courtney would each spend one day in the Hole and get toilet-scrubbing duty for a week. Someone would monitor their Memoria extra carefully for a few months. Then everything would go back to normal. Even though I'd be a Level Two, I could still see my friends at meals. And they assured me no one would know I snitched.

My friends would probably assume, and they'd hate me forever. Hell, I'd hate me forever. Still, it tempted me.

But then Director Zepp said something else.

"Don't you want to go home, Evelyn?" she said, a honey-sweet tinge to her voice. "But it's okay if you don't. I guess it means you aren't as rehabilitated as we thought you were, and might need a few more years in Level One to get there." She gave me a closed-mouth smile. Her words struck me in the heart like a poison arrow.

Tears streamed down my face. The words flew out of my mouth before I could stop them. I coughed it all up like uncontrollable vomit, spilling secrets into their waiting hands—the names, the plan, everything. I felt so dirty, so vile, but I couldn't stop talking.

They thanked me for my help. They said I'd proven I was committed to rehabilitation. They each shook my hand in turn and dismissed me to breakfast.

I am the shittiest human being in the world.

In a groggy haze, I pull on a new set of stretchy peels for the second trial. Thankfully, these have a stain-free crotch. Six jacks flank our line as we march through the mazelike corridors. All sporting recovering blisters and reddened skin, the contenders traipse forward in silence thick with tension. Having passed one trial, I'd have thought I'd feel more prepared for the second, but my pulse still hammers in my ears with each step.

I keep my head down, worried the jacks will sense the deception in my eyes. I hope they won't search our room while we're gone. When the nurses gave us our morning Memoria dose, a mere three hours after last night's emergency, I hid the pill under my tongue again. No one ever bothers to check me too carefully, but my heart still thudded when I showed them my mouth. After they left, I slid the wet pill into a rip in my rubber mattress, wedging it into the foam.

Two doses missed.

Forget the trials—if anyone finds the surprises hidden in my mattress, I'm dead anyway.

The jacks lead us back to the red-and-black orientation room. Allard, the other directors, and Red Hair sit in a row of black folding chairs against the wall. They surround a long table in the center of the room covered by a silky gray blanket. Protruding bumps line the surface, as if fifty uncracked walnuts rest under the sheet.

The jacks move down the ranks and unlock our chains. I rub my raw wrists, redness from the healing burns exacerbated by the cuffs. Everyone states their names and the oath before taking seats in plastic chairs opposite the directors, a good ten feet from the table. I can't help feeling like we're all guests at the world's strangest dinner party.

"Congratulations on progressing to trial two." Allard's booming voice reverberates around the room like he's address-ing spectators at a sporting event. Clad in a hideous mustard-brown pinstripe suit, he's more apelike than ever. I clench my restless fingers into tight fists, waiting for instructions.

"You have proven your strength—an extremely import-ant characteristic of those who have reformed. However, rehabilitation does not occur solely within the body, but also within the mind." He taps his skull. "Mindfulness. Intelligence. Problem-solving skills. The desire to commit crime exists within the twisted channels of your brain. If you can master control of your mind, if you can think through situations intelligently, you can overcome these urges." He thrusts his index finger in the air. "Today, we test those skills."

Red Hair rises and struts toward the table like a game show actress. She rips off the blanket in one swift motion, revealing a bright green screen and a full keyboard of buttons—the walnut bumps.

I close my eyes. Inhale, exhale. It's a big computer. Nothing scary about that.

"One at a time, you'll answer three questions on the screen," Doctor Allard continues. "Each question requires concentration and thought. Answer all three questions correctly, and you pass your trial. That's it."

What kind of questions? Math? Science? Shit, do I remember how to do those?

"What if we answer wrong?" Bex asks.

Allard winks. "Don't answer wrong."

My stomach twists into knots. That sounds all kinds of bad.

Allard sinks into his chair. Red Hair takes her seat beside him. He shoots us a phony smile and scribbles something on Red Hair's clipboard. She giggles.

Carolyn shuffles in her seat, arms folded tightly across her chest. I catch her eye and she scowls.

Back in school, we used to compete in geography bees. The teacher would ask a question, and if you got it right you stayed up for another round. If you got it wrong, you sat down and someone else would challenge the victor. I almost always made it to the final round. At the time, I thought it was the most cutthroat competition imaginable. Of course, nobody died in that one.

"A.R.-329. You're first."

All the color drains from Andrew's already pale face. His footsteps are heavy, as if cement fills his boots. My knee bounces against my hand. I'd hope a guy with Andrew's ripped muscles has equally impressive intelligence, but given the terror plastered on his face, I'm not so sure.

Part of me wants him to mess up, to see what happens. Better to know now than when it's my turn. I hate myself for thinking this way.

"Scan your hand when you're ready," Allard says.

Andrew presses his palm to the screen. It beeps and flashes yellow. The table lets out a buzz and the screen emits an eerie blue glow. I lean forward, hands on my knees.

Miles squints, trying to glimpse the question, but the table faces such an angle that it's only visible to the contestant at hand.

Andrew watches the screen for a few moments, then rams his fingers across the keyboard in a series of clicks.

The computer glows green with a *ding!* He closes his eyes and lets out a gusty breath.

"One down, two to go," Doctor Allard says, as if keeping score at a baseball game.

The screen returns to blue. Andrew's brow furrows as he reads. Within five seconds, he's back at the keyboard.

The screen buzzes and flashes red. Something clicks. Andrew yelps, clutching his neck. The skin around his collar grows tight and pink. My heart stops—his collar tightened. I watch with bated breath, waiting for it to loosen again, but it doesn't relent.

My blood turns to ice. That's the punishment for missing three answers. You don't even get the chance to take those final, fateful steps to the Green Room—you die here, gasping in a heap on the floor.

Andrew smacks the screen and a new question pops up.

My fidgeting hands grow moist in my lap.

I'll never survive this. It's impossible.

What if he screws up again? Do I have the stomach to watch him die?

Andrew's fingers click along the keyboard, producing a green screen. I can feel the collective sigh of relief from the other hacks.

The next question comes, and soon enough, another green screen.

"Congratulations, A.R.-139. You passed your second trial."

His collar loosens with a metallic click. He nods at Miles and takes his seat, grinning at the floor. Okay, it's not impossible. I can do this.

Miles approaches the table next. All I can do is sit and watch, each second crawling as I wait for my turn.

One by one, the other hacks take the screen. Carolyn and Bex each get one question wrong. Tom misses two and almost passes out. Miles and Desirae get perfect scores.

Of course—*of course*—I'm last.

By the time Allard calls my identification number, my quivering knees knock together in my seat. I can feel the smirks and stares from the safe contenders behind me as I step into the center of the room.

I'm sure Carolyn, Bex, and Desirae would love nothing more than to watch me writhing on the floor, gasping for air. Maybe they'd make popcorn to enjoy the show.

I place my palm to the scanner. It flashes yellow and beeps, then turns blue. Black letters jumble and come into focus on the screen.

The poorest of the poor have it. The richest of the rich need it. If you eat it, you die.

A timer pops onto the corner of the screen, flashing sixty. Fifty-nine. Fifty-eight.

I read the riddle carefully. Once, twice, three times. Fuck. I'm terrible at riddles.

Food? No. Honor? That can't be right. If you eat it, you die. What does that mean? Poison? Is it about emotions? Some emotion the rich have? No, you can't eat emotions.

Mindfulness. This trial is about mindfulness.

I close my eyes. There has to be an answer somewhere in my brain.

The richest of the rich. Who is the richest of the rich?

When I was a little kid, we went to a dinner party at this man's house. He owned the entire company where my mom worked as a secretary on minimum wage. He had a mansion with a pool. His daughter had more stamps in her passport than I had books on my full bookshelf.

But what did they need? I clamp my eyes tighter.

They had everything. I remember being overwhelmed with jealousy, bitterly sitting on their overstuffed black leather couch and pouting, knowing we'd never own anything like it.

They had everything. They didn't need anything.

Wait.

They didn't need anything.

The richest of the rich need nothing. The poorest of the poor have nothing. If you eat nothing, you die. That's it.

I wrench my eyes open and pound my answer into the keypad.

The screen buzzes and flashes red. My heart jumps into my throat.

How the hell was that wrong?

The metal constricts around my neck, forcing air from my lungs. I suck in a breath, but the oxygen won't come, as if a million cotton balls plug my esophagus. My eyes well with water. I pry my fingers around my collar, scratching at my skin.

The screen jumbles again, and new words come into focus:

The more I dry, the wetter I get.

What the hell? That doesn't even make sense.

The more I dry ... a lake? Is it a play on words? Something

drying . . . hair? The weather? Taunting seconds tick by on the screen. Twenty-nine . . . Twenty-eight . . .

Come on, think.

Oil? Some kind of plastic? Umbrellas? No. Nothing makes sense.

"Ten seconds!" Allard calls, snapping me out of my trance.

No. No, no, no. I need an answer. Anything.

What dries? A towel.

Towel!

The answer flows through my fingertips onto the keypad at lightning speed.

Buzz.

The screen flashes red.

My collar constricts like a boa. I tug at its fine metal edge, my lungs frantically gasping for air that won't come. Tears streak down my face, clouding my eyes.

One more wrong, and I'm dead. That's it. No more chances.

I slam my fist onto the screen. The words jumble in a swirling riddle soup. They slither into focus like writhing snakes.

My inventor doesn't want me. The man who bought me doesn't need me. And the man who needs me doesn't know it.

I don't know it. I've got nothing. I am going to die here in this room. Right now. It's over.

All I can think of is breathing. Air. I need air. I yank at my collar, but the squeezing won't relent. Allard might as well be strangling me with his bare hands, choking the life from my eyes.

Too much. It's too much.

This is it. My final moments. Die. I'm going to die. And these hacks behind me all want that—to see me gasping for my final breath. That's what they want, and they're going to get it.

No.

I can't. I can't die here.

Thirty seconds left. Half a minute until my racing heart stops beating. I gulp air like a goldfish, sucking in as much oxygen as possible.

No. Not this close to freedom. I don't want to end up dead. Buried. I can't. Stuffed in some coffin, underground, even then I won't be free.

Coffin.

Ten seconds left.

Coffin!

My sweaty fingers fumble as I pound out the letters.

C-O-F-F-I-

"Wait!"

I jump back. Six seconds. Five seconds.

Allard races toward the screen and dials something into the keypad. Two seconds left, the timer in the corner freezes. The director furrows his brows and examines the screen. Levine and Zepp rise from their chairs and follow closely behind him. They huddle around the computer, pointing and whispering as if observing a lab rat. Allard glances up at me and back to the screen. He taps the glass and pulls up a drop-down menu, digging into the computer's settings in a delicate surgery with my life hanging in the balance.

I swallow hard, but the metal pushes back against the lump.

"It's been tampered with," Allard mutters under his breath, only loud enough for us to hear.

Levine gasps.

"What do you mean?" Zepp narrows her eyes.

Allard turns to me. "E.S.-124, what were your answers to the first two questions?"

"Nothing." I force my voice to squeak past the choke in my throat. "And towel. This was coffin."

He studies the screen, scrolling up and down over tiny text and coding too quick for me to read. He lowers his voice. "It appears E.S.-124 would have had a perfect score. But for some reason," he taps the glass, "it was set to make her fail all three questions."

My eyes grow wide.

"Now, I don't want to overreact. It could just be a system glitch." He strokes his chin. "But what I don't understand is that it was only set to fail E.S.-124. None of the other contenders."

Zepp and Levine murmur to each other in hushed tones. The other contenders lean forward in their chairs, trying to eavesdrop. Allard taps numbers into the keypad. The screen flashes green and the restricting subsides. Oxygen floods my lungs. I inhale the deepest breath I can, and it's the greatest feeling in the world.

"Guards!" He snaps his fingers. "Wheel it down to my

office. We gotta run diagnostics, the whole thing is haywire." Four jacks hoist the heavy machinery, tugging multiple wires and cords that spark as they're yanked from the wall. I wait for Allard to announce to the other contenders and directors what happened, but he doesn't.

"Congratulations, E.S.-124." Doctor Allard grins wide enough to mask the worry in his eyes. "You passed your second trial."

The other contenders aren't very good actors, attempting to hide their disappointment.

I force a smile, despite the fear churning inside me. "Thank you."

But I can't focus on the fact that I passed. Someone sabotaged me. Someone wanted me to fail. Wanted me to die in this very room.

These trials just got a whole lot deadlier.

The October before I came here, I walked in on Matt Houston making out with Allie Thompson in the library. I thought that was the worst moment of my life.

It wasn't.

Director Zepp called a mandatory rank for all Level One girls from all blocks. In the middle of the day. I didn't know why—it was during group, and Zepp always drones on about how important it is for us to attend group.

She made us all line up together, shoulder to shoulder, while she patrolled up and down the aisle of hacks. Her two jack bodyguards trailed behind, glaring at anyone who dared catch their eyes. From Ronnie's jagged breaths beside me, I thought for sure she'd screwed up yet again, and they were going to call her out in front of everyone. Make her do push-ups or something.

As Zepp and the jacks marched on, I wondered what Ronnie did this time.

But it wasn't Ronnie they wanted.

The other five directors emerged from the stairwell and joined Director Zepp in the middle of the hallway. Zepp's stern gaze met mine, and the corner of her lips curled into a grin. I suddenly felt like I swallowed a whole bucket of ice.

She sent three jacks into the ranks of hacks. They yanked

Sarah, Ariadne, and Courtney from the line and dragged them to the center of the room by their hair. The biggest jack shoved Sarah to the ground so hard, her head smashed into the cement with a crack that reverberated down my spine. Her glasses shattered, sprinkling tiny shards of glass across the floor.

Ariadne yelled as Sarah hit the ground. A jack recoiled his fist and launched it into Ariadne's face, smashing her nose back into her skull. Her blood spattered the floor like rain. Courtney dropped to her knees to help the others, but a jack sunk his steel-toed boot into her stomach, and she crumpled into a ball.

This couldn't be happening. What had I done?

I knew I should do something, help them, intervene, but I couldn't. It was like my legs were frozen in place, gluing me to the floor. I couldn't believe my cowardice. A silent scream manifested and died in my throat.

The guards shoved my friends toward the line of directors. Ariadne coughed, spewing more blood across the floor.

Zepp strolled up to them, a jump in her step, an unspoken gloat reflecting in her eyes. I half expected her to do a heel click in the air, her sick little victory dance.

Startled confusion rustled through the ranks. No one knew what was going on, why this was happening.

But I did.

The jacks cuffed the girls' hands behind their backs as Zepp announced my friends' escape plan to the entire room. Muffled gasps whispered through the line. Sarah stared at the floor, her chest heaving. Ariadne sobbed, not laboring to control her volume. Courtney kept *her head down, like someone drained the life from her eyes.*

After what felt like an eternity, the jacks paraded the battered offenders through the ranks to exit our block. Sarah caught my eye as she passed, a whole slew of emotions swirling in her face: anger, fear, betrayal. Confusion. All directed at me. I was the only one from our group of four not victim to Zepp's wrath, solidifying their suspicions of my guilt. I knew what Sarah was thinking; I read it in her eyes: How could you?

When the jacks disappeared out the door with my friends, Zepp addressed the rest of us. She called this a learning opportunity, saying rehabilitation is about moments like this. All the usual bullshit.

Zepp sent us back to our respective rooms. No one spoke. Tension loomed thick over the prisoners of Block Four. Even Ronnie was silent for once, compulsively tugging and re-straightening her bedsheets.

I twiddled my fingers on my bed, waiting for someone to tell me how long my friends would be stuck in the Hole. I contemplated what I'd tell them when they got out. Would I beg? Grovel? Fall to the floor at their feet, asking them to forgive the unforgivable thing I did?

When someone finally unclicked the dead bolt, I rocketed off the bed. Director Zepp stood in the threshold of our cell, a permanent grin scribbled across her face. She instructed Ronnie and me to follow her into the hall. The other Block Four girls filtered out, too, and a jack ushered us into our ranks. Two jacks went down the lines and cuffed our hands.

They led us out the block door, through a long corridor, and down four flights of stairs. We walked for a long time, as a unified orange-clad mass. Stunned silence hung over our lines. No one dared ask why we were walking to this strange new part of the Center—or what we'd find when we got there.

Finally, we reached a steel door. The jacks shepherded us inside, cramming thirty hacks into a tight room the size of a one-car garage. Lights flickered on, revealing a long rectangular window in the wall. We pressed forward to see.

The room on the other side of the window was empty, minus three steel chairs in the back. Chipping green paint peeled off the cement walls. Somewhere beyond our view, a door rattled open. A jack entered the room, leading my handcuffed friends to the three chairs in the back. He shoved each into a seat by their shoulders.

The three perpetrators frantically surveyed the room, seeking the answers already dawning on the spectators behind the glass.

I pressed my palms to the window, a million silent pleas trapped behind my lips.

Three jacks lined up, twenty feet from my friends, but only inches from my fingers on the glass. A raspy voice crackled over the loudspeaker, but all I heard was the pounding in my ears. All I saw was their pure, unadulterated fear.

The jacks raised their slick metal rifles, and the entire world stopped moving. I couldn't breathe, couldn't comprehend.

Then the blaze of gunfire filled the air.

I fell to my knees, right there in the center of the spectator box. All the hacks around me broke into cries and shrieks. I felt like

I was going to puke. Going to pass out. Going to do something. But I didn't.

I couldn't bear to look back through the glass at the destruction I caused. At the mutilated bodies of my massacred friends.

What have I done? What have I done? What have I done? The edges of the room blurred. I sobbed into my hands, curling into a ball on the cold cement. I wanted to shrivel up and vanish. It should've been me in the Green Room—a punishment kinder than I deserve.

After an eternity, a jack came and pried me off the floor. Zepp and some jacks led us back into the hallway. Cheeks swollen and red from crying, we followed them like obedient, broken dogs. Because what could we do but obey?

Halfway back to the block, Zepp halted the lines. Smirking, she unlocked my cuffs and directed me to step out of rank.

I knew what was going to happen before it did.

She thanked me for my service and commitment to rehabilitation. In front of everyone. She announced that for my courage, I'd been promoted to Level Two, and she presented me with my new gray peels. I blinked back a fresh curtain of tears, not daring to meet the hacks' eyes. A jack led me out the door to the Level Two corridor. I didn't need to look back to feel the hateful glares and disgust written on the faces of the hacks who shared my former block. The girls who used to be my friends.

Morning comes quick. For the first time in days, I wake up with a rumbling stomach. The other girls yawn and stumble out of bed, mumbling to one another. I hover by the door eagerly awaiting our morning tray.

It doesn't come.

Carolyn scoffs. "Where the hell is breakfast?"

"I . . . I don't know." I creak open the door and peek into the hallway. It's deserted. I press my fingers to my collar, my neck still sore from yesterday.

The jacks and nurses come to take our blood and give us pills, but say nothing about our breakfast. Our cups contain barely a mouthful of water to swallow the Memoria, which I hide under my tongue. The half sip doesn't nearly quench my thirst. I wait for the others to speak up about breakfast, but they salute in silence until the visitors leave.

At six, we head into the hall and meet our escort jack. I half expect him to be holding trays of bananas and oatmeal, but he has nothing except a fistful of cuffs to shackle us.

We merge with Andrew, Miles, and Tom and shuffle down the hall. I'm anticipating another visit to the ominous orientation room, but we take a right down a different corridor instead.

Nerves twist in my belly—or maybe it's hunger? I overanalyze every detail, scouring for signs of my would-be murderer. Hypervigilance prickles the hairs down my neck. Was it a director? Another contender? A guard?

The jack stops abruptly at a set of double doors. He scans his forefinger into the keypad. The doors swing open. "Welcome to the Stephens' Center Banquet Hall."

I can't hold back my gasp.

Before us sits the most elegant wooden table I've ever seen, topped with every imaginable food. My mouth waters at the chicken, mashed potatoes, lobster, corn, cookies, pancakes, steak, salad, apples, stew, soda, and just about everything else lying on display in the center of the room. A smorgasbord of savory aromas swirls through my nostrils. I clench my teeth, forcing my eyes away from the feast. I haven't eaten real food in two years.

Is this some kind of reward? It has to be a test. The spacious rectangular room isn't too far out of the ordinary for the Center, with the same cement walls and tiled floor.

There's no sign of Allard or Levine or anyone. Just this massive feast, laid out like the grandest Thanksgiving dinner I've ever attended. Is this part of the trial? Where are the directors? They haven't missed a trial yet.

We can't eat until they arrive. That's probably their goal, forcing us to stand beside this feast after being denied breakfast this morning and real food for years, then making us wait. Maybe they're watching from somewhere, laughing at our grumbling stomachs. That must be part of the third trial—testing good manners or some bullshit.

Carolyn must sense it, too, because her mouth thins to a line across her face. Miles folds his arms across his chest, making an obvious effort to look at anything but the food. Clearly I'm not the only one in pain right now.

"Hell. Yes," Bex mutters.

"Enjoy your feast," the jack snaps.

Desirae glowers at me, and I'm struck with a sudden urge to beg the guard not to go. But I don't, and he does. The doors slam behind him, followed by the distinct click of the dead bolt locking shut. I shuffle my feet, unease slinking through my body the second we're alone.

Andrew, Miles, and Tom take the opportunity to officially introduce themselves to the girls. I don't expect them to acknowledge me, but it still stings when Andrew walks right past me to greet Carolyn. Nice to know my reputation has found its way to the guys' blocks too.

"What is it?" Miles circles the table. "What's the point?"

"A reward before the trial starts?" Tom suggests.

"But why?" Andrew says. "That makes no sense. Why leave us here alone?"

"Maybe the directors are joining us." Desirae counts the seats. "There's room for at least a couple more people."

"I don't like this," Carolyn says.

We all watch the table like it's simultaneously the best Christmas present ever and a bomb ready to explode.

"Maybe we should sit?" Tom pulls out a seat at the head of the table. Everyone follows his lead, chair legs screeching against the tile as we take our seats.

Bex and Miles sit on my left and right. I stiffen as Bex's elbow knocks into mine. Why does she have to sit right next to me? At least Desirae and Carolyn are at the other end of the table.

A white china bowl sits on top of a fancy plate in front of me. Little gold roses adorn the rim. A glass goblet and a set of fine silverware with way too many forks frame the plate. On top of the place setting rests a pristine white napkin folded in the shape of a swan. I carefully unfold it and spread it across my lap. They probably want to see if we'll lose control and act like animals the moment we're someplace nice. My hands fidget in my lap.

I survey the room. A door in the back seems to lead to a small bathroom. On the right wall, a white analog clock ticks every second in time with my heartbeat. In the top left corner, a red light on a security camera blinks. Watching us.

I swallow hard. What are they hoping to see?

"How long do we have to wait?" Desirae asks.

"They better hurry up," Andrew murmurs. "I'm starving."

The smell of roasted chicken floats through the air. I inhale as deeply as I can, relishing the scent to sustain my hunger with imagination. Steam wafts from the hot food, and my belly lets out another yearning grumble. I don't care how early in the morning it is—I'm hungry, and this feast looks amazing. I've gotten so used to cafeteria gruel, my mouth almost can't fathom the taste of real food.

Whoever else is coming, I hope they hurry up and join us. I can't stare at this feast much longer. My stomach rips out a loud gurgle.

Maybe this isn't part of the trial at all. Maybe Allard will feast with us and explain the third trial as we eat. That wouldn't be so bad. At least my stomach would shut up.

Bex glances left to right, then plucks a grape off the nearest stem and pops it into her mouth.

"What are you doing?" I whisper under my breath.

"What does it look like I'm doing?" She snags another grape. "I'm fucking hungry."

Miles and Andrew glance at each other, their fingers clearly itching to copy her. My eyes dart up to the camera, blinking down at us.

"Maybe we're supposed to start," Tom says. But he doesn't reach for the serving spoon wedged into the mashed potatoes in front of him.

Bex sneaks a slice of cheese off a platter to her left, stuffing it into her mouth like a chipmunk. "Sounds right to me."

"You're not supposed to start yet," I whisper.

"Says who? The jack told us to enjoy the feast." She rolls her eyes. "I'm enjoying the feast."

"I really don't think we should." Carolyn drums her fingers against her thighs. "There's got to be more to it. They wouldn't just leave us in here. What's today's trial again?"

"Three," Andrew answers.

"No. What's the theme? The third principle?"

Bex has given up on being covert at this point. She shoves an entire eggroll into her mouth in one bite. "So fucking good."

Self-control, I answer in my head. But how would they test—

My stomach drops. "Bex. Wait a second. I don't think you should—"

"Shut up, slinger." She reaches over me, greedily eyeing the plate of fudge brownies. "No one cares what you think."

Desirae laughs, and I slink down in my seat. But Bex's hand freezes mid reach. Something in her face changes.

Desirae narrows her eyes. "Bex? What's wrong?"

Bex stops chewing and wets her lips. Her eyebrows lower. She cocks her head to the side, as if deep in thought.

"Bex?" Tom rests his hand on her arm. "Rebecca? You all right?"

She doesn't reply.

Miles leans closer, his hands flared out on the tabletop. "Bex?"

Bex's eyes grow wide. All the color drains from her already pale face. She presses a hand to her stomach and nearly falls over herself pushing away from the table.

"Bex!" Carolyn rushes to her side. "Holy shit!"

Bex doubles over. Her hacking cough echoes around the tiny room.

"It's poison!" Andrew shouts. Everyone jumps up from their seats as if their legs are springs. But I can't move. All I can do is watch, my mouth hanging open, my butt planted to the chair.

A red tinge spreads across Bex's face. She retches, slowly turning a sickly shade of purple. Spit spews down her chin. Veins glow red in her eyes and track blue webs beneath her pale skin. Her body convulses with heaving breaths. She stumbles, nearly falling into Carolyn but collapsing to the floor instead, her brown hair fanning across the other contender's legs. With a final sharp intake of breath, Bex's body goes still.

An eerie silence blankets the room. Carolyn hesitantly presses a shaking hand over her mouth. "Holy shit."

Miles dry heaves. "I'm gonna be sick." He sprints to the bathroom at the back of the room and slams the door.

My body goes numb. I can't look away from Bex's glassy, red eyes, as if she's still staring into my soul.

"Fucking trial." Andrew kicks the wooden table leg.

A bowl of flan on the surface jiggles at the impact.

A couple of jacks burst into the room to remove Bex's lifeless body.

"So that's the third trial?" Tom calls at them. "Just sit here, starving, and don't eat anything?"

The guards dump Bex's corpse onto a gurney and haul her from the room without so much as grunting a response. They click the dead bolt behind them, leaving us alone with the table of tainted food and the ghost of a fallen contender.

"Well, shit," Carolyn mumbles. "So much for breakfast."

We amble around the table in silence for a while, watching the platters with a unified sense of disgust. The taunting food aromas make my stomach roll.

Part of me is thankful for Bex's impulsivity. If she hadn't gone right for the food, how long would it have taken me to cave and sample some myself? I shiver at the thought.

"Mors vincit omnia," Tom says softly.

Andrew's brow wrinkles. "What the hell is that?"

"It's Latin." Tom's ears turn pink. "I took it in school. It means death always wins."

Andrew shakes his head. "Should be the motto of this fucking prison."

I close my eyes, letting their words wash over me.

Maybe the trials will claim us all.

//

Andrew, Desirae, and Carolyn drag their chairs to the side of the room, putting distance between themselves and the tainted food. They huddle together, their hushed voices echoing incoherent buzzing sounds around the room. It's kind of messed up how fast everyone moved on from Bex's death. I guess that's just par for the course here. Still, I wish I could hear what they're saying.

Miles heads into the bathroom for a few minutes and returns covertly holding what looks like a stretchy black tank top. "I didn't sleep at all last night, man," he mumbles at Tom, tugging at his peels. "Gonna pass the fuck out for the whole trial."

Tom nods at the fabric in Miles' hand. "What's that?"

Miles hesitates. "My chest binder."

"What's a chest binder?"

"It's . . . I wear it. I'm . . . trans." Miles fidgets. "But I'm not supposed to sleep with it on."

Tom looks taken aback, but shrugs. "Oh. That's cool, man. I wish I was tired enough to sleep through this bullshit."

"Wake me up if anything happens."

Miles curls up on the tile floor, facing the wall. Maybe he's onto something with his sleep-through-the-trial strategy. Maybe he'll wake up and it'll all be over.

Tom crouches alone on the floor at the other end of the room. Releasing a bored huff, he scrubs his hand through his dark hair. It crosses my mind to go talk to him—of all the contenders, Tom and Miles seem the least likely to pummel me—but I'd rather not draw attention to myself. I wish I were used to the loneliness by now, but it still hurts. So I sit alone and space out instead.

I don't know how much time passes before Andrew plops down on the seat beside me. I startle, jerking up my head. I've never spent any time with him before. Weird that he left his party with Desirae and Carolyn to come sit with me.

His biceps bulge through his tight white peels, and I'm guessing there's a six-pack hidden under there too. Okay, I'll say it—he's hot.

"You're Evelyn, right?"

"Um. Yeah. You're Andrew?"

He nods.

I keep my eyes in my lap, but I can feel his gaze raking up and down my body. It makes me fidget.

"Can I ask you a question?"

"Um, sure." I rotate to face him. "What's up?"

Across the room, Carolyn and Desirae's conversation lowers to silence. They crane their necks in my direction. Their attention makes me bristle.

Something's up.

Andrew's mouth curls upward. He leans closer to me and perches his elbows on his knees, chin on his hands. "Why'd you do it?"

I glance at the girls in the corner, then back to Andrew. "Do what?"

"Get those three slug girls killed."

My chest tightens. Oh. That. "It wasn't my fault. I didn't . . . do it on purpose."

"Well, you ratted them out. So, technically, you did do it purposely."

Carolyn and Desirae huddle closer together, whispering furiously and watching me from the corners of their eyes. Tom nudges Miles, who props himself up on his elbows. My ears burn. Everyone wants to watch the show.

"I didn't exactly have a choice."

He snorts. "There's always a choice."

"Not in this case."

"I beg to differ."

"That's your opinion, then." I fold my arms across my chest and turn to the side. "You weren't there. You don't understand what happened."

"Tell me honestly." Andrew leans back into my line of vision. "Were you just looking for an easy way out? Skip a few steps, become a Level Two, even if it meant becoming a slinger and killing three people?"

I raise my brows. "Wouldn't you find a way out if you could?"

"Not like that. Not putting my fucking level before three hacks' lives."

"Well, I didn't know, okay? It wasn't my fault. Zepp lied to me. I wouldn't have told if I knew that was gonna happen. That they were gonna . . . gonna . . ."

"Are you that stupid?" He raises his voice. "Thought

your so-called friends were gonna get a slap on the wrist and then back to normal? Get away with it unscathed?"

I don't answer. I have nothing to say.

He narrows his eyes. "If you weren't suffering through the trials with the rest of us, I'd have thought for sure you were a plant."

"I'm not a—"

"No. You're not a plant." He stands up. "You're just a bitch. Y'all were right!" he calls to the group. "This one's a big slinging asshole. No remorse at all. Don't trust slingers. Never have, never will." He kicks me hard in the shin. I flinch but force myself not to make a sound louder than a grunt. I won't give him the satisfaction.

My assailant strolls back toward the others, who nearly fall over themselves hooting and laughing. Heat radiates from my cheeks.

Four and a half trials to go.

///

Several hours pass. How long are they going to keep us in here? Miles scoots over to join the clique but rests his chin on his knees and closes his eyes once more. Wild laughter from the corner dies into occasional buzzing, and the group wilts slightly against the wall. Carolyn lets out a lofty sigh that carries around the room. Desirae drapes herself over Andrew in an obvious attempt to flirt.

I shift my weight around, my butt growing sore against the hard chair. As uncomfortable as I am sitting still, I don't risk standing and drawing attention to myself. The others seem to have taken a hiatus from harassing me, and I'd prefer to keep it that way. With all their yawning and sighing from apparent boredom, I bet tormenting me would be a fun and distracting activity for them.

My eyes catch a silver bowl filled to the brim with red-and-white peppermint candies. They're surely coated in some horrible poison, but I still smile.

Back home, we always had a bowl of peppermints on the kitchen table. Neither my mom nor I ate them regularly, but they were always there.

When my mom started dating again, gentlemen in varying stages of hair loss started coming over, vying for Mom's affection. Voluptuous and naturally glowing, my mother is one of those middle-aged women who perpetually looks twenty-five. Some people assume she and my aunt Lily are the same age, despite Lily being nineteen years younger than her and only six years older than me.

Mom dated this one guy, Max, for about six months. He had a beer gut and a toothbrush mustache. I liked Max the most. On their first date, he brought me a dollar-store bag of peppermint candies. While I wasn't a huge candy eater, I was a huge supporter of getting presents. Seeping with glee, I poured the candies into the biggest bowl I could find and left it on the center of the kitchen table. Every few days, my mom or I would pluck one from the bowl, and Max would have to replenish our stash on the weekends.

They broke up after several months. I'm not sure why, but one day, Max stopped coming over. Mom still got up for work every day with a smile on her face, as if nothing was wrong. She continued refilling the candy bowl on weekends, even without Max's help.

So there it was, every day from when I was eight years old until I was fifteen and came here. A big bowl of individually wrapped peppermint candies. No matter whether it was a good month or a bad month, whether my mom's overtime paychecks were overflowing or nonexistent, the peppermint bowl persisted.

I run my finger across the smooth bowl surface, vowing that the moment I get back home, I'll indulge in a mint or two. I'm so busy daydreaming, I don't notice the shadows creeping up behind me until one speaks.

"You hungry, slinger?"

Carolyn, Desirae, and Andrew encircle my chair, cornering me against the table.

My shoulders tense. "No."

"Why don't you take a big bite?" Desirae sticks her finger into the mashed potatoes and flicks a glob at me. No longer steaming, the cold food plops onto my sleeve. I wipe my arm on my pant leg. My heart thuds for a moment, but nothing happens. The poison must only work if you swallow it.

"No, thanks."

"You know, we could make you eat it," Desirae says.

I inhale a shaky breath. "I won't do it."

"Hold the mudslinger's mouth open. I'll funnel it all in," Andrew says. The others giggle.

"You know, that's not a bad idea." Carolyn saunters around me. "Big last meal for the slinger."

"Don't touch me, Carolyn." I clench my fists in my lap.

"It's three against one, what're you gonna do?" Desirae asks, a silky-sweet tone to her voice. "Gonna run your mouth again and send us to the Green Room?"

"I—"

"I don't remember Allard giving us any rules for this trial." Andrew smirks. "Didn't say anything about not hurting the slinger."

"Leave me alone. All of you." My heart races. They couldn't . . . could they?

I watch the camera in the corner, a silent plea for help.

Desirae whispers something to Carolyn, who bursts out laughing. "You know what, that would be funny."

My arms tighten. "Don't touch me."

Carolyn whispers to Andrew, whose mouth stretches into a wide Cheshire cat grin. Against the wall, Tom squints at us and cocks his head. At first I think he's going to help me, but he slinks back down and closes his eyes. Miles's grumbling snores break the silence, solidifying what I already knew; I'm completely alone. Me against them.

I swallow hard, pressing my hands to my lap to keep them

from shaking. I scan the table for weapons: stew, potatoes, chicken; food everywhere, but no knives or forks. Thank God.

They can't attack me. Not in front of the cameras.

"You know," Andrew says, "if you're gonna act like a dirty, mudslinging bitch, maybe you should look the part."

He digs his hands into a nearby bowl, emerging with fistfuls of brown beef stew. "Open wide, slinger." He smooshes it into my peels, smearing glop all down my front.

"Don't forget the mashed potatoes." Desirae flings a handful at me, pelting me in the chest. I swat at her, but Andrew grabs my ponytail with his stew-coated hands, yanking me backward.

"Stop!" I brush my hands down my front, trying in vain to remove the food. "You're gonna get in trouble."

"Why?" Carolyn flicks bits of macaroni and cheese at me. "You gonna tattle on me?"

"Levine's not here to save you now," Andrew says.

"Dirty snitching slinger!"

"Hold her down!"

I try to stand but Andrew pins my shoulders, holding me in the chair. Desirae and Carolyn run up and down the table, giggling and grabbing whatever they can. Food splats me from every angle, drenching me and staining my white peels. Desirae chucks an apple, which smashes into my arm.

"Stop! Please stop!" I press up against Andrew's vice-like grip with all my strength. He pushes down harder, laughing.

"You deserve worse, slinger."

"She looks like a watercolor painting." Desirae pelts me with blueberry pie. "Don't you like art, slinger?"

"You brought this on yourself," Carolyn says. "Oh look, soup!" I fling out my arms to shield my head, but Carolyn's too quick, dumping the bowl and dousing me in tomato soup.

I yelp and bury my face in the crook of my elbow, mashing my lips shut so no poison can seep into my mouth.

Finally, Andrew relents, shoving me down and releasing my shoulders. I sink to the floor and curl into a ball under the chair, but the attacks don't stop. Applesauce rains down on my head. They pitch casseroles, potato salad, buttery peas, lobster tails dripping in oil, everything they can find, soaking me to the bone. Sticky bits and crumbs glue themselves to my peels, congealing in my hair. There's nothing I can do but lie in the fetal position and force the tears not to pour out. Finally they pull back, hands dripping, doubled over with laughter.

Every inch of my body is soaked in soup and sauce I can't eat. Tears sting my eyes as I wring ketchup out of my sleeve. I paw at my stained peels, wondering if I'll get new ones or be stuck in these for the next four trials.

Carolyn mimics me, pretending to cower behind her hands.

They're not reformed. They're assholes. I'm better than that, and I'll show them.

Mustering every last ounce of dignity I can manage, I pull myself up, feet sloshing in my soaked boots. Crumbs tumble from my lap onto the floor.

"Oh hey, she's up." Carolyn bounds toward me. "You want seconds?"

I brush straight past her, keeping my head up. Their cackles follow me to the other end of the room. I walk as gracefully as I can, chin raised, still dripping.

Miles jerks awake and cocks his head. "What'd I miss?"

"Fun new game," Desirae says. "Wanna try?"

Carolyn breaks down laughing. "It's called Slinger Splat!"

I let their words drift over me.

Tom glances at me from his seat on the floor. For a second, I catch a glimpse of pity in his eyes, but I keep walking.

I enter the bathroom, push the door closed, and click the lock. The moment I'm alone, I relax.

Solitude. Why didn't I do this in the first place?

I don't want to see them. Any of them. Ever again. They're monsters.

I slump to the cement floor and the tears break free. I'll stay here, right here in this bathroom, until the trial ends. Wait it out. I'd be nuts to go back out there with them, anyway, so they can invent more fun ways to torture me. The lingering scent of food on my clothes tantalizes me, leaving behind a wave of nausea when I remember it's deadly. I clutch my aching belly.

I'm safe now. At least for this trial. Then three down, four to go, and freedom.

Albeit cramped, the bathroom is a fine hideaway for

one person. There's a single shower stall, a toilet, and a small closet. I rip open the closet door to find several fresh sets of peels.

I tear off my ruined peels and get in the shower, scrubbing every last bit of poisoned macaroni salad and tainted buffalo sauce off my skin. A couple of noodles slither out of my hair and down the drain. Feeling the water drench my skin is agonizing when I haven't drank anything in hours, but I don't dare risk it. It would be just like the directors to taint the shower water too.

I pat myself dry, free of food and humiliation, and pull on a fresh set of peels. I use my wet towel to scrub the remaining bits of food off the floor, then close the toilet lid and take a seat.

Much better.

I twist my wet hair into a bun and lean my elbows against my knees, letting my mind wander.

I've been off Memoria for two days now. The potent pill's effects must be starting to wane, although I expect it will take time, given I've been on it steadily for over two years. The longer you're on the pill, the harder it is to bounce back. They say after the five-year probation period after release, you don't have to keep taking the pills—the memories are gone.

Several hours pass, during which I count back and forth to one hundred about forty times to keep my mind active. I count grout lines and cracks in the tiles, and every square in the drop ceiling. I analyze and dissect each miniscule detail of the hallway dream until my brain goes fuzzy from thinking too much. I'm in the middle of reciting random song lyrics forward and backward in my head, when—

Bam bam bam.

"Open up, slinger, I gotta go!" Carolyn's voice rings through the door. She bangs again, the sound echoing through my solace. I clamp my fingers around the closed toilet seat beneath me. "Unlock the door!"

It dawns on me: I hold control over the single bathroom. A grin explodes across my face.

"Sorry, I'm busy," I shout back. "Guess you'll have to pee on the floor."

She raps again. "Open the door right now, you sick, twisted little shit."

I ignore her.

"Open the fucking door," Desirae's voice joins Carolyn's, slamming what I imagine are fists into the metal.

"God, I'm so hungry," Carolyn says, presumably to Desirae. "Let me in, slinger! I need the bathroom!"

"Guess you shouldn't have attacked me," I call through the door. "My, how the tables have turned."

More pounding. *You wanna play? I can play too.*

"If you don't open the door, you're gonna regret it, slinger," Andrew says. "I'll beat you to a pulp."

"That isn't very good motivation for me to come out."

"Shut it, slinger! Open up!"

What sounds like several pairs of hands pound into the door like angry percussionists. I lean back on the toilet and shake my head.

"Seriously Evelyn, I'm gonna kill you," Carolyn says. "I have to piss."

"Now, those threats aren't the words of someone who is reformed, are they, Carolyn? Andrew? I'll have to tell the directors your rehabilitation failed—"

"I have to pee!" she screams, pounding harder.

"There's a big floor out there, take your pick of spots." I twist a couple stray hairs around my fingers. "No one's stopping you."

Someone body-rams the door, and the whole frame shakes. For a second, I shiver, wondering how strong steel really is, but it doesn't budge.

"Funny, you sure are brave when you're hiding behind a door, slinger."

She's got a point. But I'll take any upper hand I can get.

"Have fun cowering in there, slinger. Wait till we're out of this trial. You won't have anyone to save you, and you've got to come out of there sometime."

"I don't have to come out till the trial's over, Desirae. As you all kindly reminded me, there are no rules in this game."

Silence.

I startle as one final fist slams into the metal. Someone on the other side swears, presumably from injuring his or her hand.

I sink back down, fold my arms across my chest, and prepare for a long standoff.

This is the last day they get to screw with me.

//

EVELYN SUMMERS: PRISONER E.S.–124
REHABILITATION DIARY
DAY 112

I'm burned. Literally. It's like the worst sunburn ever, only without the sun part. I want to rip my skin off. Ariana Cooper keeps saying she's going to dump a bottle of red Gatorade over my head because it'll match my skin tone. Then everyone laughs at me. You'd think Level Ones, Twos, and Threes wouldn't want to crowd together in a desegregated mass in the cafeteria. But I guess ganging up to mock me, the resident slinger, brings hacks of all sorts together. I'm so glad I have that effect on everyone. Today they chanted "medium rare" as I carried my tray to my empty table in the back. Ha ha. Very funny. I'm burned and red. It's hilarious.

I don't even know why this is happening. I guess it's my fault. All I wanted to do was take a shower, wash the dirt from floor-scrubbing duty off my knees, and go to bed. But of course, Director Hannon assigned me to third showers, and several girls were already in the bathroom when I arrived. One was bent over the sink, washing her hair.

Chatter and laughter filled the room, but the moment they saw me, they stopped talking. I mean, why would they want me to hear their conversation? I'm the slinger. The snitch. The asshole.

I stripped off my towel, not meeting their eyes, and proceeded to the farthest shower. The other girls promptly gathered their things and left. Sink girl still had soap in her hair. That's how despicable I am. She'd rather deal with clumpy hair than be anywhere near me.

Or so I thought. I waited until they were gone before I let myself cry and decided some privacy wasn't the worst thing in the world. I don't blame them for hating me—I hate me too.

All of a sudden, every toilet in the bathroom simultaneously flushed. I was washing suds off my armpits when the water pressure cut in half. I blinked up at the showerhead, wondering what happened, when scalding spray sputtered all over my shoulders and face.

I yelped and leaped out of the shower gasping for air, just in time to hear giggling and pattering footsteps.

That's when I noticed my towel was gone.

Because if giving me second-degree burns wasn't enough, now they wanted to humiliate me.

Tears mingled with the shower water and shampoo dripping down my face. Soaking wet, barefoot, burned, and stark naked, I traipsed back into the Level Two corridor, pressing one arm over my boobs and the other over my crotch. Six jacks lined the halls, taking the opportunity to rake their eyes up and down my naked body. Which is super gross, because they're, like, forty.

Cell doors creaked open and giggles erupted at the sight of the naked slinger. Cheeks burning as red as my shoulders, I sprinted to the end of the hall, where Director Hannon glared daggers at me for causing a commotion.

AND, if that wasn't the perfect day, guess who progressed to Level Two? Ronnie Hartman. My evil former roommate. I'm sure it won't be long before she meets my bathroom friends, and then they can all join the fun and torture me together.

That's it. I'm not showering for a month.

My tongue is rough as sandpaper by morning. At least, I think it's morning. I lick my lips, hoping for moisture, but nothing comes. My mouth is a desert. So thirsty.

I'm crouching in the corner of my bathroom hideaway when voices fill the room beyond the door. I press my ear to the metal just in time to hear footsteps clacking toward my lair.

Bam bam bam.

"Evelyn, it's Director Levine." Her curt voice penetrates the thick layer of steel. "Your trial's over. It's noon."

Relief washes over me. I wobble to my feet and force my arm, which grew surprisingly weak from a couple days' fasting, to yank open the door.

The director pops her head into the room and raises her brows. "Well, E.S.-124, I'm impressed. You always were resourceful."

"Sorry, ma'am. I didn't mean to take the jumpsuit hanging in here. My old one was, um—"

"I know what happened," she says, with the slightest glimmer of sympathy. "I'm afraid they didn't technically break any rules—as you probably realized, the only rule was to not eat the food. But I don't blame you for wanting to be alone in here. We'll have your old uniform washed, but you can keep the spare one for now."

I follow her back into the banquet hall where a puddle of urine festers in the corner, permeating the room with a biting odor.

Serves them right.

Clenching her teeth tight enough to shatter them, Carolyn narrows her eyes when I exit the bathroom. Director Levine calls everyone into the hall, where the other directors join her in a clump. The mingled stench of body odor, sweat, and piss hits me like a wall as I approach the other contenders. It's like someone dragged a mound of dirty socks through the sewer, then left them out to bake in the sun. My nose crinkles.

Red Hair passes bottled water to each of us, and I gulp mine back in three swigs.

"Congratulations, contenders," Doctor Allard says, in his eternally jovial voice. "You all passed your third trial."

Every hack smiles at him but scowls at me the moment he looks away.

You're dead, Desirae mouths, the inseam of her pant leg tainted with a suspicious wet stain. I fidget, not daring to look at the others.

"That was quite a show in there." Allard beams. "We've been taking shifts watching the footage."

I rub my forehead. Great.

"You have a busy day tomorrow at trial four. So for now, rest up. If you'll return to your rooms, you'll find lunch plates and more water waiting for you."

The others shove past me toward the waiting jacks, luckily too enticed by the promise of food to do anything worse. I take a deep breath, dreading facing Carolyn's and Desirae's wrath in our isolated room, when Director Levine steps forward.

"E.S.-124, I'd like a word."

I pivot, mid-step. "Yes, ma'am."

A jack approaches with a pair of handcuffs clanking at the ready, but Levine shakes her head. "That won't be necessary."

Head down, I follow her past the other contenders, who don't dare attempt to touch me as the jack shackles their ankles. I trail behind the director in silence, the hollow pit in my belly growing with each step.

Wherever we're going better have food.

We round a corner and the familiar aroma of lemon-scented cleaning chemicals swarms my nose. A slew of slugs in orange peels crouch on their hands and knees, scrubbing the cement floor with sudsy brushes. Levine steps around them, dodging through the throng of Level Ones, her black pumps leaving wet footprints on the freshly mopped surface.

The notorious elevator shines ahead, a metal jewel encrusted in the cement wall. The single jack who monitors this hallway struts back and forth, guarding the elevator's massive doors. Levine makes a beeline for him. I carefully slalom around slippery puddles of cleaning solution to keep up.

Embedded in the wall beside the elevator is a flat computer screen no larger than a license plate and a black numbered keypad. Levine approaches the elevator doors, and as if tripped by a sensor, the giant threshold parts. I hesitate, but the director motions for me to step inside.

Ten-foot-tall mirrors surround us, plastering the space with a million reflections of my spandex-clad body. White lights line the edges where the walls meet the ceiling, illuminating the entire area when multiplied by the mirrors. It's eerily akin to a carnival fun house.

The jack watches from the hallway, tilting his head in an unspoken question. I half expect the elevator to instantly launch upward toward the surface, but the doors stay open and the platform remains firmly on the ground.

"Have you ever seen this elevator from the inside, E.S.-124?" A million reflections of Director Levine watch me squirm.

"No, ma'am. The elevator is off limits to prisoners, ma'am."

"I know. But I'm not too concerned about bringing you here. Any idea why?"

I scan the smooth wall, reigning in my desire to stroke

the surface—a cold, smooth mirror with nothing else on it.

"There are no buttons, ma'am. No way to move it up or down."

"Exactly." She peeks into the hall. "Morris, can you bring us up?"

I freeze.

Up?

The jack swipes his ID down the keypad like a credit card. A metal screen slides across the doorway with a clatter. He taps the buttons and the heavy steel doors glide shut, sealing us inside.

The floor beneath us jolts and begins to rise. My fingers brush the hard mirror behind me.

"This elevator can only be operated from the outside. It was designed specifically for our facility." A smile creeps across the director's tight face. "As you may have heard through the grapevine, it is the only entrance and exit in and out of the Stephens' Center." She taps the mirror with her long fingernails, tracing the outline of her reflection on the glass. "Without a guard controlling the elevator from the hallway, escape is impossible. Hence, we've never had a single successful breakout."

"Yes, ma'am."

My stomach sinks. So their plan wouldn't have worked anyway. The Stephens' Center has one way in and no way out.

She crosses her arms. "The only reason I'm telling you this is because I don't want you to get any ideas. This is a one-time thing, and attempting to access this elevator again prior to your release will result in your death, and that is a promise. You are so close to your freedom already. Do not try it."

I swallow. "Yes, ma'am."

Seriously, why is she showing me this? I've never heard of anyone stepping foot inside this elevator, and now she's taking me for a joyride in it—for shits and giggles?

"I'm trusting you, E.S.-124." Levine clasps her hands behind her back. "Do not break that trust."

The elevator jerks to a halt with a *ding!* I wobble, steadying myself against the wall and leaving fingerprint streaks across the mirror.

The doors slide open with a metallic grating noise. Director Levine steps out into the darkness, tripping another sensor that floods the room with fluorescent light. Cement, wooden panels, and dusty shelves surround us, as if we arrived in an old basement.

With a rumble, the basement wall slides upward like a garage door. I step back. A sliver of natural light licks my boots, then stretches up my body.

My breath hitches in my throat. I shield my eyes with my hand, blinking furiously as the sunlight—actual sunlight!—meets my retinas.

Levine steps outside. "Come here." She snaps her fingers and points to the ground beside her like she's commanding a dog.

I follow her through the wide, square opening—outside,

into the wild, the sunlight, the beautiful place I haven't seen in years.

We stand at the crest of a cracking driveway, leading to who knows where, shaded by the branches of towering pine trees that line the decrepit road. The building from which we emerged appears as innocuous as a household garage. No one would guess the strange wooden structure is a fortress housing an elevator portal to an underground juvenile prison. Even seeing it with my own eyes, it's still weird as hell.

Sarah was right. There's no barbed wire, no fence, no guard tower, nothing. It seems an awfully weak defense for a prison, but no one's ever escaped, so maybe they're on to something.

For a moment, I forget how hungry I am. My squinting eyes absorb the natural light they've been denied for over two years. I inhale the fresh air, savoring the scent of natural pine that doesn't come from a cleaning chemical. Sunlight warms my arms, yet goose bumps still prickle down them. I thrust my palms up, soaking in as much light as possible. Overcome with happiness, I long to dance, twirl, scream with joy.

Freedom. This is what it feels like. This is what it looks like.

Levine clears her throat, her face upturned to enjoy a dose of sunlight of her own. An impulse shoots through me while her attention's turned. I could push by her and bolt into the woods. I'm a strong runner, I could—

"When you complete your trials, we'll escort you to the surface, through this very elevator," Levine says. I snap back to reality. Guilt for my criminal thoughts burns across my cheeks.

"It's nice to feel the sunlight, isn't it?" She inhales a deep breath of fresh air and releases it with a gust. "You may not realize it, but being underground all the time isn't always fun for the staff either."

I catch her eye and sense a glint of something there. Something human and real.

A gunshot blasts somewhere in the distance. I jump back, hand over my heart. We dart our eyes toward the sound.

"Okay, E.S.-124, time to go back." Levine herds me toward the garage with her outstretched arm.

So soon? "Y-yes, ma'am." I trudge back toward the elevator, dragging my boots across the cracked asphalt. I want to plant my feet into the ground and never leave, but I force myself to follow Levine back into the garage.

The overhead door slowly descends, and the vast sunlight thins to a wedge, a sliver, then nothing, trapping me once again in a world of darkness. My empty stomach cramps with a yearning that can't be quenched with food.

Levine calls to the jack with her hand radio, and the elevator shakes to life. We lower back into the depths of my personal hell.

"D-Director?" I keep my eyes glued to my drooping reflection in the mirror.

"Yes, E.S.-124?"

"Why'd you take me here?"

Levine sighs. "I don't know. You had a rough day. I thought you needed some fresh air." She shrugs, shifting her weight between her feet.

Her logic perplexes me. I've had a lot of rough days, and I could have used fresh air every day for the past seven hundred plus.

"But why didn't you cuff me? What if I tried to run?" The words burst from my mouth before I can stop them. I step back, hoping Levine doesn't punish me for rudeness.

The elevator slams to a halt, and the doors wrench open, dumping us back in the lemon-scented glory of this hellhole. The walls close in around me, and I swallow back the urge to cry.

Levine rests a hand on my shoulder and smiles. "Because I know you, E.S.-124. You're a good girl." She strides back into the hall. "I knew you wouldn't."

///

Two jacks handcuff me and lead me back to my quarters. After a grueling five-minute walk, during which my grumbling stomach broke the uncomfortable silence multiple times, they unclick my cuffs and leave me stranded in the contender hallway alone.

My hand hesitates over the doorknob to our room. Are Carolyn and Desirae waiting inside, eager to beat me to a pulp? I linger, but my empty belly wins. I take a deep breath and push open the door, unprepared to face the wrath of my cellmates.

Carolyn lies on her bed, the remains of her demolished

lunch discarded beside her. She catches my eye and smirks, dropping a second clean plate on top of the first with a clank.

"Where's my lunch?" I ask.

She grins. "It was delicious."

I close my eyes and inhale a quivery breath. "You ate my lunch? I haven't eaten in two days, and you ate my lunch?"

She shoots me a phony pout. "Guess you'll have to wait till dinner."

Why? Why, why, why? Why can't they leave me alone?

I ball my hands into shaking fists. "You know, you're just—"

Desirae strolls into the room in clean peels, her black hair wet from the shower. Before I can stop it, her fist plows into my nose with a crack that fogs my eyes with water. I yelp and double over, blood leaking into my fingers.

"What the—"

"That's for not letting me piss," she says. "And if I get a bladder infection, you're getting worse."

Carolyn roars with laughter, pulling herself up to enjoy the show.

A trail of red seeps through my fingers.

"You can't keep . . ." My voice falters. "Or I'll . . . I'll . . ."

"You'll what?" Carolyn folds her arms across her chest.

Desirae plops into a chair facing me, leaning it back on two legs against the wall. She beckons me with her fingers, welcoming a challenge.

Tears that have nothing to do with the punch spring to my eyes.

I can't handle this. I can't.

I sprint back through the door and run, past the dark window, all the way to the door at the end of the hall.

Doors. Locked doors. That's all I find in this awful place.

Blood and tears stream down my face. I pound against the steel, longing for someone, anyone. Food. Water. Sunlight. Companionship. Memories. Answers.

Succumbing to sobs, I sink to the floor, my back against the metal, and ram the back of my head repeatedly against the door. I bury my face in the crook of my elbow and cry into my sleeve.

Something clicks, and the door swings open, knocking into me. A jack stares down at my quaking body with a look of pure hatred. Still sniffling, I pull myself up and salute, blood gushing from my nostrils. He wrinkles his nose, jaw clenched. I can't help noticing that he's not much older than me.

"State your name."

"E.S.-124, sir. I don't know what I have done; I just know that I am bad. I am here because I deserve to be here, and I am here because I must be fixed. I seek to reform under your guidance." Blood drips onto the neck of my peels.

"What was all that pounding?" He grits his teeth. "And why are you bleeding?"

I gape at him.

I'm starving. I'm locked in here. I'm one mistake away from being shot in the head. I can't remember shit about my own life. And everyone hates me.

"Are you dense?" His eyes narrow.

"No, sir." I straighten my posture. "Sorry, sir. I tripped in the bathroom, and my nose started bleeding, sir."

He rolls his eyes and slaps cuffs over my wrists. "Idiot."

The jack yanks me through the hall door, which slams behind us. He drags me by my sleeve all the way to the infirmary. Unable to block the blood flow with my restrained hands, it trickles down my face, leaving patches down the front of my peels. I wipe my nose against my shoulder as he greets Nurse Ellen. "This brain-dead hack managed to wreck her face."

The nurse struts over to me, clicking her tongue. "Hello again, E.S.-124." She unlocks my cuffs.

I smile sheepishly. "Hello, ma'am."

"I'll take it from here, Matthews," she says, plucking tissues from a box. The jack shoves past me to exit.

Nurse Ellen gestures for me to sit. I sink my butt onto the edge of the same bed I slept in after the first trial. I tilt my head back, blocking the leaky nostrils with my forefinger.

"No, not like that." She thrusts a fistful of tissues at me. "The goal is to get the blood out, so you actually need to lean forward."

I wad up the tissues and press them to my nose. Red blotches seep through, spreading like an infection over the white gauze.

"Heard you had trial three today." She fills a plastic cup in the sink and passes it to me. "Important to keep yourself hydrated."

"Thank you, ma'am." I greedily chug the water, not caring about its lukewarm temperature or metallic aftertaste.

Nurse Ellen takes the dirty tissues and passes me clean ones and a refilled cup. I press the tissue to my throbbing nose with one hand and drink with the other. My face stings with every swallow, but I gulp through the pain, cooling my cracking throat.

She props her hands on her hips. "What happened to you anyway?"

"I, uh, tripped."

She arches her brows. "Honey, I've been in this field for over twenty years. I know when a patient's lying. If you ask me, it looks like you got sucker punched."

My cheeks burn. "I—"

The door swings open. Two women and a man in seafoam green nurse's scrubs rush inside. Raised voices fill the room.

"It wasn't me." The man throws his hands up. "I swear I got the right one!"

"Well, you were the last person with access to the pills. Didn't you check?" one of the women says, balancing an armload of cardboard boxes overflowing with packing peanuts.

"I thought the dose was only given to a couple blocks."

"Sharon was supposed to be in charge of that stuff. She was supposed to order a new shipment from the manufacturer last mo—"

"That's bullshit and you know it, Dominic—"

"Ladies—and Dominic." Nurse Ellen steps between them. "We have a patient."

Their bickering abruptly stops as all four sets of eyes fall on me. I slink lower on the bed. Nurse Ellen ushers the others through the swinging door to the back room. The door sways like a pendulum in their wake before slowing to a stop.

I lie back on the squishy pillow, balling the dirty tissues in my fists.

Being back in this bed reminds me of the last time I was here, and now I can't stop ruminating over the black-hole door. The mysterious words ring with clarity as if I'm listening to them now—*It's just a summer job.* With every passing hour off Memoria, the dream grows stronger and more infused with detail. It's like putting on eyeglasses for the first time, when all the blurry edges come into focus.

I want to know why my brain wants to imagine an extra door in my mom's hallway. I want to see where it leads.

I glance at the empty bed beside me. The last time I was here, Alex Martinez was in that bed, strapped to the posts and half unconscious. A chill whispers across my skin.

The same Alex Martinez who attacked me.

I prop myself up on my elbows.

The same Alex Martinez who said he knew me.

He was trying to tell me something at his intake. Something I never got to hear.

But that doesn't matter now, because whatever he knew about me—or thought he knew—is totally gone. He doesn't remember a thing. They wiped him clean.

"Whatever, Ellen, I'm leaving the expired shit here. I don't have time for this. I've got a Level Two boy on the fifth floor who won't stop puking." Nurse Sharon bursts back through the door, shaking her head. "Everyone's been given the active dose now. I say we drop it."

"What, we all have to clean up your mess, Jocelyn?" the other says.

"Take it out to the dumpster!"

"You act like we all have nothing better to do—"

"Enough!" Nurse Ellen jumps between them. "I will handle it. You will act professionally around patients, or you will find a different job." She's mastered the don't-mess-with-me glare.

Nurse Jocelyn darts past me, huffing. "Whatever."

"Now if you'll all excuse me"—Nurse Ellen points to the exit—"I've got to get dinner ready for the guy in the Hole. Y'all need to get out."

My ears perk. Food for Alex? What the hell! He gets food after assaulting Zepp; meanwhile, I haven't eaten in days. I scowl. It's so ridiculously unfair.

"Fine. Whatever you say, as usual." Nurse Jocelyn angrily gestures her hands in the air, then lets them fall to her sides with a clap. She bustles out into the hall, followed by Nurses Dominic and Sharon. The door slams, but heated bickering continues outside.

Nurse Ellen shakes her head. "Sometimes I feel like their mother." She flings my crumpled tissues into the trash.

The nurse grips my chin, forcing my face to the left, then the right. "You look a lot better. Might have a little bruising, but there's no breakage."

"Thank you, ma'am."

"I want to give you one final inspection and a little disinfectant to be sure–"

"I told you the first time!" One of the nurse's voices blares through the infirmary door. Nurse Ellen's mouth forms a tight line across her face as the shouting outside reaches a new decibel level.

"Give me five minutes. I'll be right back." She clicks cuffs over my wrists. "I need to make sure those three don't burn the place down, excuse me."

"Yes, ma'am."

She clambers into the hall, leaving me alone on the bed.

I can't help stewing. Alex gets his dinner soon—that bastard. Meanwhile, I have to wait. I follow all the damn rules, and here I am, starving. He almost kills two directors, but, whatever, let's feed him first.

"I know you're a good girl," Director Levine says in my head.

If she hadn't taken me on that pointless detour, I'd have eaten lunch.

My stomach erupts in a rumbling growl. A surge of

anger ripples through me.

As if someone has stabbed me in the heart with a syringe of adrenaline, I jolt upward and burst through the swinging doors to the back room. A plate sits on the counter, with two open pieces of wheat bread, waiting to be made into a sandwich.

Alex's dinner? Ha. Soon to be my lunch.

I grab for the bread with my cuffed hands, but stop mid-reach. Beside the plate sits a clear orange canister, half filled with bulbous blue pills. Someone scribbled HOLE on the side in permanent marker.

Alex's Memoria?

I click my teeth behind my lips.

I scan the room. There's a sink, a bunch of cabinets, and a roll of paper towels—and the cardboard boxes abandoned by the flustered nurses.

I teeter on my feet, then rip open the closest box, struggling to maneuver with my cuffed hands. Dozens of orange plastic Memoria bottles are stacked inside, their white caps stamped with red EXPIRED labels.

A dangerous idea prickles in my mind. If I want answers, there might be only one way to get them.

I pluck a bottle from the box, sandwiching it between my cuffed wrists. The pills rattle against the plastic in my jittering hands.

This is illegal. This is so illegal.

I dart my eyes back and forth, from the door to the active

medication in Alex's bottle. My pulse pounds in my ears.

I unscrew both bottles, spilling slightly with my limited mobility, and dump the contents into two piles—expired and active. Closing my eyes, I clench my fists as tight as I can bear around the plastic canisters.

Just do it!

The door creaks in the next room, and my heart leaps into my throat. I brush the expired pills into Alex's bottle, dump the rest into the empty bottle, twist on the lids, and toss the active pills into the cardboard box. The canister hits the other bottles with a clatter, and I cringe.

"Who's there?" booms a male voice. My pulse threatens to rocket out of my skin.

I slide the expired pills toward Alex's plate, silently praying Ellen won't remember their exact position.

"On the ground, hands behind your head!"

The swinging door flings open with the kick of a steel-toed boot. I jump back, throwing my hands up. A jack plows through the doors, aiming his rifle at my chest. I fall to my knees, cuffed hands clasped tight behind my head.

"What the hell are you doing back here?"

"I was . . . uh . . ."

He slaps me in the face, shoving me backward and rereleasing the flow of blood.

"What did you steal?"

"Nothing!"

Growling, he pats his meaty hands down my peels.

"Then why were you back here?"

"I was—"

"What is the meaning of this?" Nurse Ellen bursts into the room. "What are you doing to my patient?"

The jack snarls. "She was back here by herself!"

"I was just—"

"Shut up!" He slams the butt of his rifle into my side. I flinch but don't dare move my hands.

"This is a medical treatment facility." Fire blazes in Nurse Ellen's eyes. "When she's out in the Center, you're in charge, but in here, we follow the Hippocratic oath—first do no harm."

His cheeks flush crimson with rage, knuckles growing white around the barrel of his AK-47. Nurse Ellen doesn't falter.

She's right; she does act like a mother.

The jack kicks the filing cabinet and stomps out. His foot leaves a dent in the metal.

Nurse Ellen glances at me from the corner of her eye and unlocks my cuffs. "What *were* you doing back here?"

"I was looking for food, ma'am."

She raises her brows. "You really couldn't wait five minutes?"

"I'm super hungry."

"I see."

She's not buying it. I grimace, waiting for her to call the guard back to teach me a lesson. "I'm sorry, ma'am."

"Well, you know better for next time." She clicks her tongue disapprovingly and tilts my head back. "The bleeding is pretty much done. I think you're ready to return to your room. I'll have someone escort you back." She turns on the faucet and lathers soap up to her elbows.

"Yes, ma'am."

She turns off the faucet and flicks water off her hands. "Oh, and E.S.-124?"

"Yes, ma'am?"

"The next time someone sucker punches you, you punch them right back."

EVELYN SUMMERS: PRISONER E.S.–124
REHABILITATION DIARY
DAY 221

Someone scribbled something on the bathroom mirror last night.
When I say "someone," I mean Maura Trindley. The thick, black
marker lines paraded a message for anyone who came within ten feet
of the Level Two Girls' Block Four sinks: HANNON IS AN UGLY BITCH.

I was in the stall doing my business when I heard the bathroom
door squeak open. Two sets of gray tennis shoes clomped inside. I
quickly scooted my knees up to my chest, perching my toes on the
edge of the toilet seat.

Ever since the shower incident, any company in the restroom
makes me anxious. I squeezed my eyes shut, praying it wasn't
Ronnie and her cronies eager to torment me—Ronnie had already
led a chorus of "shoot the slinger" during morning chores, while
the other hacks showered me with spit and dirty mop water until
a jack broke it up. I hoped whoever was in the bathroom would
finish up quick and get the hell out so I could make it back to my
cell without any trouble.

The two mysterious prisoners hovered by the sink, whisper-
ing and giggling about something. At first I didn't know who they
were—and therefore, whether or not I should start to really get
scared. But the more I eavesdropped on their conversation, the more
I knew; Mom always said I have ears like a bat.

Director Hannon had made Maura and her cellmate, Rachel

Harding, each do fifty push-ups after lunch because Maura's shirt was untucked. And, being her cellmate, Rachel did her a disservice by not pointing this out before afternoon inspection. Maura and Rachel were really pissed off at the block director, cursing her out behind the safety of the heavy bathroom door.

That's when I heard Rachel's voice. "Don't write that there, c'mon, someone's gonna see." Followed by a snort, and "I don't give a shit." The two whispered and laughed another moment, then hightailed it out of the bathroom. When I was sure the coast was clear, I ducked out of the stall.

I saw the graffiti on the mirror and swallowed down a lump, praying no one would see me exiting and assume I did it. Luckily, I slipped out of the bathroom unnoticed.

That was last night.

Ronnie hip-checked me into the wall today as we lined up for morning inspection. I didn't dare confront her, even when she smirked and flipped me off. Director Hannon had seen the graffiti and, of course, was less than amused; I think irate is the appropriate word. She forced all the Level Two hacks into two straight lines and patrolled the ranks, trying to sniff out guilt like a bloodhound. She asked us calmly to identify the culprit.

No one fessed up.

I clenched my arms at my sides, doing my best to maintain my "at attention" position, despite the fact that my insides melted into a puddle of nerves. My cheeks grew warm as Hannon passed me in line. Could she somehow sense that I knew something? I was terrified of the answer. No way could I spill this mud—I was hated *enough already.*

Hannon lectured on and on about how these types of offenses will keep us locked up forever. She mentioned that they were going to put cameras in the bathrooms now—I admit, I was a little relieved—and then disappeared back into her office.

At first I thought that was it—lecture over. But the jacks wouldn't let us break rank. No one knew what was going on.

Director Hannon emerged from her office a minute later with a dangerous glint in her eyes, holding a sleek black device that looked like a remote. She asked one more time for the graffiti artist to come forward.

No one did.

Director Hannon shrugged. She pointed the remote at a random hack and lazily swiped her thumb across the buttons. A red beam of light flashed from the device.

The girl fell to the ground, screaming and writhing on the floor. Her collar buzzed and crackled. I froze. A terrified murmur swept through the ranks as the same revelation dawned on all of us—it isn't a rumor, our collars are actually electrified. Hannon pressed the button again and the crackling stopped, leaving her victim shivering in a heap on the floor.

But, still, no one came forward.

Hannon pointed her remote at the next hack, activating the prisoner's shock collar. And then another. Each victim's screams grew louder and more visceral, sending goose bumps down my neck. Moving down the ranks, Hannon let out a roaring yawn, sending a clear message—she could do this all day. I watched, helpless.

More screams. More sparks. Each time louder, longer. Each time looming closer to me. With every passing second, the desire to snitch threatened to spill from my mouth. It was like the altruistic part of my brain telling me to keep my mouth shut had to fight the equally strong sense of selfish fear boiling inside me.

I was staring at my gray tennis shoes when Hannon stepped in front of me. My teeth chattered as I waited for the oncoming pain. But instead of zapping me, she sent the beam to my left and nailed Ronnie. My former cellmate's wails drowned the block in terror.

I couldn't be a snitch; I just couldn't. Couldn't be a mudslinger, not again. Not when everybody already loathed the mere sight of me. Not when I risked assault each day just by using the bathroom. I could only imagine what would happen if I once again proved myself the director's pet. Hannon scared me, but the hacks' escalated wrath would surely be worse.

I darted my eyes to Maura and Rachel, who stood still as corpses, their eyes fixed on the ceiling. Maura bore a smug expression on her freckled face, indifferent to my ex-cellmate's pain.

I counted seconds in my head, inhaling and exhaling sharp breaths, looking anywhere but at the convulsing and screaming girl on the floor. I clamped my eyes shut, waiting for the screams to end.

But this time, Director Hannon didn't stop. Her game became clear; either someone was going to confess, or Ronnie was going to die. That would be our punishment for holding our mud—watching another hack, a fellow resident of Block Four, get shocked to death before our very eyes.

I couldn't breathe. Couldn't think. Wisps of smoke billowed from Ronnie's collar. Sparks flew from the metal. The smell of burning flesh swirled into my nostrils, and I gagged.

I don't like the girl. But could I let Hannon kill her?

No one spoke. No one looked at Ronnie. Everyone held their best vacant-eyed, teeth-clenched expressions. Maura and Rachel were going to let Ronnie take the fall for this. They were going to let her die.

I couldn't. I couldn't let her.

Eyes squeezed tightly shut, I burst out Maura's name.

The screams stopped. I released the biggest gust of air, finally daring to open my eyes.

Director Hannon asked me how I knew, and I admitted I was in the bathroom stall at the time. Two jacks handcuffed Maura. Hannon sentenced her to two weeks in the Hole.

Ronnie shivered on the floor, still shaking. A crooked smile brimmed across the director's face at her plan's success.

Hannon dismissed us to our afternoon group. Whispers of "slinger" followed me around every corner, louder and angrier than before. But there was one voice that was oddly silent—the voice of the one person who hated me above all others.

Ronnie Hartman.

"Welcome to your fourth trial!" Allard strokes his chin. "Congratulations on making it this far."

I stare at my lap, not daring to meet the angry glares of my fellow contenders. My swollen nose greeted me in the mirror this morning, parading a shiny purple bruise. Desirae and Carolyn called it my "badge of dishonor," and broke into their typical hyena cackles.

Now, sitting in these black chairs, the familiar dread of the unknown churns inside me. Will my saboteur make a reappearance today? My knee jiggles against the chair leg.

If I get through whatever they throw at me, I need to speak to Alex. He's been off his Memoria for a day. Is that long enough? He hasn't been on the medication nearly as long as me, so I'm guessing he'll get his memories back sooner.

Will he remember what he said to me at his intake?

Will he remember me?

Six jacks march into the already cramped orientation room, each one toting an enormous white helmet. They remind me of the memory-erasing helmets I saw in my pre-req.

"Accountability"—Doctor Allard shuffles his feet at the front of the room, unable to pace due to the number of people crammed into the small space— "is a key trait required to succeed in the real world. Therefore, it is also our fourth principle of rehabilitation."

Carolyn perches her chin on her hand, deep in concentration over Allard's accountability lecture. The image of her roaring with laughter at my expense makes me roll my eyes; she obviously lacks this particular trait.

"Taking responsibility for your actions is not only wise but right. If one is not held accountable, they'll be more inclined to commit crime." Allard unfolds his red glasses from his shirt pocket and tips them onto his nose with his forefinger. "But accountability does not stop with yourselves. You must also hold others accountable. That's what it means to be a productive member of society. Now, one of you . . ." He winks at me. "Has already proven her commitment to holding others accountable."

My shoulders tense.

Carolyn and Andrew sneer. The tension in the room thickens around us. I keep my head down, knee bouncing so high I worry it might take flight.

The closest jack thrusts a bulbous white helmet into my arms. It looks like the devices old women sit under in hair salons, only with buttons and flashing lights.

"Before we get started, I need you all to do something for me," Allard says. "I need you to each take a helmet and place it over your head, so we can measure your brain waves and pulse. Then, when I instruct you, you may remove it, and we can get started on your trial."

Measure our brain waves? What the hell does that have to do with anything?

I assume questions aren't allowed, so I don't bother asking. With a deep breath, I slide the slick white helmet over my head. It envelops my face, drowning me in darkness. The bulky device reeks of fresh plastic.

Two beeps sound in my ears, followed by a line of red lights prickling in the darkness ahead. A soft hum vibrates over me. I only half hear Doctor Allard's voice instructing us to remove the helmets.

I jerk it back over my head, laying the heavy headgear in my lap. Each contender now sports matted helmet hair and a dumbfounded expression.

"Very good, your results are being tabulated," Allard says, as if we just finished a math test.

My forehead crinkles. That was fast.

"Now, to begin your fourth trial." He steps back.

The red wall creaks. Two panels slide open with a rumble, revealing a secret opening in the back of the room.

Darkness obscures whatever lies beyond it.

"All rise," Allard says, "and come to the gate."

Jeez, this is ominous. I join the other contenders by the entrance to the dark passage. Fog swirls on the other side. A cold draft of stale air blows in my face.

I squint into the dark abyss and can barely make out a solid gray wall about twenty feet beyond the entrance. It spreads left to right with a single skinny gap in the middle. I look up, but there's no ceiling—only darkness.

The directors form a semicircle behind us, blocking our only escape from whatever waits ahead.

"Beyond this room is what we call the Labyrinth of Accountability." Allard's voice eerily echoes, amplified in the misty darkness.

I bite my lip. It's dark in there; I don't do dark. A wave of fear ripples through the line of contenders like falling dominoes.

The six contenders stand at the threshold, squinting and leaning in a vain attempt to see beyond the distant gray wall. Tom clears his throat beside me. Carolyn's uneven breaths rattle from three people away. I close my eyes, concentrating on my quickening heartbeats.

"Remember, absolution can be painful. But to atone, sometimes pain is the only way. You have one hour to complete the maze." Allard waves. "Good luck."

I reluctantly follow the other contenders through the door. The panel slams shut behind us, stranding us alone in the darkness. As if triggered by the slamming door, the cement wall illuminates, shining fluorescent green light. The gap glows blue, alerting us to the maze entrance. It's like the whole labyrinth is a giant glow stick. This is such a huge, random thing for the Center to be hiding.

The glowing green wall stretches at least ten feet high. It continues left and right in the distance as far as I can see.

We hover, bunched together in a pack. Then Tom takes off into the maze. The colossal walls swallow him whole, and his pattering footsteps fade into nothing. Desirae bolts after him, followed by Miles and Andrew. Carolyn grabs my shoulders and shoves me backward, then darts down the path, out of sight. Determined not to give them a head start, I take off running after them.

I speed down the first corridor. The green glow from the walls eerily reflects on my skin and white peels. Everything above the maze is pitch black, creating an illusion of being smothered by night sky.

Twenty feet in, the labyrinth breaks into two halls. I randomly choose the left path, which curves and breaks into three more possible turns. I pause a moment, wishing I had a better sense of direction, then haphazardly run down the middle.

I power through the ache in my calves, forcing myself not to stop. My footsteps echo between the walls.

With each turn, my heart rate spikes at the chance of meeting another contender alone in the dark, but no one appears. The only foe I meet is thick fog.

I turn and find myself at a seven-way intersection. Studying each potential path, the endless sea of glowing green passages and massive walls overwhelm me.

How did they fit this here? It's almost implausible that it exists. Then again, the Center could be huge—I haven't seen much beyond the blocks.

With no sense of direction in the winding roads, I go with my gut. Right. Left. Left. Straight. Right. I take another left, and slam head-on into Andrew, colliding at top speed from an intersecting path.

We each shout at the impact, my muffled scream disappearing into his chest. Damp patches of sweat dapple the underarms of his peels. I splay my hands over my face to shield myself from his wrath, but he doesn't move. His body shakes furiously, his mouth open but not uttering sound. Fear pulsates in his wild eyes.

I recoil when I see it. Andrew's sleeves bunch up at his elbows. Bits of shredded skin hang from his right arm. Blood leaks from his open wounds, dripping down to his fingers. It looks like he got pushed through a cheese grater. Okay, so this is definitely more than just a creepy, glowing maze. But what the hell happened to him?

Andrew grunts and shoves past me, sprinting down a corridor to the right, leaving me alone in the intersection. A trail of blood marks his path like breadcrumbs.

I squint in the direction he came from, but there's only

darkness. I shudder, rubbing my arms at the thought of meeting a similar fate. No, thanks.

I turn and race in the opposite direction. The walkway grows narrow as I dart to the left, then to the right at full speed, almost too late to see the clear plastic wall blocking the road ahead.

My boots screech to a halt on the cement floor, and I throw out my hands, an inch away from ramming into the dead end. I press my palms to the smooth, almost invisible plastic barrier serving as a window to the unreachable foggy corridor ahead.

Damn it.

I turn back, but another plastic panel juts out from the glowing cement behind me. It fuses with the opposite concrete wall, sealing the exit and trapping me inside a half-plastic, half-green cement box.

Something beeps. Red letters scrawl across the clear blockade, as if burnt into the plastic with a laser: PAY THE PRICE.

What price?

I slam my body against the former exit, but it holds firm, locking me inside a cramped square trap. I can brush both walls with my fingertips if I spread my arms wide. Spinning in circles, I pat my hands up and down both plastic panels.

Each second wasted in here counts against the allotted hour, ticking like a deadly time bomb.

"Help!" I scream at the top of my lungs, barreling against the immovable wall. My shoulder throbs as I throw myself against the hard barrier again and again. I pry my fingernails in the corner where the cement meets the plastic, trying in vain to wrench it open; I wince as my fingernail cracks in the cement.

Sweat beads across my forehead. I wedge my body between the two plastic surfaces, pressing my hands to one side and my feet to the other, but slip and crash back to the hard floor. My sweaty palms leave wet handprints on the plastic.

"Help!" My voice grows hoarse but draws no one. "Please!" I beat my fists against the wall.

There has to be a way out.

My mind races.

Accountability. This trial is about penance and account-ability.

"I'm sorry!" I throw my hands above my head. My words echo around me. "I'm accountable! I take all responsibility for my crime!"

Silence.

The glowing walls flicker for a moment, then fade back into gray, stranding me in complete darkness.

Shit.

I wave my hand in front of my face but can't see a thing. This isn't good.

I force my hands into fists, bracing myself for whatever they'll throw at me now.

A spotlight clicks on above my head, illuminating the

box with white light. I blink furiously, shading my eyes with my hand.

Something rumbles.

I squint upward to find the source of the noise. The gray cement ceiling comes into view in the distance. It grows bigger, moving slowly toward me with a mechanical grumble.

It's a compactor.

They're going to crush me alive.

I frantically claw at the walls around me.

"Help! Get me out of here! Please!" My heart slams, on the verge of exploding, in my chest. I ram against the plastic with all my strength. My palms slide down the surface, slippery with sweat.

There has to be a way to make it stop.

I slide my fingers around the sides, into every crevice and corner, seeking some sort of emergency latch. The ceiling drops farther and farther, ready to crunch my bones into the cement floor.

Standing on my tiptoes and stretching my arms over my head, I use all my force to press against the unrelenting descending concrete. It weighs on my outstretched arms, forcing my elbows to bend. I sink lower, kneeling to avoid the encroaching ceiling.

My eyes catch the mysterious red-lettered words scribbled across the wall. They seem to magically lower as the ceiling drops. Sharp breaths rip through my lungs.

My price? What price? Is my life my price? Are they

going to kill me?

I wedge my crouched body between the walls, pushing with all my strength and crying out pleas to nonexistent ears.

It creeps farther by the second, swallowing inches and forcing me lower into a squat.

Price. I need to pay a price.

Allard said absolution is painful. This is their way of punishing us.

Andrew was bleeding.

I sprawl flat on my stomach on the cold ground as the cement reaches three feet from the floor. Two feet.

Blood.

I dig my fingernail into my arm and scrape it across my skin as hard as I can.

The ceiling touches my back. A shallow breath dies in my throat.

I frantically claw into my skin again and again until red blossoms in the searing cut and blood oozes from the stinging scratch. I press my bleeding arm against the bottom of the plastic wall.

Ding!

Everything around me explodes with sound. The plastic barriers retract, sucked back into the maze walls. The ceiling freezes, sandwiching my body between concrete slabs. A heavy breath escapes my lips.

I shimmy out, gasping for air. The rough, cold floor scrapes my legs through my pants, but I don't care; I'm alive.

The white spotlight shuts off with a click, and the gray walls morph back into glowing green.

This place gets weirder and weirder.

Back on my feet, I stretch my cramped arms over my head. A few blood droplets seep from my scratch. I wipe it on my peels, leaving a red skid down my pant leg. I allow myself a moment to catch my breath before I break off running back into the maze.

"Attention, contenders," a voice crackles through the air. "You are halfway through your allotted hour. You have thirty minutes remaining to complete the labyrinth."

I curse out loud, forcing my sore legs to race around corner after corner. They all look the same. Each time I reach a dead end, I shudder and jump away but meet no more traps.

Two more turns, and someone's white-booted heel disappears from view around another wall. I follow, darting to the right, and find myself in a long corridor.

The maze walls stretch at least a hundred feet in the distance with no other passages or potential turns jutting off the sides. Maybe a good sign. At least it's new. I race straight ahead.

A pixelated yellow wall flickers into view, blocking my path. I skid to a halt and throw my arms over my face to block an attack. Nothing happens.

The yellow wall flickers like an electric hologram at risk of short-circuiting. A soft buzzing hums around it. It's bizarre. It doesn't match the rest of the maze; instead of glowing like a highlighter, it's a subdued pastel. The whole thing looks like a glitching computer program.

Suddenly, it blinks, and rows upon rows of coding appear, all displaying the same message: ERROR.CODEX_80209_ERROR-BOX. I cautiously poke it; the wall zaps my finger. I wince and whip my hand back. The wall flutters and blinks one final time before flickering out and disappearing altogether. I eye the empty space suspiciously before running through it.

Nothing happens.

That was too easy.

But I don't waste time ruminating. Straight ahead, a white screen shines through the darkness proclaiming FINISH in blocky red letters.

My heart somersaults.

That's it. I did it. It's over.

Picking up speed, I race down the corridor, a giddy smile erupting across my face. I holler out a victory cry, pumping my fist in the air as the finish line gets closer.

Carolyn bursts from a side opening and slams into me.

"Out of my way, slinger!" She shoves me to the ground and limps toward the finish. A long red streak stains her pant leg.

I pick myself up and chase after her. Carolyn jerks to a halt in a clearing, and I almost crash into her again.

Andrew sits cross-legged on the ground, head in his hands. "Hope one of you guys can figure this shit out." Caked blood coats his arm like a sleeve. "Or else we're trapped in here."

Six crimson doors wait under the glowing finish screen,

each sporting a bronze doorknob. One door is propped open, revealing darkness on the other side; the others are closed.

Behind us, against the maze wall, stand six wooden posts about seven feet tall. I squint in the dim light, not believing what I'm seeing. A different prisoner slumps against each post, each wearing Level-One orange. They're knocked out cold—eyes closed, chests rising and falling with steady, even breaths. Some kind of glowing yellow twine wraps around their torsos and legs, binding them to the wooden stakes. My nose wrinkles. How much bug juice did Allard use to sedate them so badly? Why are they even here?

I approach the nearest tied-up hack. She's a girl with jet-black hair, at least a couple years younger than me. A single blade lies at her feet, right beside a tag labeled C.P.-680: Carolyn's number.

"Hey, Carolyn?" I tap the unconscious prisoner's shoulder, but the Level One girl doesn't move. "Do you know this hack?" I cast a glance over my shoulder, a tad concerned about the fact that Carolyn and Andrew have access to knives in here, but they ignore me.

Carolyn's too busy examining the line of doors. She's probably on to something. These chained prisoners could be distractions intended to throw us off.

Cautiously, I step toward the doors. A silver plate engraved with a different contender's name glints from the top of each. I walk past Andrew's door, then Miles's. Smack in the middle of the line is the door labeled E.S.-124. Embedded in the door, a blue light blinks from a fingerprint reader similar to the ones the directors and jacks use to get between rooms. That seems awfully simple.

I press my right index finger to the pad; the light blinks red. I gently push the door, but nothing happens. "The hell?"

I shake the handle, but it doesn't budge.

Carolyn rattles her own doorknob beside mine. Her face grows tense.

"Forget it." Andrew cradles his injured arm. "They're locked. I tried. Fingerprints don't work."

"They wouldn't have fingerprint scanners if they didn't work," Carolyn says.

I cock my head. "Maybe our fingerprints unlock each other's doors?"

"Did I stutter, slinger?" Andrew rolls his eyes. "Tried them all. Nothing works."

"Well, what the hell good is that?" Carolyn snaps. "I had to slice my fucking leg open. I did my time." She yanks up her pant leg, revealing a wide gash. I swallow back my gasp.

Andrew snorts. "Yeah? They made me reach into a barbed wire cage to get a key." He brandishes his torn arm.

"I . . . I had to scratch blood out of mine," I say. "They trapped me in this box, and the ceiling kept lowering. It was gonna crush me alive."

Carolyn shakes her head. "I'm done. I can't do this shit anymore. I just wanna get out." She kicks her door with a crash. It doesn't relent.

"There's a way out." Andrew stands and points to the open door. "Desirae must've done it first, she's gone."

I scan the line of unconscious, tied-up hacks. Each one has that same blade by their feet and a label naming a different contender. One post is empty; Desirae's hack must have been removed when she completed the trial.

My mouth scrunches to the side. "Maybe we're supposed to free them? We untie them and bring them with us?"

"Good luck with that," Andrew says. "I tried it. Whatever that rope shit tying them up is, it's not meant to be undone."

I move down the row, studying each prisoner. They're different ages, but all Level Ones. I don't understand. Why have random hacks tied up in here?

Carolyn scrunches her mouth to the side. "What if we go out through Desirae's door?"

"Don't," Andrew says, "you'll fail the trial; I know it. There's one for each of us for a reason."

I stop at the hack labeled E.S.-124. She's got a pale face full of freckles, wildly curly red hair that clashes with her orange peels, and that same slick blade resting at her feet. Heavy, sleeping breaths rock her whole body.

Soft footsteps echo behind us. Miles limps into the opening, cradling something in his arms. Tears stream down his cheeks. His dark skin is several shades paler than it should be.

I step closer to see what he's holding but jump back and clap my hand over my mouth.

He's missing a hand.

Miles's left arm supports his right, which now ends in a blood-spurting stump.

"Holy shit!" Carolyn's upper lip curls in disgust. "These directors are sick."

Andrew's jaw drops. "What happened to you?"

"I just . . . want . . . to get . . . the hell . . . out of here." Miles convulses with shivers.

Something screeches, and we jerk our heads up. Tom skids into the room, trailing a black scuff mark across the cement. He's doused in sweat, dark hair splayed over his face, but he appears uninjured. Andrew updates the newcomers on the door situation.

Tom nods at the Level Ones. "Who are they?"

"Beats the hell outta me," Andrew says.

Miles's jaw clenches as he scans all five fingerprints from his remaining hand; the light on his scanner flashes red, his door stubbornly remaining closed.

I pluck at the glowing twine wrapped around my hack's torso and legs, binding her to the wooden post. It's deceptively thick. That has to be the knife's purpose.

I gently saw the dull blade into the twine. A loud screech fills the air, like the world's loudest seagull on crack. I drop the knife, and it clangs against the cement.

Andrew slams his hands over his ears. "Would you stop that, you dumbass bitch? It doesn't work."

"I'm just trying to get out of here," I snap back. "I don't

see you trying."

He jumps to his feet. "I told you twice, slinger. I already tried everything. Don't make me tell you a third time."

"I'm just trying to help!"

"Come on. Come on!" Tears spring to Carolyn's eyes as she swipes her fingerprints again and again. "I am not dying in here."

I gently nudge the hack again, but she doesn't wake; her head lolls against her shoulder. With the movement, something shiny glimmers against her collar.

I pull out the silver chain necklace I hadn't noticed before. An engraving on the dog tag marks three words: DISCIPLINARY REFORM NEEDED.

"Shit, we're almost out of time." Andrew scrubs his hand through his hair. "There's gotta be a way out. Desirae did it."

"What about them?" Miles nods at the unconscious hacks. His eyelids droop, shading the pain reflected in his eyes. "It's gotta involve them."

You'll need to hold others accountable. Allard's voice rings in my head.

A sick thought crosses my mind. Maybe the fingerprint scanners weren't for us.

Stomach crawling as if swarmed with a million bugs, I approach the hack labeled E.S.-124. She's propped directly parallel to my door.

I don't want to say my idea. I'm probably wrong, and the others will think I'm a sick piece of trash just for thinking it. The words roll like a wave of nausea inside me. Holding my breath, I grab the blade, my knuckles going white around the hilt.

"I think." I close my eyes and steady myself. "I think the fingerprint scanners might be for them."

"What do you mean?" Carolyn asks.

"They can't." A vein pulses in Andrew's forehead. "I tried picking up my hack to bring him to the scanner, they're bound too tight." He raises his voice. "Doesn't. Fucking. Work."

I hold up the knife, letting it speak for me. The message must get across, because Carolyn's face scrunches in disgust. "No. What the hell? That's fucked up."

"That's the answer?" Andrew says. "We have to cut off their fingers?"

"Count on the slinger to come up with that," Carolyn mutters. My face gets hot.

Tom holds his fist in front of his mouth but doesn't speak.

"We're supposed to hold people accountable, and Allard's one sick bastard." I throw my hands up. "I don't know what else it could be."

"I'm not staying here." Andrew plows toward his unconscious hack—a boy no older than thirteen—and greedily grabs the knife. He yanks the boy's arm. I can feel the other contenders holding their breath. Carolyn looks away.

"Sorry, man," he mumbles. With a sickening swipe, Andrew hacks into the boy's hand and chops his forefinger clean off.

Not even bug juice can soften that blow. The boy's eyes shoot open and his piercing scream fills the room. He strains his arm against the twine, blood gushing from the wound and dyeing his maimed hand red.

My stomach rolls. I double over, at risk of vomiting my breakfast all over the floor.

Andrew holds the amputated finger to the scanner at his door. Something clicks, a light flashes blue, and the door creaks open. He grimaces, dropping the finger to the cement. "There's your answer. Just do it." He plows through his door, disappearing into a shroud of darkness.

"Guess you didn't try everything," I mutter, too low for anyone to hear.

Tears stream down the mutilated hack's face, his cheeks pallid and clammy. Jumbled words come pouring out of his mouth, but I can't understand any of them.

The rest of us look at one another, our mouths hanging open. I can't believe I was right. I'm horrified I was right. What the hell is wrong with Allard? How can he force us to permanently disfigure these poor slugs?

Miles hobbles up to his hack, about ready to pass out himself. "S-sorry." Miles takes his blade in his remaining hand and cuts his hack's finger. "I'm really sorry. It's not my fault." The hack's screams drown out the sound of Miles's door clicking open and the contender's footsteps exiting the maze.

The room spins around me. I feel lightheaded. I can't

believe I have to do it.

"Five minutes remaining," a voice booms over the intercom.

My pulse races. Carolyn tilts her head back, inhaling and exhaling deep, steady breaths.

Tom shuffles in place, not daring to look at the lanky little boy strapped to his post.

I can't do it. There's no way.

All the emotion leaves Carolyn's eyes. Her face blank and empty, she strides toward her hack. For a second, I wonder if she'll throw up. Carolyn buries her face in the crook of her elbow, her chest heaving. With the precision of a surgeon, she takes the knife in steady hands and smoothly cuts off her hack's finger. Something hardens in my chest. Carolyn doesn't even look back over her shoulder at the sobbing hack as she plows through her door. Cries and anguished screams from the three mutilated prisoners echo in my ears.

Tom's usual brown face is pallid.

I swallow the biggest gulp of courage I can muster and approach my hack. That poor girl. What did she do to deserve this? Screw up her chores? Punch someone? No one deserves to be maimed like this. I tell myself I don't have a choice, but deep down, I know I do. I force my brain to go numb and take her delicate fingers in mine. Her skin is so soft, so young.

I have to do it. It's the only way.

Acid churns through my stomach. I squeeze my eyes shut. If I don't do it, one of the directors will—or worse.

The blade slices through her dainty bone in one swipe. Warm, sticky blood soaks onto my skin. I mash my eyes shut, forcing myself not to feel it. Not to look into her eyes. Not to hear her screams. I stumble over to my door and hold her finger to the scanner; the light blinks blue.

I take a deep breath. *I'm so sorry*, I want to say, but the words come out as a gust of air. Hot tears flood my eyes, blurring my vision.

I push open my door, one foot through the threshold. Tom steps up behind me.

I freeze. "What are you doing?"

"Exiting the maze."

"Aren't you going to go through your own door?"

"No."

"You're not gonna do it?"

"I'm not going to permanently disfigure someone to pass a stupid trial. It's not worth it."

I blink. "They'll execute you."

Tom looks away. "Maybe not."

I step over the threshold into the darkness. Tom follows, leaving his hack unharmed.

A cold chill envelops my body. Something hard presses against my face with the overwhelming scent of sanitized plastic.

What's going on?

Someone tugs my hair and light floods my eyes.

I'm sitting in a black chair, in the middle of the orientation room. A jack stands a foot away, gripping the huge helmet in her arms.

Allard winks. "Welcome back."

The skin on my arm healed, leaving no evidence of the scratch. A solid red wall covers the secret maze entrance.

Two chairs away, Miles clasps his shaking hands together, his eyes glued to the appendage he thought he lost. Andrew holds his head between his knees. Desirae primps the helmet head from her hair.

"The maze you completed was a simulation," Allard says. "I'm sorry we lied to you, but we needed you to think—and feel—like it was real."

I open my mouth, then close it. It was fake?

I can't absorb it. My hands won't stop shaking.

"The . . . the Level Ones?" Carolyn watches Allard through the corner of her narrowing brown eyes. "They weren't real?"

"Holograms. Very realistic ones at that."

Relief floods over me. I cradle my head in my hands. I didn't do it. It wasn't real.

That technology was ridiculous. I never would have even suspected—it was so realistic. Well, almost everything, aside from that pixelated yellow wall. A glitch must have sneaked through their otherwise perfect coding.

It seems unlike Allard to produce a trial meant to trick us and then allow a glitch. He's a lot of things, but sloppy isn't one of them.

For some reason, it bothers me. I shouldn't speak out of

turn, but the words spill from my mouth anyway. "What was the yellow wall for?"

All the directors set their eyes on me.

"Yellow wall?" Allard cocks his head.

"In the final stretch. A yellow wall sprung out in front of me." Except, it didn't look solid. It didn't look like it was supposed to be there at all. "It kept flashing an error message."

I glance at the other contenders, waiting for one of them to show signs of understanding, of seeing the wall with their own eyes, but no one does.

The directors eye me suspiciously, and I have my answer: The wall wasn't supposed to be there. "It was . . ." I shake my head. "Never mind."

The wall only showed up for me. It tried to block my path. If the directors didn't program it that way, that means only one thing: My saboteur struck again.

Doctor Allard laughs, wagging his finger at me. "Why, E.S.-124, you must have quite the active imagination." I catch a nervous glimmer in his eyes, as if he, too, suspects foul play.

I force a laugh. "I must have imagined it."

"Stress can do that to a person. Be sure to get a good night's rest tonight, E.S.-124."

The jack sets my helmet at my feet and slides cuffs over my wrists.

Four trials down. Three trials to freedom. Three chances for my anonymous enemy to get in my way.

Jacks walk down the line of recovering contenders and

cuff everyone's hands.

"It's time to celebrate!" Allard says. "You're more than halfway done with your Freedom Trials." His gaze hardens. "Well . . . some of you. T.P.-129, you will not be returning to your quarters."

Tom quivers in his seat. He doesn't speak.

No. I should've stopped him. I shouldn't have let him exit through my door.

"Prisoner T.P.-129, you have failed your fourth trial," Allard says. "You are hereby deemed unsavable."

The jacks yank Tom to his feet. He doesn't make a sound as they shackle his ankles.

"Enjoy your last walk," a jack says, as they stride into the hall. "Because it ends in the Green Room."

EVELYN SUMMERS: PRISONER E.S.–124
REHABILITATION DIARY
DAY 223

Today took an unexpected turn.

I wished my cellmate, Kara, a good day, and as always, she ignored me. I slipped into my gray peels and headed down to breakfast with the line of Level Twos. As usual, I sat by myself and scarfed my goopy porridge alone.

Then came chores. Today, I had dish-washing duty. The jack instructed me to scrub all the dirty pots and trays from breakfast. Considering the amount of cookware required to make breakfast for a couple hundred hacks, this took hours. By the time I neared the end of the dirty pile, my stiff hands were raw and red.

I only had a few spatulas left when Maura and Rachel drifted past me with their brooms and dustpans. I didn't want a confrontation—the only jack monitoring us was at the other end of the kitchen, reaming out Amanda Daniels for spilling sudsy water on the floor.

I looked up just in time to see their dirty dustpans emptying onto my stack of clean dishes, coating the wet pans in dirt and grime from the cafeteria floor. Maura and Rachel dashed back into the cafeteria, giggling, before I could stop them.

I groaned. What the hell could I do? I wouldn't dare turn them in again. Rachel's BFF with my cellmate, Kara, and I'd rather not wake up with a pillow pressed over my face.

I got halfway through re-cleaning the formerly spotless dishes when the clock struck noon. Of course I hadn't finished my chores, since I had to clean double what I was supposed to.

The jack flipped out and forced me to do fifty push-ups in the middle of the cafeteria, right as everyone was filtering in for lunch. The whole Center witnessed the jack screaming and berating me, while I struggled through my punishment on the hard floor.

When I was finally allowed to eat my lunch, sweat seeped from every pore in my body. Arms burning, I kept my head down and fought back tears. I took my usual empty table and forced myself to nibble the stale bread. I was about to succumb to the urge to cry when another tray slammed down onto my table.

Ronnie Hartman sunk onto the bench beside me. I didn't know what to do. Someone was sitting with me? And, of all people, Ronnie? My former roommate who could have single-handedly led the Evelyn Summers Hate Club? It must have been a cruel joke, a prank. Surely this breakfast was going to end with Ronnie's food dumped over my head or something.

She didn't talk. She sucked milk from her straw and gulped down her pea soup, shoveling it all into her mouth as fast as possible.

I didn't cry; I was too dumbstruck. I mumbled out a "hi," but she didn't respond. She just ate her lunch in silence beside me. When 12:30 p.m. came, she rose from her seat without a word.

For the first time in months, I didn't sit at an empty table.

We retreat to our quarters after the trial. Desirae and Carolyn don't speak at all. No one wants to acknowledge that Tom won't be joining us tomorrow. Carolyn's mattress squeaks as she collapses onto her bed, kicking her shoes to the floor.

Desirae gathers her towel. "I'm showering." It's her usual tendency to announce her bathroom plans like they're evening news. She flips her hair behind her shoulders and strides from the room. Carolyn doesn't reply.

I lie on my bed. My feet tap together, but I force the rest of my body not to fidget. The longer I prolong the inevitable, the more knots twist inside me.

It has to be done. I pull myself to the edge of my bed and tug my boots back on.

"I'm going for a walk," I say to the quivering lump on Carolyn's bed. She remains curled in the fetal position, facing the wall.

"Carolyn . . . are you . . . okay?"

Nothing.

I step toward her bed. "Do you need anything?"

"Leave me alone." Her pillow muffles her words, but I still catch the hint of pain in her voice.

I rest my hand on the edge of her bed. "Carolyn . . ."

"I said, leave me alone!" She flips over and hurls her shoe at me; it misses, smacking the wall instead. Tear tracks mar her puffy cheeks. She turns her back once more, hiding her raw, red eyes.

I slink down. "Okay."

Carolyn? Crying? Big, tough, bully Carolyn? I shake my head, struck with a stab of pity.

I push Carolyn's tears to the back of my mind and slip into the hallway, pressing my back to the cement.

Don't show your fear. Don't think. Just do it.

I take a deep breath and approach the dark window. The white, corded phone looks innocuous enough. I recognize the six-inch metal square in the wall from when Levine brought me to see the Hole. I pry open the panel, revealing a selection of three light switches.

Here goes nothing.

Covering them with my palm, I flick all three switches at once. White light drowns the room.

Alex startles in the corner, blinking furiously at the burst of bright light. I pluck the phone from its dock and gesture to him.

The prisoner cocks his head, narrowing his eyes in my direction. He grabs his phone off the wall like it's a stick of dynamite ready to detonate.

"H-hi, Alex."

His eyebrows knit together. "Hello."

I can't help feeling like I'm observing a zoo animal locked in a cement-walled cage. Peering into Alex's cramped room, it's easy to forget I'm a prisoner on lockdown too.

I force a smile. "How's it going?"

"Fine."

Our eyes meet through the thick glass. Something inside me jolts.

Alex rolls his head back laughing, raking a hand through his long, black hair.

"It's not funny!" I shove his arm but can't fight the smile off my face.

He clears his throat.

I snap back to the present.

What the hell was that?

"Is there something I can help you with?" Alex twirls his finger through the phone cord.

My mouth opens, but nothing comes out.

He rolls his eyes. "Or are you just gonna stand there?"

"I-I just want to talk."

Alex sinks to the floor, slouching with his shoulder against the thick glass. "So talk."

I sit beside him and lean against the window. If there weren't a good four inches of glass between us, our shoulders would rub together.

Up close, the Hole isn't much of a hole; it's a cement pit, housing only a white ceramic toilet fused to the concrete floor. They didn't even provide him with the bare essentials, like a mattress or a blanket. That sucks.

I run a finger around my collar. "I want to know more about you."

I want to know if you really know me. If I ever knew you.

"Not much to tell." He thumps the side of his head against the glass. "I'm stuck in here."

I run my hands up and down my pant legs, sandwiching the phone between my ear and shoulder. "Yeah, it sucks. You get used to it over time."

"How long have you been here?"

"Two years. Plus."

"Great." Alex pinches his forehead. "I'll be here a while, then."

"Yeah, probably."

"So what's your name? And if you don't mind me asking, how did you know mine?"

"Evelyn. Evelyn Summers." An idea pops into my head. "But some people call me Eva." I glance at him, hoping for a reaction. He doesn't budge. I scrunch my mouth to the side.

"Well, it's nice to meet you, Eva. I'd shake your hand but, you know . . ."

"Yeah, the glass might make that challenging."

He taps his fingernails to the back of his phone, clicking in my ear. "Well, Eva, you never answered my other question."

"Right." My cheeks burn. "You don't remember? You were lying on the infirmary bed next to mine a few days ago."

A half smile twitches across his lips. "That's where it was. I knew you looked familiar, but I couldn't place from where."

My heart leaps. Familiar.

I scratch my neck in a forced attempt at playing it casual. "Are . . . are you sure that's the only way you know me?"

"Should there be another place I know you from?"

I sigh. "Nope."

He's got to have something. He's been wiped less than a week and off Memoria for a day.

Alex tangles his hand in the cord. "It's nice having someone to talk to."

"Yeah, it is." Especially someone who doesn't know the word slinger. I scooch my knees up to my chin. "Wanna play a game?"

"What sort of game?"

"Well, my friends and I used to play this game where we'd try and guess each other's crimes. You know, we'd each say the last thing we remembered, and go from there."

Worth a shot.

"Hmm . . . I don't know if I'll be very good at this game. My memory tanked."

"Welcome to the club." I rest my chin on my knees. "What's the last thing you remember?"

He thinks for a moment. "I was in the car with my mom and my two sisters. My sister Cora was being a royal pain in the ass. My mom was . . . upset? I think?"

"Where were you going?"

"I . . . I'm not sure."

"Well, where does your family usually go?" I lean closer, hoping he can't sense how desperate I am. "Where does your mom work?"

"She manages a Wegmans."

"What's Wegmans?"

Alex mock gasps. "You've never been to Wegmans?"

"I don't even know what that is."

"It's, like, the greatest grocery store on the East Coast."

"Well, I live on the East Coast, and I've never heard of it."

He groans. "Okay, fine. As soon as we get out of here, I'm gonna take you to Wegmans."

"A grocery store?" I shoot him an amused grin. "That's so weird."

"You'll love it."

"How do you know what I'd love?"

He shrugs. "Everyone loves Wegmans."

"Fair enough."

"So, what's the last thing you remember?" he asks.

I tell him about being almost done with freshman year, and the math exam, and the flyers on the music room bulletin board.

"There was a pamphlet on the board about not smoking pot, so I'm wondering if maybe I used to be a druggie."

"You don't look the type."

"Yeah, I feel like if I tried to smoke something, I'd cough everywhere."

Alex raises his right shoulder in a half shrug. "Maybe you're better off not knowing."

"What do you mean?"

"Well, think about it. If you did something so bad, so vile and horrible that they had to lock you up for years and make you wear a collar and erase your memory . . . Would you really want to know?"

My forehead crinkles. "Yeah. I do want to know."

"You have a chance to start over. Clean slate. And you want to be haunted forever by whatever horrible thing you did?"

I weave the phone cord around my fingers. "I don't want there to be any secrets about my life that I don't know."

"That's fair."

The door clicks open in the hall behind me. Two jacks stride in carrying dinner trays.

"I better go." I stand. "Dinner's here."

And I'm not letting Carolyn and Desirae steal my food again.

"Did they say how long you'll be in the Hole?"

He laughs. "The Hole? Is that what they call this place?"

"If by 'they,' you mean the other prisoners, then yes."

"It doesn't feel like a hole. It feels like a piece-of-shit box. And no, they didn't. They said for as long as they need to monitor me."

"Monitor you? For what?"

"I don't know. Eating, I think. Fat mustache dude threatened to stick a feeding tube in my arm."

"That sounds like Director Marewood. So are you eating again?"

"Yeah." He scowls. "But they drag me to the infirmary for meals."

"That sucks."

"I guess."

One last try. "Before I go, I need you to do something for me."

Alex stands and stretches his arms behind his head. The phone slips off his shoulder, and he fumbles to catch it before it hits the ground. He presses it back to his ear. "Sorry. What?"

Do I really want to know?

"I want you to look at me. Look really carefully." I close my eyes. "And think. Just concentrate. Please."

I expect him to object, but he doesn't. He presses his left palm to the glass and leans forward, cradling the phone with his other hand. I place my right hand against the window over his, and his fingertips peek out behind it.

A crease wrinkles at the edges of his brown eyes when he stares into mine. His gaze pulls me in, as if latched by an invisible rope.

"Alex." I labor to keep my voice steady. "I need to know. Do you know me?"

He blinks, his dark eyelashes sweeping down, then back up.

"Yes."

My breath hitches, leaving a foggy cloud on the window.

"It's fuzzy," he says, "but . . . I think we . . . we worked together."

Wind rattles through the curtains.

"Don't leave me, Eva," says a quivery voice.

"Don't be afraid." I blink back a sheet of tears. "It's just a summer job."

"Prisoner A.M.-624!"

I snap back to attention. Three jacks clomp into the Hole and rip the phone from Alex's hands, slamming it back onto its dock.

"Dinner, let's go," a jack roars, cuffing Alex's wrists.

The three men drag Alex behind them. He casts a final glance at me over his shoulder before they exit through the back.

The room behind the glass goes dark once more.

//

EVELYN SUMMERS: PRISONER E.S.–124
REHABILITATION DIARY
DAY 241

Ronnie and I sit together every day for meals now. For a while, we didn't talk. She'd eat her lunch and I'd eat mine, in silence, across the table from each other. I kept taking my usual empty table, expecting another meal alone. But Ronnie would plop down beside me within a couple minutes. She always let out a huff before sitting, like she was paying some obligatory price for not dying at the hands of Hannon's remote.

Hacks have started giving her crap for sitting with me. They call her the "Slinger Sympathizer." I can see in Ronnie's eyes that she's pissed, but she stays with me anyway.

I didn't know how long Ronnie intended to sit with me, how long she thought she had to pay off whatever debt she thought she owed me. It was weird. Part of me thought it was a trick. Like one day she was going to jump up and yell, "Just kidding!" and trip me or something.

Then last week, a bunch of us were assigned sweeping duty in the hall. The jacks unlocked the shackles binding us to one another, but left our individual ankle chains, turning sweeping into a shuffling dance routine.

I was brushing some cobwebs into the dustpan when Maura sneaked up behind me and shoved me to the floor.

All the hacks laughed, asking, "Did you slip, slinger?"

I tried to hoist myself up, but with my ankles tangled in the mass of chains, I ended up wobbling in place. The shackles pinned me to the floor.

That's when Ronnie shuffled over. She tapped Maura on the shoulder, and when the hack turned, Ronnie punched her in the face. Maura doubled over, clutching her nose, which spewed blood onto the freshly swept floor.

The other hacks surrounded their injured comrade, but Ronnie came to me instead. She offered me her hand. I met her eyes with disbelief, then laced my fingers with hers and let her pull me up.

The jacks sentenced Ronnie to five days in the Hole.

Of course, since she's been gone, I've spent the last five days eating alone. Not that I'm not used to it.

I knew Ronnie was being released from confinement today. I figured she'd want nothing more to do with me. She'd paid her debt, took one for the team, and now she'd go back to living her life. I'd resigned myself to lonely meals for the remainder of my sentence.

But today at lunch, she clacked her tray down beside me anyway.

I took a deep breath. "Ronnie, you didn't need to hit her like that. But . . . thank you. I—"

"No." She interrupted me, holding up her index finger. "I need to talk to you."

I shifted, slightly terrified of what might come out of her mouth.

"When I was a kid, I wanted to do something big with my life. I wanted to be someone that everyone knew—not some jackass celebrity but, you know, someone important. A scientist or something, like that guy who invented Klaurivex. I wanted to travel to every continent, see the world. I wanted to write about it and bring the world to people who couldn't see it themselves. I just . . . I don't know." She shook her head. "I don't know how I got sentenced to this shithole. And I probably never will. But I have a million things to do with my life. Six more continents to see. I have two little brothers—they're shitheads, but I love them, you know? I wanna see them grow up, attend their weddings, all that shit. And I almost lost it all. I almost lost that chance," she snorted, "because some bitch decided to scribble graffiti in the bathroom."

I didn't know what to say.

"God, Evelyn, I know I've been a bitch to you. Maybe you deserved it—at least a little, I don't know. But . . . you saved my life. And honestly, if someone treated me the way I'd treated you for months, I don't think I would have saved them like that. So . . ." She twiddled her fingers in her lap. "Thank you."

I opened my mouth, then closed it. I didn't have the right words to say, so I didn't say anything.

We ate the rest of our lunch in silence.

I stand in front of the bathroom mirror, pulling my hair into a tight bun. Trial five looms a mere hour away. No matter how many challenges I pass, my heart still thrums when the next one approaches.

I hesitate in the hall, rocking back and forth on my heels. I don't know why, but I approach the window and flip on the lights.

Alex jerks awake from where he lies, curled in a ball on the floor.

"Good morning," he says through a roaring yawn into the phone receiver.

I slide my hand down the back of my neck, over my collar. "Hi."

His eyes rake up and down my body. "You look . . . disheveled."

"Thanks."

I need to pump him for more information. What was our job together? Does he remember? If I really did work a summer job, it would've been after eighth grade—I got sent here May of freshman year. Middle school seems awfully young to be working, and plus, I recall the summer after eighth grade with perfect clarity. I would have remembered having a job. And since there's only an hour or so missing from my memory, my crime occurred during that time. What kind of job could have possibly only lasted an hour?

I swallow hard. The worst kind.

A million questions about Alex's memory boil inside me, but I blurt something else out instead.

"How'd you break your cuffs?"

He scratches his head, still blinking away sleep. "Break my what?"

"You don't remember your intake?"

"No. Are we supposed to?"

Well, technically no, but you've been unintentionally cheating the system for three days . . . "Never mind. Sorry." I pick at a loose thread on my sleeve.

Alex leans against the glass. "How would you know about my intake?"

"I don't." It's an event I'd rather not relive. And somehow I doubt the directors would be thrilled if they found out I told him what happened. So I lie. "I was just asking."

He gives me a half smile. "You know, for someone about to be released, you're very curious about the people still stuck inside."

"Slinger, let's go! Jacks are coming in five minutes!" Carolyn hollers from our quarters. "If I have to do push-ups because you're late, you're dead."

"She's lovely," Alex says.

I roll my eyes. "Oh, you don't know the half of it. I guess I gotta go."

"Hey. Knock 'em dead today."

"I'll try. How'd you know what I was doing anyway?"

He shrugs. "This dude Tom comes to talk to me sometimes, at that window over there." He points across the Hole. "Said you're all in the Freedom Trials. Lucky bastards."

A knot tightens in my chest. "Yeah, Tom's . . . a good guy."

At least, he was.

"Will you come back and visit me tonight?" he asks.

I sigh. "If I'm still alive tonight."

"You will be," he says. "I believe in you."

"You don't even know me."

"No. But I think I did once."

He presses his palm to the glass. I press my hand over his, four inches away. A strange sense of calm floods me.

The jacks come to line us up, and the feeling disappears.

The shrinking ranks of contenders arrive at the orientation room. Seven folding chairs form a semicircle around a giant standing mirror in the center. Red Hair sits in the farthest one, scribbling notes on her clipboard. Four jacks flank the door as we take our chairs. Sandwiched between Andrew and Desirae, I squeeze my elbows tight at my sides.

Directors Hannon, Agarwal, Zane, Zepp, and Marewood whisper among themselves, in the line of black chairs against the wall. Director Levine sits with them on the end, but remains quiet, twirling a pinch of copper hair around her finger. She meets my eyes and nods.

A jack escorts Doctor Allard into the room. He enthusiastically greets all six directors with a handshake before addressing us.

"Good morning," he says, a wide smile plastered across his face. "And welcome to your fifth trial."

Fabric rustles from the other contenders shifting in their seats. I fidget my cuffed hands in my lap.

Eight prisoners started the trials, but only five remain. Three trials to go. How many will pass them all?

Will any of us?

Will this be my last moment with Andrew? Carolyn? Miles? Desirae?

"Reflection"—Doctor Allard wraps his arm around the standing mirror like it's his prom date— "is your fifth principle of rehabilitation. Now, some previous contenders have called this the easiest trial." He gestures his hand in the air.

"However, others find it the hardest. So I'll leave that determination up to you."

Wow, way to be ambiguous.

"Reflection is what happens when you think about the past. Analyze it. Examine it. Look at it critically to improve the future. You cannot change the past, but you can learn from it."

He reveals a small hand mirror. Holding it outward at arms' length, he circulates the room, giving us each a quick glimpse at ourselves in the glass. I straighten my spine as he passes.

"Today is a day many of you have waited for, some of you for years, without realizing it." He snaps the hand mirror up to reflect his own face, and his grin widens. "Today is the day you will get answers to at least some of the questions you've been harboring throughout your sentences here."

My knee bounces against my bound hands.

"As you all know, you were tattooed upon admittance to the Stephens' Center. While all major details of your crimes are wiped, this tattoo serves as an eternal reminder of the crime you committed. Everyone you meet on the outside will know you once served time here, and you will probably have some explaining to do." He clasps the hand mirror's stem with both hands. "Today, to prepare you for this, we will temporarily remove your collars, and you will each see your tattoos."

The contenders inhale a unified gasp.

No. Way.

"One by one, the guard will remove your collars, and you will approach the mirror." He indicates the six-foot mirror beside him. "Once your crime is revealed to you, you will reflect upon why you believe you committed the crime and how you intend to prevent yourself from repeating it in the future. You'll share your answers with the group, so that we may all learn from one another."

Doing this with spectators who hate me isn't ideal.

"You'll be hooked up to a lie detector, so if you're dishonest in your remorse"—he wags his finger at us like we're little kids—"we'll know about it."

I'm pretty sure everyone stopped listening when he mentioned the whole collar-removal thing. Miles's eyes flick back and forth, his twitching feet pattering on the floor. Desirae leans forward in her chair, elbows perched on her knees, ready to pounce. Carolyn subconsciously tugs at her black braids. Andrew sports the toothiest smirk I've ever seen on his smug face.

"So to begin, let's start with . . ." Allard jabs his pointer finger around in the air. "Contender M.A.-402."

The jack unlocks Miles's cuffs, and the contender runs his hands through his close-cropped black hair. Another jack approaches him, armed with a black remote. My stomach flips at the all-too-familiar device.

The jack thrusts Miles's head down and scans the remote against the back of his collar. Something clicks and beeps, and the band unclasps itself, falling limply into the guard's waiting hands. Another jack quickly fastens a lie detector around the contender's wrist like a blood pressure cuff.

Miles brushes the indent in his dark skin, running his fingers around his bare neck. His lip trembles at the newfound taste of freedom.

Doctor Allard claps Miles on the back. We all lean in to try and catch a glimpse of the contender's exposed tattoo.

"When you're ready." Allard passes him the hand mirror.

Miles turns his back to the tall mirror and positions the handheld glass to reflect the back of his neck. I can almost hear the other contenders holding their breath as we wait for our comrade's dirty little secret.

"It says . . . armed robbery. I can't even imagine. . . ." He trails off.

"Tell us what you're feeling right now," Allard says, eager to act as ringleader for our big reveals. "Give us a peek into your brain."

 Well, this is rather touchy-feely, considering the other trials tried to kill us.

Miles chokes, shaking his head. "I . . . I don't feel like a robber. Maybe . . . maybe before I came here, I got in with the wrong crowd, and I felt like robbing was the right thing to do. But . . . I'm different now." The little needle on the lie detector points due north. "Armed? I don't even wanna look at a weapon. I don't feel like that anymore. I'm gonna work for what I want, not steal it."

Allard and the other directors break into hearty applause.

The contenders join in, weakly clapping with cuffed hands. Miles smiles, his cheeks flushing pink.

"Very good, M.A.-402. You have passed your fifth trial. Please pass the mirror to contender D.I.-119."

The jack refastens Miles's collar around his neck. It locks shut with a *thwiss*. Desirae slumps to the side as the jack unclicks her cuffs and straps the lie detector over her wrist. Her collar slides off, revealing her crime: arson.

She rattles off a spiel about regret and changing her life for the better. I'd love to know her secret for fooling that lie detector. If every director in the Center wasn't watching, I'd probably roll my eyes at her phony words.

Andrew goes next, and I'm not at all surprised when it's revealed that he physically assaulted someone. Hell, he almost physically assaulted me three days ago when I wouldn't let him pee. Rehabilitated, my ass.

He rambles on about how he'd never, ever, ever hurt anyone again, and I call foul on that little charade. I don't know how he cheats the lie detector, but the little needle doesn't budge.

Just get on with it, damn it.

Allard calls Carolyn next, and one jack removes her collar and cuffs while the other re-collars Andrew.

I force myself to keep still in my chair, despite my rocketing heart rate threatening to launch my body into the air.

Carolyn raises a brow when her tattoo is revealed—drug trafficking. "I . . . don't know what to say." She opens her mouth, then closes it. "I don't remember trafficking anything. I'm so, so sorry that I did, though. Jeez." She rubs a hand down her face. "I mean, someone could have gotten addicted to something because of me. That just sucks. I can't even believe it. It's . . . weird . . . being asked to apologize for something you don't remember doing—I mean, not that we shouldn't be remorseful about it," she corrects quickly. "But it's, like, it doesn't even feel like me who did it. It feels like it was another lifetime, another person. My nana didn't raise me like that. I feel like . . ." Her voice breaks. "I feel like I let her down."

I can't focus on anything but the fact that I'm next. I drum my fingers against my thighs.

"But I'm done now. I'm not going near so much as a poppy seed again. I wanna make my nana proud."

Applause ensues, and Allard commends Carolyn on her heartfelt words. I leap to my feet and stand awkwardly beside them, bouncing in place, waiting for permission to take my turn.

Finally, the jack approaches, brandishing the remote and mumbling at me to "keep my panties on." He uncuffs my wrists, and I wriggle my free hands. Not even the snug clasp of the lie detector around my arm can scare me; I'm too excited. The jack beside me snaps Carolyn's collar back on.

Something beeps. The metal slips off my neck, and for a second, I forget the trial completely. I close my eyes and inhale as deeply as I can, relishing the lack of constriction around my throat.

Carolyn gasps, clapping her hand over her mouth.

"What?"

She takes a step away from me.

I frantically paw at the back of my neck. "What is it?"

Carolyn thrusts me the mirror.

I hold it up to catch the reflection of my tattoo.

My heart stops.

The mirror slips from my hand and falls to the floor, shattering into a million pieces.

MURDER.

//

EVELYN SUMMERS: PRISONER E.S.–124
REHABILITATION DIARY
DAY 312

I don't know what I'd do without Ronnie. Between the glares from the other hacks, the constant shouts of "slinger," and the endless push-ups, I'd probably have given up by now without her. Plus, the other hacks are so afraid of her, no one assaults me anymore.

But I've got to be honest: Ronnie bugged me today at lunch. She wouldn't stop talking about this guy prisoner. There's a hot hack with a big 'fro across the cafeteria, and Ronnie's convinced she's going to have his babies when we get out of here. When I tried to change the subject, she asked me that dreaded question: "Have you ever had a boyfriend?"

Matt Houston was not a can of worms I felt like ripping open. "Nope," I stuttered between bites.

"Girlfriend?" she asked, her cheeks bulging with food.

"I'm into guys. I've just never dated anyone." Not officially anyway.

So of course, she had to make it a zillion times worse by not-so-quietly adding, "Wait, you're still a virgin?"

Maura's clique giggled at the next table until Ronnie shot them a death glare over her shoulder. I thought my face was going to ignite into flames. That girl has no filter. I nodded, wishing I could vanish into thin air.

Ronnie took this as an opportunity to regale me with tales of her sexual exploits, with a double helping of TMI.

There was a time I almost had a boyfriend. Maybe Matt Houston would've eventually been my first, if I hadn't become a criminal. When they first locked me up, I pictured us getting together the moment they released me. But he's a good guy. He'd never want anything to do with a convicted felon.

My aunt Lily used to ask about my love life—or lack there-of—incessantly when she was wasted. Maybe that's why Ronnie's question irked me so much. Lily used to pelt X-rated questions at me, critiquing my body and laughing when I blushed. She'd call me a slut, a virgin, a bitch. Then she'd steal mom's stuff and beg her for cash. Mom would get pissed and kick her out.

Two years ago, Mom told Aunt Lily she couldn't sleep over anymore. I mean, she only stayed with us when whatever scumbag of the week she was living with kicked her out. It always felt weird calling Lily my aunt when she's barely older than me. Mom's half sister is six years older than me but half as mature. Honestly, I couldn't blame my mom for wanting her out; Mom caught Lily sneaking into her medicine cabinet and stealing her Xanax. When Mom confronted her, Aunt Lily went ballistic and smashed my favorite picture frame on the kitchen floor.

I remember that caused crying. I don't remember if Mom cried or me, but I remember tears. That photo was my absolute favorite. I don't know why I like it so much. It's not even a full picture; the bottom half got ripped off over time, and now there's an ugly jagged edge.

I don't know the date it was taken, or even the occasion—I was only eight at the time. It's a picture of me, perched at the end of a bed, with the widest, most sincere grin on my face. I look like the happiest kid in the world. There's a vase of sunflowers on a table behind me and a heart-shaped balloon tied to one of the table legs. Happy stuff, for a happy day. Everything below my waist cuts off at the tear, but the top remains intact and pristine. If I close my eyes, I can almost pretend to be the little girl in that photo again—happy, without a care in the world. It's such a foreign feeling when you never see the sun.

Mom bought a new frame. She didn't talk to her sister for almost a month.

They've gone through phases of loving and loathing each other for as long as I can remember. Sometimes I don't understand why Mom allows Aunt Lily to stay in our lives—she's nothing but trouble. But whenever I asked, Mom shook her head and said she's her sister, and she'd do anything for her. I guess I'll never understand; one of the many pitfalls of being an only child.

The walls and corridors blur together in a mass of gray cement. The six-letter word circulates through my head on repeat, as if stamped into my brain instead of my neck. Desirae and Carolyn's suspicious stares sear into me like witch-hunting torches.

Five minutes ago, I blurted out answers to Allard's ridiculous questions about reflection. I closed my eyes and made some shit up. How could I even begin to justify the horrible crime I'd committed? Nothing I say could atone for the act of taking someone's life.

I don't remember everything I said to appease them, but I passed the fifth trial. I mumbled about how murder is wrong under any circumstances, and I'm so horribly ashamed of my past. That doesn't even begin to cut it.

My crime sits on my shoulders like barbells, weighing me down with every step closer to our quarters.

Murderer.

Killer.

Criminal.

The jacks abandon us in the female contender quarters. Carolyn slips past me, scooting her elbows to her sides to avoid the slightest brush against my arm, as if I'll lash out and kill again without warning.

Desirae jabs her thumb over her shoulder at Carolyn's retreating back. "I don't know why she's so shocked. We already knew you killed those three girls." She smirks and follows Carolyn to our room.

I want to scream that it wasn't my fault they died. I was tricked, and Zepp lied to make me tell. But I don't. I'm too drained.

I told Alex I'd stop by, but I need to be alone to think.

Seeking solitude in the bathroom, I sit on the edge of the closed toilet-seat lid, grasping my hair in fists.

Why would I kill someone? And more importantly, who was it?

Was my victim a stranger?

I can't stop picturing names and faces of people I love.

Or someone I knew?

The answer must be hidden somewhere in that dream.

If the black-hole door is a memory that only came back with the defective Memoria, that means they erased it on purpose. Whatever lurks in that dream is a clue. There's something in there they don't want me to know.

What would I see if I went through that door?

//

I lie awake with jittery hands and a restless leg that won't stay still. The more I try to force my brain to sleep and enter the dream, the more it stubbornly refuses to do so. Instead, it conjures gruesome images of murder and death.

Me, holding a knife, standing over a slashed body gushing blood on the carpet.

Me, holding a smoking gun, blowing a gaping hole in my victim's chest.

Me, with a pinch of powder, spiking someone's drink and watching their eyes go cold. With each new horror, I jerk up, gasping for air.

Our alarm won't ring for two more hours, and at this rate, I'll never sleep that long. Ironically, the one night I actually want the dream could be the first night I don't get it. Plagued with insomnia, I trek into the hallway and slump to the floor. It crosses my mind to flip on the light for some company, but I don't want to wake Alex. There's nothing I can do but wait for morning and whatever horrific new challenge that brings.

Two trials from freedom. Two trials from home.

I count squares in the drop ceiling, scuffs on the floor,

anything to force my mind from wandering into violent territory.

It doesn't work.

The short, six-letter word haunts me. Maybe the memory wipes are a form of mercy. Maybe it's better to have a clean slate, to not know the truth about who you are. If you don't know what you did, it can't follow you around like a shadow, always looming over you.

I always thought I had myself figured out. I thought I was a decent student, a great friend, a good person. But that's not the truth. I'm a felon; I snitched out three of my closest friends; I'm a killer. Killers definitely aren't good people.

Maybe I'm meant to be locked up. Maybe I don't deserve to get out.

Before long, my eyelids grow heavy, and I feel myself drift away.

//

Back in my mother's hallway, a chilling shudder rips through my body. I steady my breath and collect myself. Tonight is the night I suck it up and take the plunge.

My heart performs its usual drumroll routine, but I swallow down the fear and force my feet forward.

With a whir, the wall beside me ripples and expands, swirling into the mysterious doorway. I brace myself to face it head on. . . .

"Wake up!" Carolyn's shouts ring out in the distance. "God, I'm gonna kill her!"

The hallway dissolves, whisked away pixel by pixel.

"Wake up, you jackass murderer!" Someone jostles my elbow.

I jolt awake. Carolyn and Desirae hover over me.

"Sorry to interrupt your beauty sleep, your highness," Carolyn snaps. "We've been shouting at you. You should've been up twenty minutes ago."

I rub my groggy eyes.

Desirae slaps me in the face. "Get with it, slinger. If I have to do push-ups 'cause your sorry ass isn't ready, I'll turn our quarters into my own personal Green Room."

The hallway clock proclaims the time: 5:20 a.m.

Shit.

I shove past them before they can berate me further, to dress for our sixth trial.

///

EVELYN SUMMERS: PRISONER E.S.–124
REHABILITATION DIARY
DAY 404

I celebrated my sixteenth birthday today. At least, I think I did. There are no calendars here, so it's easy to lose track of months and seasons when you never go outside. Unlike old prison movies, no one actually scratches tally marks into our cell walls. But I've been trying to mentally track the days. I don't know the exact date they arrested me, since that part of my brain is all fuzzy.

Today felt like July 27, and the math seemed accurate, so I declared myself sweet sixteen. Plus, sometimes they give us semi-stale cookies at lunch, leftovers discarded by the directors, and today was a cookie day. So why not make it a birthday cookie? If I couldn't have my usual birthday cake, this would have to do.

Despite being my self-declared birthday, I was feeling kind of mopey. I missed my mom so bad it hurt. We always had a big pink cake on my birthday back home. Cake was a big deal in my house. It was a special treat we only had three times a year: on my birthday in July, on Mom's birthday in September, and some years, an extra cake a few months later. Just because.

Ronnie sat beside me at lunch with a sly grin on her face.

"Happy birthday, bitch." She tossed me two additional stale cookies.

"How'd you get these?"

"I owed Maura and Rachel some payback for, you know, being

responsible for my near-death experience. And I really wanted to. So I stole them."

"You're going to get in trouble. You shouldn't have done that." I shook my head. "Haven't you been busted for shitty bed making, like, four times in the past three weeks? Do you really want to get caught thieving?"

"Please. What are they gonna do? Throw me in the Hole? I could use a break from my chores anyway." Ronnie stacked the three cookies on my Styrofoam plate. "It's not a cake, but best I could do. Close your eyes and pretend they aren't hard as a rock."

When I'm out of juvie, I know people will judge me for meeting my best friend in prison. But I don't care. She'll still be my best friend on the outside; screw what people think.

I closed my eyes and made a birthday wish on my imaginary candles—I wished to get to my Freedom Trials ASAP, so I could get out of here and see my mom again. If I could have one thing in the world, right now, that would be it. I know they say telling someone your wish means it won't come true, but writing it down doesn't count, right?

I hope it happens before I'm fifty.

We reach the orientation room, but the jacks lead us past the door, down an unfamiliar corridor. The single fluorescent bulb over our heads flickers, threatening to burn out at any moment. A metallic odor bites my nostrils, and I wrinkle my nose.

They halt our line at a blue steel door. A jack slides her ID into the slot and the dead bolt clicks. We walk into a cramped square room with two long, black couches covered in clear plastic. Chipped white paint streaks the cement walls, with a black analog clock near the ceiling. Embedded in the back wall is another rusty door, painted with red lettering that has almost completely rubbed off; all I can make out is a B, a V, and a DE. Doctor Allard lies sprawled out on one of the couches but springs to his feet like a tiger when we enter the room.

"Good morning, contenders!" His eyes are practically bulging out of his head. "And welcome to your sixth trial. Congratulations on making it to your second-to-last challenge." I wonder if coffee runs through his veins instead of blood.

The jacks uncuff us, and we offer Allard a salute before huddling in a circle around him.

"The theme of this trial is justice." He rotates, meeting each of our eyes in turn. "When your crimes resulted in a sentence to the Stephens' Center, that was an example of justice. Justice is required for society to run smoothly and without crime." He flairs his fingers out as he speaks, embellishing the dry words.

"Justice is our sixth principle of rehabilitation. Today, we will test your ability to balance, determine, judge, and serve justice."

I shuffle back and forth on the balls of my feet.

"For this trial," Allard continues, "you will not be with the other contenders. One by one, we will call you into the next room, where you will complete your trial individually."

Relief courses through my veins. The others won't be watching, waiting for me to fail.

"You'll learn more when you begin your trial." A grin bursts across Allard's wrinkly ape face. "So, without further ado, today we're starting with Contender C.P.-680. The rest of you, please make yourselves comfortable." He gestures toward Carolyn. "C.P.-680, if you will." They both disappear through the back door, which clanks shut behind them.

Andrew and Desirae each collapse onto a couch, not bothering to leave room for Miles or me. Andrew's long frame engulfs the entire sofa; he rests his head on one armrest and his toes brush the other. Desirae perches in the center of the other couch, draping her arms like wings over the cushions to mark her territory. Miles paces back and forth between the two sofas, mumbling to himself.

Two jacks guard each door. I lean against the wall, arms folded across my chest, waiting.

Twenty minutes pass when the back door swings open. Doctor Allard saunters into the room alone. "A.R.-329, you're up."

Andrew rises from the couch and follows the director. Miles plops down in Andrew's spot, knee bouncing against his hand.

Fifteen minutes later, Doctor Allard reemerges. "Okay, E.S.-124, we're ready for you. Right this way."

I take a deep breath and trudge toward Allard. He holds the steel door open for me, and I have to duck under his arm to pass through.

We enter a short, dimly lit hallway, with a second door at the end. I follow him down the corridor, into the next room.

All six block directors and Red Hair sit around a circular faux-wooden table in the center of the room. Aside from a ceiling spotlight illuminating the directors and the table, pitch darkness engulfs everything else. It reminds me of interrogation chambers from old movies, like someone's going to shine a hot lamp in my face and ask me whodunit. I gulp down the nerves twisting inside and wipe all traces of emotion off my face.

Director Levine pulls out an empty chair beside her. "Evelyn, have a seat."

"Yes, ma'am." I sit and splay my hands flat on the table like they taught me. My shields are down at the mercy of the directors.

Doctor Allard takes the other empty seat between Directors Zane and Hannon, filling the crowded table. Red Hair's elbow knocks into Marewood's arm as she scribbles across her clipboard.

Director Agarwal speaks first. "Hello, E.S.-124. Nice to see you again."

I force my voice not to quiver. "You too, sir."

"Today, as you know, we'll be testing you on the sixth principle of rehabilitation: justice. Now, I'm going to read a list of three hypothetical scenarios we've come up with." He thumbs through a stack of papers on the table. "Your trial is to determine the best course of action in response to the given situation—an action that best exemplifies justice. Each scenario will require critical thinking on your part."

"Yes, sir."

"Think of them like case studies, if you will. As directors, we make these decisions every day. Imagine you're a director and must think and act as we would in each proposed scenario."

"Yes, sir."

Agarwal smiles. "Okay. Let's begin." He plucks the first sheet of paper from his stack. "First we have—"

"Wait." Hannon reaches across the table and rips the papers from his hand. She flicks through them, tugging three sheets from the middle of the pile. Marewood leans over her shoulder and nods. Levine narrows her eyes and leans in, but Hannon tilts the papers away from her. "These are Evelyn's assignments." She thrusts the pages back to the youngest director.

Agarwal skims the sheets. "Yes. Very good. Okay, E.S.-124, we'll start with Hypothetical Prisoner A. Prisoner A is a male who has been at the Stephens' Center for six months. Lately, he's been getting into physical altercations with other prisoners and recently made a lewd joke about a female guard. How would you respond with justice?"

Okay. That's not so bad. I can do this. "Well, I think I'd have a discussion with him about the Center's expectations and assign him a really awful chore for a while, like toilet scrubbing. And I'd make him do it under the command of a female guard, so he'd learn some respect. Maybe force him to eat his meals in solitude for a few days, so he can't get into fights."

Red Hair scribbles on her notepad.

"Very good," Director Levine says. "That's a similar course of action to something I might recommend myself."

"Thank you, ma'am."

"Yes, a just punishment indeed," Agarwal says. "Now, let's move on to Hypothetical Prisoner B. Prisoner B, a

Level Three, has demonstrated perfect behavior since day one. He follows every rule, has never exhibited violence toward a guard or another prisoner, and works toward his full potential in both group and chore time. His behavioral modification therapist says that he appears to deeply regret his criminal past and has a genuine desire to reform. He has been incarcerated for nine months, which is considered the minimum sentence for an offender of his crime." He leans forward. "How would you respond with justice?"

"Well . . ." I run over the facts a few times in my head, tapping my finger to my lips. "Honestly, it sounds like his rehabilitation was successful. I'd say he's probably ready to begin his Freedom Trials."

Director Agarwal grins. "Well done. I do believe you're right."

Red Hair's pen dashes across her notepad.

"Okay, last one." Agarwal pulls out the third sheet. "Hypothetical Prisoner C has spent several years serving time for a crime that generally results in rehabilitation within a few months. She has repeatedly slacked on her chores and demonstrates a severe lack of respect for authority. She has responded to both guards and other inmates with violence and vulgarity. While she completes her chores, they are always halfheartedly done. Her block director believes she has shown no improvement and questions if she has the capacity to reform at all." He places the sheet neatly on top of the stack. "How would you respond with justice?"

I fidget. I know the answer they want to hear. It's shitty, and never something I'd actually agree with, but I know it's what they're looking for.

"I would conclude that rehabilitation has failed and sentence the criminal to execution."

I meet Director Agarwal's eyes, not letting my gaze falter; he has to believe this is sincere.

"You would sentence her to die?" He cocks his head. "Really?"

"Yes, sir."

"Fascinating." Director Agarwal leans back in his chair. "Excellent. Just responses for all three cases. Congratulations, E.S.-124, you passed your sixth trial."

I close my eyes and release a heavy sigh.

Doctor Allard stands. "A fine judgment indeed, displaying a high capacity for understanding how justice truly works. Well done, E.S.-124." He shakes my hand; my thin fingers disappear in his gorilla grasp.

"All right." He claps his arms to his sides. "Let's get on with it."

I blink. "Get on with what?"

"Prisoner A is on my block." Director Zane rises to his feet. "I will ensure his sentence is carried out this afternoon. He's got a week's worth of toilet scrubbing in his future, lucky guy."

The other directors don't hide their chuckles.

"Wait . . ." I furrow my brow. "This was hypothetical."

"And Prisoner B is the star member of my block," Director Marewood says. "He'll be thrilled to hear he'll be starting his Freedom Trials next round."

I freeze.

But that means . . .

The lights flash on. An eerie sense of déjà vu falls over me as I survey the room.

I've been here before.

I scramble to the massive window in the back. It peeks into a dingy space with chipping green cement walls. My mouth runs dry.

No.

A door creaks open in the Green Room and two jacks march in, dragging a handcuffed prisoner by her armpits. She flails and thrashes but can't fight the guards' firm grips.

It's Ronnie.

No, no, no, no, no.

I press my palms to the window, my breath fogging against the glass.

"I changed my mind." My voice cracks. "Make her clean toilets. Put her in the Hole."

Hannon clicks her tongue. "Not how it works, E.S.-124."

"But—"

"Justice is not simply making decisions but acting on them and sticking with your choices," Director Zepp snaps. "There are no buts."

"What's done is done," Allard says. "You cannot change

your answers. There are no easy choices on the path to just—"

"This isn't justice! You lied to me!" I grab Director Levine by her upper arms. "You can't do this!"

The nearest jack rips my hands off her and slaps me in the face. "Keep your hands to yourself, or you'll be the next one down in that room." He shoves me toward the window.

Hot tears sting my eyes. The directors mumble to one another behind me. A female jack unlocks Ronnie's cuffs. My best friend's eyes grow wide, frantically darting around the room.

She does a double take when she catches my gaze, and a chill shoots down my spine.

Evelyn? Her mouth forms the word but no sound comes out.

"Veronica Hartman," Doctor Allard says into the microphone, his crackling voice broadcasting into the Green Room. "It has been decided by our Center Board of Directors that you have not completed your rehabilitation to our standards. As part of her Freedom Trials, contender Evelyn Summers was given the task of determining your punishment to demonstrate her knowledge of justice."

Ronnie's eyes pierce mine, her trembling lips parading all the betrayal and fear swirling behind her gaze.

No. Not again. I can't do this again.

"Ms. Summers has concluded that the just response to your actions is execution. Therefore, you have hereby been sentenced to die."

My thudding heart drowns out his words in my ears.

No. Stop it. I have to stop it. I have to do something.

A million protesting words rise and die inside me.

Ronnie's body shakes under intermittent sobs. "No, please . . . I'll do better . . ."

"It's too late," Doctor Allard says. "The time has come and gone for you to demonstrate your willingness to rehabilitate. Our decision is final." He switches off the microphone.

I press my palms to the window, a helpless spectator behind the glass. Shallow breaths catch in my throat.

"Ready!" a voice thunders.

Four jacks raise their rifles.

No.

"Aim!"

Ronnie's eyes lock with mine, her open mouth quivering with silent screams.

No, no, no, no, no. I'm sorry. No.

"Fire!"

//

EVELYN SUMMERS: PRISONER E.S.–124
REHABILITATION DIARY
DAY 518

When I was in sixth grade, we had to read this short story called "The Tell-Tale Heart." In the story, a man commits murder, chops up the body, and buries his victim under the floorboards. Looking back, it was kind of a creepy story to make a bunch of eleven-year-olds read, but whatever.

After a few days, the cops show up and search the man's house, but they don't find any evidence. The murderer covered his tracks well. Then suddenly, he swears he can hear the dead man's heart beating—pounding—right under his feet. Faster, louder, until the murderer finally freaks out and confesses.

I remember thinking that if the man had kept his mouth shut, he never would have gotten caught. Obviously the heartbeats were only in his head, and he should have just lived with it. It could've been so simple. He could've led a normal life. Then I remember thinking how messed up it was that I was contemplating how to get away with murder. What was wrong with me?

I get it now.

I don't hear heartbeats under my concrete cell floor. But I can feel them. Everywhere I look, Sarah, Ariadne, and Courtney are there. Sometimes I'll do a double take in the hallway when a girl with short dark hair and glasses walks by. For half a moment, I'll swear it's Sarah. Then sometimes, someone in the cafeteria will laugh a certain way, and for a split second, I'll hear Courtney. This is going to sound super weird, but one time I heard a girl crying in a bathroom stall, and my heart leapt, because it sounded just like Ariadne that day she started crying at breakfast. I almost called out her name.

They're everywhere and nowhere all at once. I feel them, heavy in my chest, a weight I can't get rid of.

Sometimes, when I'm stuck washing floors, I imagine I have a time machine and can go back and save them. Or that I make a bargain with some sort of higher power—maybe it's a god, or the devil, or someone else—and my friends magically reappear. I picture them as ghosts, watching me as I recite my lines or suffer through my chores. Not really gone; that feels too final.

They are my tell-tale heart. Always there, always beating—soft as a whisper or loud as a cannon—in the back of my mind. Following me. A shadow, trailing behind.

Some days I wish they'd go away. I wish the Center would wipe them from my mind like they never existed. But most days I hope they never leave me.

And then there are other days I reach out and grab Ronnie by the arm. I pretend to brush a piece of dust off her peels, just to touch her. To feel her warmth and realize she's there, solid and fleshy and alive. She scowls at me every time, but I don't care. For the brief moments in the cafeteria the Center lets Ronnie and me hang out together, I feel normal. I feel human. I feel like I am surrounded by people and not by ghosts, even though "people" is really just one. Maybe one is all anyone needs.

I will not let the Center take away my humanity. I will do whatever I can to redeem myself until all the ghosts go quiet. I will prove to whichever souls of Sarah, Ariadne, and Courtney that haunt me in the hallways that I regret it all. I will never hurt anyone again.

I never told them I was sorry.

I hope someday I can prove it instead.

I storm into my quarters and kick off my boots, flinging them into the wall. A piercing scream rockets through my body, draining my lungs and drowning the room. I scream until I can't scream anymore, then I collapse onto my bed and sob into my pillow. My cries probably echo past the locked door and into the bowels of the Center, but I don't care.

She's gone. She's really gone. She's dead. And it's all my fault.

Just like Sarah.

Just like Ariadne.

Just like Courtney.

And just like the other person I murdered.

I'm a murderer. I'm everything they think I am. Everything my tattoo says I am.

My best friend's final thought was of my betrayal.

I sacrificed her life to earn my freedom.

I press my soaked pillow to my puffy face and scream as loud as I can, slamming my fist into the mattress.

The door creaks open. I force my limbs to lie limp on the sheets.

"Oh hey, slinger, I was wondering where you went," Desirae says. "They were still cleaning up her blood when they called me in. I should have expected as much, given they let the slinger pass judgment. Must've been your favorite trial!"

I roll over and face her, not caring if she sees my tears.

"You're crying?" Her tone is sickly sweet. "That's funny." She sinks into the metal chair. "I thought this trial would've been right up your alley. I figured you'd enjoy adding another kill to your list."

My mind goes blank.

I launch myself off the bed.

Desirae shrieks as I crash into her, plunging my fists into her stomach. The chair tips backward, and we tumble to the floor. I pummel her with every drop of strength in my arms, fists meeting fabric with rustling thumps.

Desirae flings her knee up to kick me, but I pin her to the floor with my weight, raining fists onto any part of her I can find, hollering with rage. She yanks a fistful of hair from my skull, whipping her other fist into my jaw.

I grip my stinging face for a nanosecond, but she elbows me in the stomach, knocking the wind from my lungs. She shoves me off of her and rolls on top of me, plowing her fist into my chest. We roll, one on top of the other, ripping each other's peels and sending fists and knees flying. Clumps of hair float to the ground.

Somewhere behind us, I'm half aware of the door flinging open.

"Oh my God, what the hell?" Someone pries me off of Desirae and throws me to the floor. Hair splayed across her face and panting, Desirae charges for me. Carolyn throws out an arm to stop her, thumping her in the chest.

"Both of you, stop!" Carolyn thunders, her cornrows hidden beneath a shower cap. "We're gonna get in trouble!"

"Keep her the hell away from me," Desirae snarls, her shoulders rising and falling with heaving breaths. She presses her finger to her split lip. Bleeding fingernail tracks mar her face.

Hatred floods my body. I ball my fists, daring her to try anything.

"Now cool the fuck down." Carolyn glances from Desirae to me.

Desirae's eyes shoot me with invisible bullets. I turn on my heels and stomp from our quarters, channeling every ounce of anger into slamming the door behind me.

My whole body aches. Warm blood leaks from the scratch on my cheek. I kick the cement wall, barely feeling the sting as the hard surface meets my sock-clad toes. All the violent things I'd like to do to Desirae course through me.

That bitch. That horrible fucking bitch.

Maybe once it was "us versus them." And maybe I never truly fit into either category. But now I know the truth: there is no "us" or "them." There's only me. I am alone, and it's me against the world. I am the only one who can get myself out of this mess.

I clomp toward the dark window and snatch the phone, flicking on the lights.

Alex startles from his corner in the back.

He collects the other phone. "You okay?"

"No."

"Your stare could melt ice right now."

I roll my eyes.

"What the hell happened?" he asks. "You look like you were out in a hurricane. And what happened to your face?"

"I don't wanna talk about it."

"Okay."

I sit cross-legged on the floor, fuming, ready to punch anything that dares get in my crosshairs.

We sit in silence for a while, and my pulse slowly decelerates.

"Sorry," I mutter. "I needed to be out of that room."

Alex gestures his hands at the confined Hole around him. "I know the feeling."

We share an awkward laugh, and my anger melts into an overbearing sense of loss.

A heavy weight drops into my chest, knotting and pulling at everything inside me as if the bullet that killed

Ronnie also tore a hole in my heart. I can atone forever, I can rehabilitate until I'm eighty; I'll never make up for what I've done. I am a killer. I sacrificed my best friend to save myself. I am lower than a criminal.

"Hey." Alex's eyebrows knit together. "You look like you're gonna cry."

I swallow down a hard lump. "It's nothing, really." Tears burn behind my eyes, threatening to spill out. I can't talk about this anymore. I'll completely break down. "Tell me . . . tell me something about you." Something to distract my mind. Anything.

"Um." He thinks for a moment. "Let's see. I bake a mean strawberry layer cake."

I smile.

"I have two little sisters. Cora and Abby. Cora's going through a preteen too-good-for-everyone phase, so she's become a little brat most of the time. Abby's still cool—at least for now. But they're good kids. I love them, you know?"

Something about his words stab me in the gut. My mind flashes to Ronnie and her twin brothers. She'll never see them again. And it's all my fault.

My face scrunches, and the tears pour out. Before I can stop myself, I'm convulsing with sobs.

"Eva, shit." Alex's voice softens. "What did I say? I'm sorry."

I can't talk, can't think. I collapse against the window and let the sobs shudder through me. "She's gone." The words come out a gummy, incoherent babble, but I don't care.

The finality of it all guts me. "She's really gone." I let the phone slip from my fingers and fall into my lap.

For an hour, I let it out. The world goes on around me, but I'm frozen in a moment of pain and tears that wrecks me to the core. I sob until snot runs from my nose and my body goes numb against the glass. I cry until my eyes sting and my chest burns and I can't cry anymore.

She would want me to keep going. She wouldn't want the Center to win.

I wipe my face on my sleeve.

When I look up, Alex is still sitting there, behind four inches of glass that might as well be a football field. A mask of worry shadows his gaze, but it fades slightly when I meet his eyes. I'm surprised he's still here. He hasn't gotten up and left this whole time. It's weirdly comforting, seeing him there beside me. Like I'm not so alone anymore.

I sniffle, pulling myself up and pressing the phone back to my ear. "Sorry."

"Don't be sorry."

I wish I could touch him—just to feel the warmth of another person. It's so wrong. Everything in this foul, cement-walled shithole is wrong. "This is all so fucked up."

"They literally stole memories out of our heads and locked us up for something we can't even remember." Alex gives me a sympathetic smile. "Fucked up is the right phrase."

I wish Ronnie were here. She'd have answers. She'd probably bring up Center spies and conspiracy theories and all that stuff I used to roll my eyes about. Now I'd give anything to hear one of her theories again. She'd tell me the Center had planned this whole thing, and my black-hole dream is yet another peg in their scheme. That maybe everything they've done had a reason.

I sit up straighter.

Is it so outlandish a theory?

"Do you ever feel . . ." I fidget, uncomfortable. "I don't know. Like all of this is somehow connected? That we're all playing a part?"

"Is that some sort of conspiracy theory?"

I sigh. "No. I just . . . I just miss my best friend."

"She on the outside?"

I close my eyes, fighting back another wave of tears. "I don't wanna talk about it." But now that I'm thinking about it, I can't stop. What would Ronnie say if she were here? She would have something to explain it all. I know she would. "I just wish I could remember."

"What's going on?"

"What's going on?" Alex brushes my cheek with his fingertips, his eyes crinkled with worry. "Something happened, didn't it?" He takes my shaking hand in his, lacing our fingers together.

"I need to go back. It all went wrong." My voice falters. "I should never have come here. I never should have dragged you into this."

"Stop." He pulls me into his arms. The leathery scent of his jacket overwhelms me with a familiar feeling of safety. "I already told you. We're in this together."

"Eva?"

I startle, heart racing a million miles a minute. My mouth opens, but closes again.

"You okay?"

"I just . . . had a . . . I don't know, a flash of something." I hide my flushing cheek behind my hand. That was weird. Why was I being semi-romantic with Alex? "A memory."

"What was it?"

I close my eyes and rest my forehead on my palm, trying to grasp at the fading images. "I don't even know." And I'd never tell him what I just saw.

"Eva . . ."

"I just . . . I can't right now." I rub my hands down my face. "Something's changing. The memories come back without warning, like a movie I can't shut off or make any sense out of."

"Sorry." He sighs. "Eva, I have to . . . I should probably tell you something."

"What?"

His eyes flick up to the camera in the corner of the Hole, then back down to his phone. He cups his hand around the receiver, shielding his mouth to avoid a lip-reading jack. "More memories came back a couple hours ago. Like someone opened the floodgates, and they came spilling back."

"You . . . you remember everything?"

"Not everything." He shakes his head. "I don't know what job we had. But I remember our last night together.

You said you needed to find . . . someone. Desperately. I didn't catch the name. We were hugging goodbye. Like, permanent goodbye, the type where you don't know if you'll ever see the person again. Any idea who you were looking for?"

"No." I rub my forehead. "That's gibberish."

Alex and I were hugging?

"There's still a lot I don't remember," he says. "But I do remember some other things. About . . . you."

So he knew stuff about me before I did? What the hell?

"Stuff about me?" I throw out my hands and the phone flies to the floor with a smack. I snatch it back up. "And you didn't feel the need tell me this the moment I sat out here?"

"You seemed so upset, I didn't wanna make it worse. Listen to me. There are still big empty patches I can't put together. Like, things that don't make sense. And the things I saw . . . they weren't good, Eva."

"It's not looking good," a male voice says, shaking his head. "She only has about four months to live, five if we're lucky."

I clap my hand to my mouth. "No. That can't . . . no."

"There is one option."

"Eva?"

I snap back to the present. What? Who has four months to live?

"Eva, are you okay?"

"What? Now you wanna talk?" I pick at the raw scratch on my face, not meeting the eyes of the boy I was beginning to trust. This is getting ridiculous. I'm sick of seeing half-second fragments of memories I don't understand. I can't even deal with this shit anymore. "This is the worst day ever. And that bitch marred my face, and I'm ninety-nine percent sure I'm gonna get bruises from the fight, and—"

"Wait, what fight?"

"I was in a fight, with another contender who's had it out for me since day one for something that wasn't even my fault. And my whole body is sore because we hit the ground pretty hard, and honestly, I want to go home, pretend this whole two-year shit show never happened. I just want to go back to living with my mom."

Alex blinks.

I roll my eyes. "What is it now?"

"You really don't remember . . . do you?"

"No, I don't." I huff. "Like I already told you, I don't remember shit about my own life. How can I possibly be clearer?" I punch the window, grimacing at the throbbing in my knuckles afterward.

"Eva, you don't live with your mom." He lowers his voice. "You live with your aunt."

His bizarre words strike me, and I can't help it—I burst out laughing.

"What's so funny?"

"My evil aunt Lily? Yeah, okay. Good one, Alex. Seriously, my mom can barely tolerate that woman, I don't know why you'd think I—"

"Eva, stop. Your mom's dead."

EVELYN SUMMERS: PRISONER E.S.–124
REHABILITATION DIARY
DAY 605

At lunch today, Ronnie asked about my first kiss. I lied and told her I'd never kissed anyone, because I couldn't bear to explain. She already thinks I'm super innocent, so she bought it. Her question felt like ramming a knife into my heart, so let's not also twist the blade.

Matt and I kissed once. We were at Sherri Sherman's New Year's Eve party, the winter before I came to the Center. She'd made all these awesome little cheese cubes, mini sausages, and hummus. It was the first New Year's Eve I didn't spend at home. We sipped sparkling cider and watched the countdown on TV.

Sherri's dad was stuck in the hospital over the holidays, held prisoner to whatever new experimental drug of the week they thought would be "the one" to cure his ALS. It was his seventh try or something, and not looking good. I think her mom thought the party would help cheer Sherri up, because her Christmas blew, sitting in white-walled hospital waiting rooms for hours, praying for a miracle.

Matt had on this navy blue shirt, unbuttoned at the top to expose a few tantalizing inches of chest. His jeans sagged a bit at his waist, and damn, he looked hot. Seeing him made my insides go all mushy. Even though he was a senior and I was a lowly freshman, I wasn't going to throw away my shot.

I hovered awkwardly near him, occasionally brushing his arm in an awkward attempt at flirting. My face got hot when he turned to talk to Allie Thompson instead. Everyone knew they'd broken up in November, but it still stung seeing them together. Allie's family is tied at the hip to the Shermans, so I should have known she'd be at the party. I don't actually mind Allie. She's nice. But it still hurt.

I couldn't stop stewing. Someone like him would never want me. I should have picked a sexier outfit for the party instead of a blue sweater and jeans. Matt and Allie would probably be back together by the end of the night, and I'd be stuck watching them make out again.

I'd been getting these awful migraines for a few months, so I wasn't surprised I had a pounding headache. But when the dull ache escalated to a throbbing pain behind my right temple, it sent a surge of anger through my core. Because on top of playing second fiddle to Allie, now I couldn't even focus on enjoying the party.

I simultaneously tried to tune out Allie and Matt's conversation beside me and my oncoming migraine.

Midnight ticked closer. The ball was dropping, and most people were coupled up, huddling around the TV. When I looked up, Allie was in Corbin Michaels's arms, lips locked on his before the clock even struck twelve. I think Matt noticed them at the same time, because when I glanced over, his eyes were glued to the new couple.

Some people blew those obnoxious party horns when the clock struck midnight. Matt whirled around, grabbed my forearms, and kissed me, right there in the center of the room. My headache faded into nothing as my heart somersaulted through my chest.

Within two seconds, Matt jerked back. He scratched his neck, suddenly fixated on Sherri's beige carpet.

The party ended, and I grinned the whole way home.

I remember feeling like things were finally going to turn around. A win for Evelyn. I'd get a boyfriend, and my life would be awesome.

The next week at school, Matt told me he didn't want a relationship. He'd met an older girl at a party and wanted some casual fun before leaving for college in the fall. He threw the classic "it's not you, it's me" bullshit in my face. My heart sank, but I smiled and told him I understood, and I didn't want one either. The lies clumped in my mouth as I spoke. An older girl. Of course. Because I was just innocent little Evelyn, the girl everyone wanted as a friend but no one wanted to kiss.

At least Sherri Sherman had a good day. She sat beside me at lunch with happy tears in her eyes and told me her dad had made a full recovery. He was one of the first patients to be cured by Klaurivex. I listened as she chattered, but I couldn't relish in someone else's happiness. All I felt was resentment, which made me feel worse, for being a shitty friend.

Four months later, Matt told me he'd made a mistake and wanted to start over. I embraced his words as eagerly as I embraced him, in the foyer outside the school library.

We made plans to go to the lake for a day that summer. He said he'd take me to the burger place he used to take Allie, and it all sounded so amazing. My life had done a one-eighty, and in that moment, I could have floated in the air. I thought all my dreams were coming true.

But they didn't.

Because that's what happens when you get arrested. Everything changes.

Alex presses his hand to the glass. "I'm so sorry."

"Is this some sort of sick joke? You're lying."

"Eva, I—"

"You're full of shit. How could you even know that anyway?"

"Because you told me yourself!"

"Stop it, Alex! Just stop!"

It's not true. It can't be true.

A veil of knowing dread cascades over me. I get a flash of something—Mom's brown eyes, wide and vacant and empty. Nausea rampages in my stomach.

It's the truth.

I jump to my feet and throw the phone to the ground; the curly cord catches it, bouncing it back up like a bungee cord, two inches from hitting the floor. It dangles in the air, tapping the glass as it sways back and forth. I dash down the hall, leaving Alex alone in the blinding light.

Desirae and Carolyn don't acknowledge me when I plow through the door to our quarters. Desirae presses a wet towel to her eye, nursing her wound from our fight. She rotates her back to me.

I face-plant on my bed. My whole body aches from Desirae's fists, but that's not the pain I feel the most.

I'm queasy. I'm tired. I'm wracked with a level of devastation I've never felt before.

My mother's dead. My best friend is dead. I'm a murderer.

Could I have killed my mother? Could something have driven me to murder her? My own family?

I wrap the coarse sheet around me like a burrito and tug the blanket over my head.

Why would they erase her death? Why let me spend two years believing I'd have a family to go home to when I finally got out of this shithole? I have no one. I have nothing left.

Someone had four months to live. I saw it in that messed-up memory. Was it Mom? But why? What was wrong with her? If my mom was sick, I would have remembered it. Klaurivex would have cured her.

The jacks bring our lunch, and then several hours later, our dinner. I don't move an inch. Carolyn and Desirae try to provoke me, but I don't let them. I stay curled in bed while they divvy up my meals between them. Food won't quench the ache in my stomach.

I stare at a crack that's spiderwebbing across the nearest cement brick in the wall. The tears dry, but my eyes still burn. I shift my legs under the covers, but the movement is foreign and numb. I feel like my heart got thrown into a wood chipper, and it now lies shredded in bits in my chest.

Nothing about these memories makes sense.

"Last trial tomorrow," Carolyn says. I almost don't catch her words, but unfortunately, the pillow doesn't block out everything—it just muffles. I press it harder to my ears, longing to drown out the harsh voices of the Center's finest.

"Yeah, about time," Desirae says. "I need to get out of here before that thing attacks me again."

I don't need to look up to know she's talking about me.

Hours slip by, and one of the hacks shuts off the lights.

It's at least two in the morning before my eyelids finally close and I drift off to sleep.

///

Darkness swallows me whole, spitting me out at the mouth of my mother's hallway—is it even her hallway anymore? Whatever, I'm still in this same damn place. This awful, ugly place that's haunted me night after night.

I don't want to see this right now. I don't want to be here. Let me wake up.

My knees buckle, and I sink to the ground.

Why bother walking to the end? Mom isn't there. She's dead.

"I don't wanna play this game anymore," I call to no one through the empty dreamscape. "I'm not walking another step. I give up."

Nothing happens.

The door at the end stretches farther away from me, taunting me with the mother I'll never reach again. The mother who should be waiting for me in her room but isn't there anymore. I've been foolishly chasing that door for the past two years.

Because, for some sick reason, they erased her death from my brain.

They. They did this.

They put me here. They erased the very last moments I had with my mom, and it has something to do with that imaginary door.

Poison courses through my veins, inflating me with rage.

I rise to my feet. Whatever is behind that door, good or bad, I need to know.

No more trembling. No more fleeing. Whatever it is, I'll meet it head on.

My pace quickens down the dark corridor.

The black hole warbles to my left. I spin toward it, ready to face the darkness. It stretches upward, materializing into the third door my mind invented in the hallway. I stand ready, with my right foot slightly in front of my left.

The doorframe ripples and bends until the uppermost line thickens and solidifies. Two walls on either side of the gap freeze in time, creating the mysterious opening.

Now or never.

My foot hovers over the dark threshold. I put up my fists, poised to fight whatever nightmare monster lies beyond the entry. The skeletons in my closet.

I take a deep breath and step inside.

Nothing happens. It's dark.

I bring my foot down another step, and it crunches on something hard. My shoulders tense. I bend over and retrieve the plastic action figure wedged between the carpet and my boot.

What the hell?

I examine the toy, running my fingers around every edge of the plastic soldier before letting it fall back to the floor.

Darkness floods the room, but as my eyes adjust, shapes and colors come into focus.

Not just a single toy—toys—tons of toys. Everywhere. Stuffed animals, plastic rockets, LEGO bricks, building blocks, and dinosaurs lie strewn across the floor at my feet. Some are broken, lying in plastic shards ground into the carpet. A red-and-blue wooden airplane spins over my head from a dangling mobile.

It's like a graveyard of childhood.

I pluck a fuzzy teddy bear from the floor and hug it to my chest, longing to absorb comfort from a dream-induced stuffed animal. It pings my heart with familiarity I can't place. I feel like the answer to a big riddle hovers in front of my face, but it's out of focus—like my mind needs glasses to see it.

I walk around the room with the bear. A pint-size bed with superhero sheets sits in the corner. A rocket ship–shaped lamp lies cracked on the floor beneath a dresser coated in dust. Fluttering blue curtains frame a rectangular window. It looks like an abandoned child's bedroom.

But why did I imagine this in my mother's house?

My gaze drifts around the room, searching for something. Anything. A clue.

Why was I supposed to see this?

My eyes catch something on the dresser. I step closer to investigate. An overflowing clear baggie spills white powder onto the faux-wooden surface. It seems out of place in a child's room. One of these things is definitely not like the others. I poke it with my finger. Drugs?

The closet door is propped open a couple inches in the back corner of the room. Breaking my own rule not to tremble, I step toward it.

Dark red blotches dapple the carpet like paint. The splatters grow larger as I inch closer, leading a deadly trail.

Against my better judgment, I grab the doorknob and twist.

My eyelids flick open. I'm staring at the ceiling in my quarters. And, suddenly, I remember. It's the clearest truth I've ever known.

I didn't imagine that extra door, that child's bedroom. It actually exists.

They erased an entire person from my memory.

//

EVELYN SUMMERS: PRISONER E.S.–124
REHABILITATION DIARY
DAY 740

Today, I did something I swore I never would. I went back and reread my old diary entries. I'm not sure why I did it. It hurt more than I expected it to. If I had a fireplace blazing right in front of me, I'd pitch this whole journal in and watch it go up in flames, burning up my old mistakes with it. The past is ugly sometimes. And when it's written down, it's a big ugly mirror I'd be better off never seeing again.

That's why I've decided to stop writing in it. This will be my last entry. I don't want to look back years later at all the bad stuff I've done, the things I regret. Isn't that what rehabilitation is all about? Starting over? A clean slate? If new beginnings weren't important, they wouldn't erase our memories.

Maybe someday I'll tear all these pages to shreds. For now, all I want to keep are the simple things about my past that I know for a fact will never change. Things that bring me happiness. Facts I can cling to when I don't even know who I am anymore:

I am Evelyn Summers. I am 5'10." I loved basketball. I got good grades. I had a good life, even if I didn't know it. My mom was my best friend. She worked hard to give me everything she had before I screwed it up. I know she'll always be there for me. Just the two of us against the world.

That's the only truth I know.

The dam breaks, and it all comes rushing back.

My baby brother, David. My brother, David, the product of my mom and Max.

David, whose bedroom door stands halfway down the hall between my mother's room and mine.

David, who single-handedly polished off all the peppermints in the bowl and forced my mom to replenish them every week.

David, whose March birthday always led to that third cake.

David, who cried when Aunt Lily shattered the framed photo of eight-year-old me holding newborn David at the hospital.

David, who was seven when I came here. Who is nine now.

It comes crashing back, a tidal wave of memories flooding over me.

I slide my back up against the wall, using the cold concrete to ground me back in reality. Tears prickle in my eyes as my brother's sandy-haired, blue-eyed face comes into focus.

How? How did they do it? How did they erase a whole person from the past nine years of my life? And why? They didn't erase my mom, Matt, or any of my friends from home. Why David? It doesn't make any sense. It's like they snipped him out of my mind, a surgical photoshop procedure in my brain, leaving empty patches in memories where my brother should have been. But they did it in such a way that I never saw the holes. Their wipe was flawless.

They wanted me to believe he never existed. And I did.

I'm awake for hours, ruminating over every freckle on David's face. By the time my spine grows stiff against the cement, the alarm clock ticks from 4:59 a.m. to 5:00 a.m. and wails our morning wake-up call. The lights click on.

"Last one!" Carolyn rolls over and kicks off her sheets. "Last trial! Whoop!" She pumps her fist in the air.

Desirae grumbles and hauls herself out of bed, sporting a shiny black eye. She scowls at me. "Good. Let's get on with it."

The jacks and nurses come with Memoria, but we're already at attention in a terse line. Swiping the pills under my tongue is second nature to me now.

David. David. David. David. David.

I chant his name in my head, burning his image into my brain so I can't forget him again.

As the shock wears off, a thought sneaks in: If Mom is dead, where's David now?

//

"Welcome to your seventh trial!" Allard throws his hands in the air like he's tossing confetti.

I clamp my arms tight at my sides, between Miles and Desirae. No one fidgets. No one moves a muscle. We stand stoically in the orientation room for the last time. This is it. The end. Game over. Freedom or death.

The six directors crowd in a semicircle around Doctor Allard, their hands clasped behind their backs. They watch us like scientists, studying their latest collection of expendable lab rats.

Which one of you did it? Which one of you took him from me?

"Fear is a basic human emotion. Fear is healthy." Allard paces down the line of contenders, nodding at each of us in turn. "Because it's such an integral part of life, fear is our seventh and final principle of rehabilitation. Fear of the unknown causes the desire to commit crime."

That sounds like a stretch, but okay.

Five jacks file into the room, each toting a sleek red

helmet. They're as bulky as the white helmets, yet somehow twice as menacing.

"Please sit." Allard gestures toward the line of black seats. The chair legs scrape against the tile as we practically jump into them, eager to get started. "Look at your directors. The Center Board consists of these incredible men and women who seek to help you, to guide you. We created these trials for you, to make you realize your full potential."

Is that what they call these death traps, and erasing my brother from my mind? Guiding us to potential? Please.

The jacks distribute the shiny red helmets.

I'll do it, David. I'm going to finish. I'm going to do it for you.

And then I'll find you.

"If you complete the challenge, we will see each other again, and discharge will begin," Allard says. "Helmets on, now."

"What's the trial?" Desirae asks. "What do we have to do?"

A sinister glint gleams in Allard's eyes. "For your seventh trial, you must conquer your darkest fears."

Before I can overanalyze what he means by that, Allard claps his hands.

"You may begin."

Desirae whips her helmet over her head in one smooth motion. Andrew and Miles follow, their tough exteriors faltering as the plastic descends over their faces. Carolyn takes a deep breath and buries her face in the monstrous device. Determined not to give them a head start, I ram the helmet down over my eyes, smothering my face in plastic.

Four long beeps sound in my ears. A string of red lights flashes in the darkness.

I blink.

Brightness floods my retinas. I shield my eyes, blinking at the sudden burst of light.

I'm standing inside a giant gray dome, my back against the wall. I feel like an ant in a football stadium.

A curved ceiling stretches over my head, as high as I can see, like I'm trapped inside a giant metal bubble. Fluorescent light drowns this part of the dome, but everything beyond twenty feet away is enveloped by darkness. I squint but can't make out anything outside the lit area.

My heart rate quickens. I flare my hands out, ready to defend myself. The other contenders appear around me, frantically studying the massive arena. We wait in silence, backs to the wall, bracing ourselves for whatever Allard plans to throw at us next.

Below our feet, a black road begins, disappearing into the unknown ahead. It shines like freshly paved asphalt painted with a glossy finish. It's some sort of path, and we're standing at the beginning of it.

A large traffic light hangs over our heads, beaming solid red. Beside the light, a giant clock ticks down: Ninety. Eighty-nine. Eighty-eight. Eighty-seven.

Thick, yellow ribbon stretches across the road, blocking our path forward. The starting line, maybe? Andrew cautiously extends a finger to poke it. It gives a sharp buzz; he cringes and whips his hand back.

I stiffen. Okay, message received. Don't cross the line until the clock hits zero and the light turns green. Got it.

I gulp, not daring to wonder what we'll meet down that road. There's no sign of cameras, but I know they're watching. I feel like a cricket trapped in a terrarium.

"What do you think it is?" Carolyn whispers to Desirae. "Some sort of race?"

Desirae shrugs. "Maybe."

A twinge of unease crosses Carolyn's face. Her anxiety makes my pulse speed up. I cross my arms and look away.

Sixty. Fifty-nine. Fifty-eight.

Miles folds his fingers together and closes his eyes, deep in prayer. It's an odd sight—a hardened criminal, standing here in a metal death dome, praying.

Desirae stretches her arms at her sides, then behind her back. Carolyn hops in place, puffing out sharp breaths with each bounce. Andrew plants his feet one behind the other beside me. He looks like he's preparing to fight in a boxing match. I better not have to outrun him. I'd never stand a chance.

Thirty-three. Thirty-two. Thirty-one.

Fluorescent rope lights mark the sides of the road like a landing strip. Stale air hovers around us like a moldy cellar overflowing with mothballs. The whole thing is so realistic, it's easy to forget I'm actually sitting in a black chair in the orientation room that might as well be a million miles away.

This is the last trial. Does that mean it's the hardest? Will they throw everything they've got at us?

I shuffle back and forth on my antsy feet.

The clock tortures us, dragging out each second that ticks by way too slowly.

Fifteen. Fourteen. Thirteen.

Whatever happens, either way, it will all be over soon.

Ten. Nine. Eight.

The knot in my chest tightens with each passing second. Maybe that's all part of their plan. They build the fear slowly through agonizing anticipation.

Somewhere in the distance, something smashes, as if a two-ton elephant crashed to the ground.

What the hell was that?

Five.

I focus on the clock.

Four.

I lean forward, ready to take off.

Three.

I'm gonna do it. I'm gonna pass.

Two.

I take a deep breath.

One.

A loud beep echoes around us, and the yellow ribbon vanishes.

The clock flashes a new message: RUN.

My heart leaps into my throat. Before I can question it,

I bolt, the other contenders at my heels. Andrew sprints ahead into the darkness, easily outpacing us. Our virtual footsteps thump against the pixelated road. Spotlights illuminate the path, following us as we run but leaving everything beyond us pitch black.

Something whirs to my left.

"Duck!" Miles shouts.

An arrow whizzes by, nearly stabbing Carolyn's thigh. With another airy whir, an arrow clips my sleeve.

Carolyn screams. "Look out!"

A hundred arrows fly from the darkness at the left, pointy tips poised to kill. Everyone shrieks and dodges, jumping and ducking. I cover my head with my arms and keep running. An arrow slices through my peels, grazing my leg.

Andrew grunts, tugging a bloodstained arrow from his bicep and tossing it to the ground.

Another blitz of arrows flies at us like a swarm of bees. I fall to the ground on my stomach, shielding my head with my hands. Nearby thumps tell me the others have done the same. Arrows whoosh through the air over my head. I clench my teeth and wait.

Finally, the attack subsides. We jump to our feet and race onward. Blood spurts from Andrew's wound, but it doesn't keep him from holding the lead.

We reach a roadblock and abruptly stop.

A twenty-foot metal wall stretches upward, slanting away from us. It appears to completely bisect the dome; the only way forward is up. Scattered footholds dapple the smooth gray surface like a gymnasium's climbing wall. Thick ropes dangle down the sides, beckoning us to grab on and work our way up.

It's an obstacle course. I breathe out a heavy sigh. Somehow, giving it a name makes it less scary.

I grab a rope and slide my foot into the nearest crevice, barely deep enough for my toes to latch into. I scale the wall like a mountain climber, with Desirae at my side. When the top comes into view, I throw my arms onto the surface and hoist myself onto the second level of the obstacle course. A new road begins, identical to the one below.

Miles and Andrew are ahead of us, taking off in a sprint. I chase after them, closing the gap between us.

"You are halfway through your allotted time," an echoing voice booms into the dome. "Fifteen minutes remaining."

I run faster, each step thudding in time with my heart. My calves burn, but I push through the ache.

The path narrows, and it drops off into an abyss below us on either side. Slimmer with each step, I race ahead until the road thins to barely as wide as my boots. We creep forward, step by step, inch by inch, single file across the deadly balance beam. I jut out my arms like a tightrope walker, not daring to look down at the plunging cliffs on either side. Desirae's foot nudges mine from behind; I flinch—I wouldn't put it past her to shove me over the edge. I quicken my pace, stumbling into Miles's back.

He loses his footing. A note of panic crosses his face.

"No!" I lunge for him, latching around his sweaty wrist. My heart races; I wobble, unable to keep my balance. He frantically grabs at me, but it's no use. Miles's sweaty hand slips right through my fingers.

"Miles!" Andrew whirls back around to help his friend, but it's too late.

Miles' scream echoes around us as he plummets over the edge, his voice fading to nothing when he disappears into a cloud of darkness.

I hold my fist in front of my mouth. Oh my God. I let him fall. What have I done?

"Slinger!" Desirae grabs my shoulder from behind. "Murderer."

I throw my hands out to steady myself. "I didn't mean to. I swear." I quickly shuffle forward to escape Desirae's wrath, but I smack right into Andrew. "He tripped."

Andrew seethes. He grabs the collar of my peels in his fist. "You'll pay for that." I cringe, preparing to be thrown into the chasm.

A booming voice crackles into the dome. "Ten minutes remaining."

"Let's go," Carolyn snaps from the back. "Or we're all dead."

Andrew sneers at me. He shoves me to the ground and keeps going. My pulse slams. I hug the balance beam, barely keeping myself from careening over the side. Surrounded by the bottomless pit, I tighten my grip. A yelp escapes my lips.

Desirae kicks my back. "Get moving! You're holding us all up!"

I force my unstable legs to push up. Arms flanking me, I tiptoe the remainder of the balance beam, breathing a sigh of relief when the path widens to a normal width again. I take off running after Andrew, with Desirae and Carolyn not far behind.

A blade swings down from nowhere, slicing the air a foot in front of us. I halt mid-step, jerking backward in a whiplash. Another blade cuts three feet ahead. The first one swings back like a pendulum. Then the second swings again.

"They're timed!" Andrew shouts.

Swing. "Go!"

We run past the first swinging blade in a wobbly line.

Wait.

"Go!"

We dodge the second blade. The path thins, forcing us into a single file line again.

Three, four, five blades: We jump and dodge in synchrony, working as a unified force, one after the other. I can feel Carolyn's heat against my back.

Desirae points. "Last one!"

Andrew jumps past the last blade. I follow, then goes Carolyn, with Desirae in the rear. But Andrew stops short as a hidden blade bursts from the ground. "Holy shit!" The knife swings up, whirring sharply through the air and missing him by half an inch.

I crash into him, and Carolyn crashes into me.

Desirae's eyes grow wide in terror. "Move!"

But the previous blade swings back, carving clean through her body. Desirae's blood spatters the metal. She topples to the ground like a blood-soaked rag doll as the blade sears back through her again. Blood sputters from her corpse.

The sight turns my stomach.

"No!" Carolyn goes rigid, but she doesn't dare step backward. "Des! Oh my God."

I can't look away from her bloody corpse, torn apart like paper in a shredder. Holy shit. None of us will survive this trial. First Miles, now Desirae. A sick, twisted part of my brain chimes in—at least she can't torment me anymore. I angrily bat the thought away. What the hell is wrong with me?

Andrew's mouth pinches together. "It's too late. She's gone. Let's go." He grabs Carolyn's hand and tugs her past the last blade. I follow.

A steel block slams into the ground, shaking the entire dome—the elephant stomp. It lifts back up, then crashes down again, eager to grind our bones into the cement.

We pause, hands on our knees. For a moment, our breaths are the only noises cutting through the eerie silence. The block lifts again.

"Now!"

We throw ourselves underneath, dashing to the other side before the block can slam back into the cement.

"There!" Carolyn points.

The yellow finish line beams in the distance, a mere two hundred feet away, like a lighthouse beckoning weary sailors. We collectively pick up speed. Huffing for air, I push my legs toward their final destination. A balloon swells in my chest.

This is the end. I did it. I'm going to finish.

Logs litter the path ahead. Okay, that's easy enough. I can do this.

Andrew gets there first and starts hurtling over them. Carolyn chugs after him, with me racing behind.

Right before Carolyn reaches the first log, a pained scream pierces the air. I hear Andrew's shout before I see the cause. A spear shot up from a log, impaling him right between the legs. Andrew doubles over, skewered like a kabob, the metal spear tip protruding out the back of his neck. Blood gushes from the wound, dripping into a red puddle beneath him. His body twitches for a moment before going still, permanently hunched like a scarecrow. I gag, my insides curdling. They got him. The strongest, fittest guy in the trials, and they cut him down like he's nothing. Bile swirls in my stomach.

It's almost as if they didn't intend any of us to finish.

"Holy shit!" Carolyn cries out, covering her mouth. "Oh my God!"

"Just go! Keep moving!" I shove her back.

We race side by side over the logs, dodging the spears jutting up all around us with sickly whooshes. I can't think. I just jump and dodge, the finish line in sight. Carolyn puffs beside me. My lungs burn, but I can't stop. Not until I'm safe.

Finally, we hurdle the last log.

I gain momentum and race past Carolyn, my eyes on the finish.

My feet pound against the black road. Sweat dampens my brow.

Fifty feet away. Forty feet.

Out of nowhere, a pixelated wall springs up around me. Before I can register the familiar buzzing, I slam headfirst into the shiny barrier. Three more materialize, trapping me into a digital box. I push against it. My pulse races. This one's not glitching; it's solid as bricks.

I slap my hands up and down the wall. *No. No, no, no. Not again.*

Carolyn races past me.

"Wait!" I pound the invisible wall. My heart slams.

"Five minutes remaining," the voice booms.

I ram my body into the virtual wall; it buzzes but doesn't break. My frantic hands search the pixels for flaws, but it's pointless. I'm sealed inside. Whoever keeps sabotaging me finally got it right.

"Wait! Carolyn! Come back!"

She doesn't stop.

"Please, Carolyn! Come on!"

Carolyn peers over her shoulder, her pace slowing.

"Carolyn. Please. Don't leave me here." Tears burn in my eyes. My saboteur won. It's over. "Please help me."

Carolyn hesitates. She glances from the finish line, back to me.

I press my palms to the box. "Please, Carolyn. Don't let them kill me. Not like this."

Carolyn throws her head back and groans. She races toward me. I release a heavy breath. Carolyn's fists pound against the box, searching for a weak spot.

Her eyes grow frantic. "I don't know how to break it!"

"There has to be a way." At least, I hope.

Carolyn slaps and kicks the barrier, growing more and more frustrated. She's using up all her time. I bite my lip. Soon she'll give up and save herself.

But suddenly her eyes light up. "It's virtual. Maybe we need something virtual to break it. Hang on." Carolyn rushes back to the hurdles and, straining against it, wrenches a log from the ground. Sweat coats her face. "Slinger! Duck!"

I barely register Carolyn's shout before she heaves a log at me. It shatters the pixels with a deafening crack. I press my hands over my ears as the wall disintegrates. The pieces hit the earth like hail and vanish into thin air. I blink, disbelieving. I could cry.

"Let's go."

"You wasted all your time." I gape at her. "Why'd you help me?"

She rolls her eyes. "Wow, really? You think that low of me? Not even slingers deserve to die in here. Come on."

I don't have time to thank her—the clock is ticking.

"Two minutes remaining."

I speed up. "Let's go!" Carolyn pushes on beside me.

We both see it at the same time and stop so short, we nearly topple over. I grab the back of Carolyn's peels to stop her from tripping.

The road breaks at a cliff. A chasm plummets into the darkness at our feet, as far down as I can see. It stretches at least twenty feet across before continuing with the road on the other side. It could rival giant craters on the moon.

The finish line taunts us, twenty feet away but just out of our reach.

We can't jump that. It's impossible.

"What the hell?" Carolyn's words come out as an airy whisper.

I start running to the right, following the cliff. It has to stop at some point. She follows behind me, but the cliff doesn't end. It stretches the entire length of the arena, blocking the finish line like a big-ass moat. There's no bottom, at least none that I can see. Just darkness, all the way down.

I swallow hard, staring into the dark abyss below. "It's impossible. There's no way to get across."

Carolyn gapes, as if she can't process this. "They can't give us an unpassable trial."

"Well, that's what they did!" I kick the ground. Anger wells up inside me at the injustice. They brought us through hell to get here, and in the end, there's no escape. What a cruel joke. After all that work, all that time served, I'll never see David again.

Carolyn grows pensive, zoning out on the cliff.

"Fuck you!" I shout into the abyss. "Seriously, fuck you, Allard!" I fist my hand in my hair, yanking out my elastic. "Fuck all of you who put us in here just to kill us!"

"Oh my God." Carolyn's eyes grow wide. "No. Hell no. I can't do it."

"Do what?"

"That's the answer," she whispers, more to herself.

"One minute remaining."

I scowl at the ceiling. "There is no answer, Carolyn. The answer is we all die in here."

"Yeah, exactly. That's what they want."

"What are you talking about?"

"Think about what Allard said." She grabs my upper arms. "We have to face our worst fears to pass the trial. What's everyone's worst fear?"

A shiver washes over me, chilling me to the core. "Death."

Carolyn nods, the color draining from her face. We stand side by side, staring down into the pit. There's no bottom—there's nothing but pitch-black emptiness.

"So Miles, Desirae, and Andrew?"

"I don't know." She swallows. "I hope so."

I close my eyes. We have to die. We literally have to kill ourselves to survive.

Maybe she's wrong. Maybe we'll just die, and that'll be

it—the end. I wouldn't put it past the directors. Maybe that was their goal all along. To make us think there's a path to freedom when in reality we're all screwed. Isn't that what I've always known about the Center? One way in, no way out?

"Thirty seconds remaining."

I clench my fists at my sides.

I either jump, or I stand here until the time runs out, and then what? I'm stuck in here? I die anyway?

No. I will not let them kill me at their whims, impaling me like Andrew, or shooting me in the head like Ronnie, or poisoning me like Bex. I will do it on my terms. I will take my power back. They will not take that from me.

My whole body shakes. I can't stop trembling. This could be the end. I could hit the ground and shatter every bone in my body.

Or I could wake up, pass my trial, and win my release.

I take a deep breath and step toward the chasm.

"I can't do it." Carolyn, wide eyed, stands beside me, frantically shaking her head. "I can't just kill myself. I can't."

"You have to. We both do."

She squeezes her eyes shut. "What if I'm wrong?"

"Then we'll both die." I can't look away from the chasm at our feet. "But we'll die on our terms. Not in the Green Room."

Carolyn nods, clearly forcing a stony mask across her face. "You're right."

"Ten seconds remaining."

My heart pounds like a bass drum. "Okay. Let's do this."

Carolyn sniffles, her eyes wet. "I'm scared."

"Me too." I hold out my hand. "Together?"

Carolyn nods, threading her fingers through mine.

"Five seconds."

I close my eyes, feeling the solid ground beneath my feet.

"Four."

The subtle wind breezing through my hair.

"Three."

The metallic smell of the arena.

"Two."

My legs work without thought, and the ground disappears beneath me, Carolyn's sweaty hand clamped over mine.

"One."

We jump.

The familiar helmet envelops my face. Something clicks. A jack tugs the helmet over my head, and I'm back in the orientation room. I slap my hand over my heart, gasping for breath. Sweaty hair clings to my face.

I can't help it; my face scrunches, and tears pour out. I'm not dead.

It worked. It really worked.

I'm here.

I'm alive.

The trials are over.

As usual, our jovial ringleader grins at the front of the room. "Congratulations, contenders. You passed your final trial."

We shift in our chairs, casting nervous glances at one another.

"It's okay." Allard says. "You can celebrate."

The room explodes in a collective cheer. Miles and Andrew guy-hug, slapping each other's backs. Carolyn and Desirae tackle the guys in a contender sandwich. A pang of loneliness twists in my chest at their group hug. I watch the jubilation unfold from my chair, drumming my fingers against my thighs. I lean back and allow the realization to wash over me.

It's over. I'm going home.

Does David miss me? Does he know where I've been these last two years?

Andrew sinks back into his seat, grinning, and stretches his legs out in front.

Will he forgive me for deserting him and becoming a murderer?

Allard winks at me. My face heats when I remember cursing him out at the end of the trial. Hopefully he'll forgive that little outburst.

Desirae chats with Miles, discussing everything they'll do back in the real world. They talk over each other in excited jabbering.

Will I have to explain the tattoo on my neck, when I don't have any explanation to give?

Carolyn steps toward me, her mouth in a tight line.

I swallow. "Carolyn."

She holds out her hand. I hesitate, unsure if she plans

to yank me out of my chair and throw me to the floor. But when I offer my hand, Carolyn gives it a firm shake.

Five jacks cart the discarded helmets out of the room, leaving us alone with the directors. Director Zane takes center stage.

"Congratulations, contenders. It was a long journey, and I'm thrilled you all made it to this point. Rehabilitation has shown its progress on you all. Now you'll be escorted to your quarters, where you'll await instructions on next steps and processing your release. Thank you for all your hard work at the Stephens' Center Rehabilitation Program."

The directors break into stiff applause. Levine, Agarwal, and Allard smile at us, but the others keep their mouths pinched and their eyes blank.

I can't fight the grin off my face.

Whatever, I'll figure it all out later. For now, I'm free, and that's all that matters.

Two jacks lead Carolyn, Desirae, and me back to our room without cuffs. I study the cement hallways, memorizing every crevice and scuff and relishing the fact that I'll never visit this hellhole again. The jacks leave us in our contender hallway and bolt the door.

Carolyn and Desirae chat animatedly as they scurry toward our quarters for the last time.

"What are you gonna do when you get home?" Desirae asks.

"See my nana and pops. And I wanna hug my dog."

"Oh man, me too. And my friends. God, it's been so long."

Carolyn tugs at her peels. "I wanna go to the mall. Get some real clothes."

The mall. For some reason, those words send a shiver down my spine.

Carolyn and Desirae disappear into our quarters, and the red metal door clanks shut behind them. I shuffle beside the dark Hole window.

I should share my good news with Alex.

My heart sinks.

And I guess I should say goodbye.

I pat my hands over the sweaty, bedraggled hair bursting from my messy bun and scrunch my mouth to the side. Maybe I should freshen up first.

I skip down the hall to our quarters. Carolyn and Desirae twirl around the room, laughing and dancing.

I grab my hairbrush and tug the mats out of my hair.

"You got someone you wanna impress, slinger?" Carolyn asks.

I expect a smirk, but she winks at me instead.

I smile back at her. "Oh you know. Gotta look decent. Not every day you discharge from the Center."

The door swings open, revealing two jacks—a girl and a guy, each no older than nineteen.

"Congratulations, everyone, on passing your seventh trial," the girl says. "It's a big day for the three of you. Now, E.S.-124, you're first. Come on."

I beam.

Desirae scoffs. "How come the slinger gets to discharge first?" she whispers to Carolyn, purposely loud enough for me to hear. I wave at them over my shoulder as I depart the room for the last time.

Again, the jacks flank my sides but don't cuff my wrists. I swing my arms, the unrestricted hands of a free woman. Reigning in the urge to skip, I walk with a jump in my step.

It crosses my mind to ask for a moment alone to bid farewell to Alex, but I shouldn't push it. I wish I said goodbye when I had the chance.

We exit through the door at the mouth of our confined hallway. Out of these shithole contender quarters for the last time!

We trek down the hall and up several flights of stairs. Each step feels lighter, like a two-ton weight's been lifted off my shoulders.

Never be called a slinger again. Never be cuffed again. Never do another trial.

I get to see David. And Matt. And all my friends. I can go home.

We round a corner and enter a cramped room. All six directors plus Doctor Allard greet me with a handshake; some grin and shake my hand enthusiastically, while others give my arm a tense jerk instead.

"Ah, Evelyn. You're the first one, welcome," Director Zepp says. Guess I have a name again! For the first time ever, the smallest hint of a smile twitches on her stony face.

"Thank you, ma'am." I force myself not to bounce up and down on my toes.

"Now come sit here. We have some paperwork for you to complete to finish everything up."

. . . And remove my collar, of course!

Director Zepp hands me a booklet called "Life After Incarceration" with information on readjusting to living on the outside. I scan through it, initialing at the bottom of each page to confirm I've read through it in depth—okay, maybe I exaggerate on the "depth" part, but I give every sheet a solid skim.

I jot answers on the blank spaces: my name, date of birth, generic crime title, and names of the block directors who worked with me. I sign on the dotted line in the back stating that I have reformed completely and will not attempt to commit another crime.

My knee bounces against the table leg. I slide the completed packet back across the table to Doctor Allard.

"Thank you, Evelyn." He shoots me his usual apelike grin and thumbs through the documents, checking each page "Very good."

All seven adults rise, and I follow.

"Now, if you'll go with the guards"—Doctor Allard points to the jacks who escorted me here—"it's time for your eighth trial."

I freeze.

"E-eighth trial? But, aren't there seven?"

Just kidding. Say you're just kidding.

Director Hannon crosses her arms. "There are seven principles of rehabilitation, and therefore seven preliminary trials, one for each principle. However, the eighth and final trial is designed to test the overall results of your rehabilitation. A final individual challenge to determine whether or not you are truly ready to lose your collar and reenter society. The final trial will test the most important trait you will have gained from us: your commitment to good."

They lied to me. Again. Why the hell did I ever think it would be this simple?

Director Hannon arches her brows, as if daring me to challenge her.

I close my eyes and take a deep breath. "What do I have to do?"

Allard sweeps his hand in a beckoning motion. "Follow the guards into the next room."

My body goes numb, but my legs carry me toward the jacks as if yanked by puppet strings.

Doctor Allard turns to his colleagues. "All right, let's go to the deck."

The what?

The jacks take my elbows and roughly direct me from the room. We round a corner and head down a flight of stairs. The male jack swipes his keycard against a towering metal door. The dead bolt unlocks with a resounding clank.

"In here," he says.

I swallow down the growing lump in my throat and step inside.

It's the Green Room.

My heart slams against my ribs. Every instinct in my body tells me to turn and run, but both jacks block the door.

They're going to kill me.

"Evelyn Summers, former prisoner E.S.-124," Allard's voice booms over the intercom like the ringleader of a circus. "Welcome to your final trial."

I whip around to see all seven directors framed in the long clear window above my head. The window where I watched four of my friends die. Watched the life drain from their eyes at the hands of unforgiving rifles wielded by jacks who didn't even know their victims' names. And for what? What did the Center gain by slaughtering those girls? What will they gain from killing me? Murdering the murderer?

Jagged breaths rip through my lungs.

I'm going to die here. Just like them.

"Haven't I done everything you wanted?" I shout up at the observers, clenching fistfuls of my hair. "I did everything you ever asked! How is that not enough?"

Allard ignores my cries. "To prove your commitment to good, you must pass your final trial. Fail this task, and you will be shot. Complete this task, and you will immediately be given clean clothes and escorted to the surface. Your collar will be permanently removed. This is your final step."

I don't believe you!

"Do you promise?" It isn't lost on me how childish my question sounds, but tears flood from my eyes, and I shout it again. "Do you promise?"

"Yes." Levine cuts in front of Allard. "I promise."

Allard narrows his eyes at her and pushes back to the front.

"For this trial"—his lips curl into a sick grin—"you must execute a criminal whose rehabilitation has failed."

The male jack exits through a door in the back. He returns seconds later—with Tom.

Tom! Tom's alive?

Tom's frantic gaze bounces around the room. Chains bind his hands behind his back. Our eyes lock, and I can see in his face that our roles in this equation have dawned on him.

The jack shoves Tom against the red-stained green wall and struts back to where I stand, frozen in place. He grabs the semiautomatic Glock from his holster.

"There's only one bullet, so don't try anything stupid." He pulls back the slide, and it clicks. I wrap my trembling fingers around the thick, cold pistol. It feels heavy and unnatural.

"All you need to do is aim and pull. That's it."

He says it like it's so simple!

My mouth runs dry. I can't do this. I can't. How the hell could I ever have killed someone before?

"Stand on the red line; that's point blank," the female jack commands.

I step up to the line of red paint smeared across the concrete like blood, a mere six feet from Tom. From his beating heart.

I want to see David. That's it. I have to do this for him.

The jacks bark more directions, but all I hear is my heart pounding in my ears—is it my heart? Is it Tom's?

It doesn't matter. David is all that matters.

"Okay, Evelyn," Allard says over the intercom. "Whenever you're ready."

I wipe my wet eyes on my sleeve and sniffle. Every director stares down at me from the window, waiting for their pound of flesh. My arms feel like rubber when I weakly raise the weapon. I hold my index finger to the trigger and aim at Tom's chest.

How do I know this is really the end? How do I know they'll keep their word this time? They lied to me—how many times now? And they expect me to trust them?

Tom's jaw clenches, but he doesn't take his eyes off me.

My friends' faces flash through my mind. The ones who died so I could live. So I could move up a level and pass my trial. Who I sacrificed to save my own pathetic skin.

If I don't do it, they'll kill me.

I swallow hard.

But maybe there are things worse than dying.

Maybe being the killer they want means dying on the inside anyway.

This is my initiation into their club. The final step to becoming "one of them." A brutal hazing into the ranks of the rehabilitated.

Aren't I already a killer? Isn't it too late for redemption anyway? Not shooting Tom won't change what I've done. If I don't murder him, someone else here will.

A sickening realization drops into my chest.

Look at me. I'm justifying killing someone. I'm making excuses for recommitting the crime that brought me here. My chest burns with self-disgust. I'm vile.

I can't change what they'll do to him. And I can't stop what they'll do to me.

But I can choose not to do this and accept the consequences. I can say no and face my own execution. I can control my own life. My own choices.

I bite my lip.

Haven't I always had that control? The power to stop the shitty and violent things I did?

Except once. When I didn't.

The memory materializes in my mind, pixel by pixel. Something happened at Alex's intake—something they erased immediately after.

My body moved without thought, and I beat the crap out of Alex. Levine said some word that sounded like Latin. It made me . . . powerful. They did something to me. Something to turn me into a monster with no control over my body.

What was the word?

I strain to think. I can visualize Levine's mouth forming the word, but it's like the memory is on mute. What the hell did she say?

Tom. Tom knows Latin. He quoted it at the third trial, right after Bex died.

But what's the word? What did it mean?

I turned on. I got strong.

It hits me: I was *powerful*.

It's blurry in my head. Like I can hear the echo of the word, somewhere in my brain, but I can't comprehend it.

F something.

Fuh . . . fah . . . fac.

I'm probably wrong. Maybe it wasn't Latin. It could be a different language or gibberish, for all I know. I have to try. It's our only shot.

My muscles tense as I square my chest toward Tom, ready to throw it all away in a game of risk. I meet his eyes and tilt my head down in a fraction of a nod.

It's a long shot.

One chance. That's all I've got. I hope I'm right. Because if I'm wrong, we're both dead anyway.

David, if I die now, I'm so sorry. Please forgive me.

I close my eyes.

Everything slows. For a moment, I savor the fact that

I'm breathing. Inhale, exhale, in and out. I'm alive, and I'm breathing.

I wrench my eyes open. "Tom!"

He startles.

My fingers tighten around the pistol.

"What's a Latin word for power that starts with F-A-C?"

He cocks his head. "*Facultas?*"

The weapon falls from my fingers and crashes to the floor. Fear drains from my body, leaving me with a hazy sense of calm. I whirl around and sink my foot into the male jack's crotch, then grab the woman by her shoulders and slam my skull into her nose. Before the male jack can retaliate, I ram my knee into his stomach. Limbs hypnotized under some sort of spell, the heel of my palm flies into the woman jack's face with a sharp crack. I jam my booted foot onto the male jack's instep, and he yelps. A jumping wheel kick to both jacks' necks, and they fall to the ground. Time crawls, but the fight is over within two seconds.

"*Desine!*" Levine shouts over the intercom.

I suck in a sharp breath. My arms fall limp at my sides. Someone in the window points the black remote through the glass, the beam missing my collar and striking the floor a foot away from me. All the directors flee the observation room, disappearing from the window.

They're coming for me.

I bolt all three dead bolts on the door.

"Tom! Let's go!" I grab the nearest jack's discarded rifle

and fish through his pockets, finding the generic handcuff key and his identification card. Tom races over, and I unlock his chains.

He stares at me, bewildered. "How'd you do that?"

"I don't know. It just happened."

Something slams into the door.

"Shit." I hand him the single-shot pistol meant to stop his heart. "Let's go."

We break off running to the back door, and Tom yanks it open. We slip through and press our backs to the wall of the empty corridor.

"If anyone comes, use that word," I say. "It does something to me. Say *desine* to shut it off."

He doesn't ask questions. "Got it."

Tom follows me into a sprint down the hallway. "Where are we going?"

Shit. I don't know.

"To the quarters, to get the others." Strength in numbers, right? And someone has to run the elevator to get us out. We break off in that direction. Camera lenses in the ceiling follow us, their watchful eyes giving away our position, but we don't have time to stop.

A shrill alarm pierces the air.

"They'll catch us," Tom shouts.

"Not yet."

We tear around a corner and smash into two jacks. They jump for their guns.

"*Facultas!*"

My rifle falls to the ground. The alarm fades to static in my ears. My hands latch around the first one's arm, and I slam it to my knee, breaking the bone with a sharp crack. I grab the other by the ears and ram his head backward into the cement wall. He topples to the ground. I leap into the air, kicking off the wall and sending my foot into the first jack's face. He falls to the floor on top of his colleague.

"*Desine!*"

I jerk out of my trance, the wailing alarm returning to its ear-shattering decibel. My chest tightens at the sight of the injured jacks, arms bent at unnatural angles. I was aware of the damage as I fought, but somehow it didn't feel real until now. It strikes me how young one of the guards is—maybe even younger than me.

Tom thrusts the rifle back into my arms. "Come on."

We keep going. Three more armed jacks race toward us, but with the trigger word, I incapacitate them quickly. I hope they regret whatever they did to make me this way. We run down the stairs, through the corridor, and back to the contender quarters.

Sweat plasters Tom's dark hair to his forehead. "What do we do?" He has to shout over the blaring alarm.

I hand him the ID card. "Get Miles and Andrew. I'll get the girls." I swap my rifle for his one-shot pistol—I can defend myself without a weapon, but Tom can't. "If a jack comes, use the gun."

He nods and dashes down the opposite corridor. I click the safety on the pistol and stuff it into my boot, racing through the door to my quarters.

Desirae and Carolyn jump up from the edges of their beds.

"What the—"

"We need to . . . get out of here . . . now." I bend over, hands on my knees, panting.

"What the hell happened to you?" Carolyn presses her hands over her ears. "Did you trigger this fucking alarm?"

Desirae crosses her arms. "What're you playing at, slinger?"

"They're gonna make you kill someone. That's the final trial."

Carolyn gasps.

"The trials are over," Desirae says. "We passed."

"That's what they want you to think. There's an eighth trial. I don't even know if that's really the end; they lie about everything. I couldn't do it. I took out the jacks and ran here. Come on, I've got Tom, we gotta go."

"Wait. Tom's dead."

"No time, come on."

I turn toward the door, but something clicks behind me.

"Not so fast, slinger."

Desirae aims a silver pistol at my forehead.

Carolyn's eyes grow wide. "Desirae, what the—"

Desirae spins toward her. "You shut it too. I'm fed up

dealing with you and your bitching. God, you're just as whiny as the slinger." She turns back toward me. "Hands up, slinger. On behalf of the Stephens' Center, your rehabilitation has failed."

I throw my hands up and back toward the wall. "You're a plant?"

"You want a medal?" Desirae steps closer with her Glock.

Carolyn gapes at her. "How long were you hiding that gun in your boot?"

Desirae doesn't respond.

"Oh my God." My jaw drops. "That's why she never got dressed in the room with us. She's had it the whole time."

I knew it! I knew she was bad news!

"But . . . but the trials," Carolyn's voice squeaks with the stab of betrayal. "You did them too. It's not possible."

Desirae stalks around me in a circle. "There are ways around the trials."

I take a deep breath, wondering how I'll shut myself off. "*Facultas.*"

Nothing happens.

Shit, shit, shit, shit.

"What are you muttering about, slinger?" Desirae lowers her brows. "Keep your mouth shut and your hands where I can see them."

I don't dare take my eyes off her. We don't have time for this; jacks must be closing in on us.

"Her rope was in the corner in trial one," Carolyn says. "She wasn't with the rest of us."

If only I could reach my gun . . . If only Carolyn knew to say the trigger word . . .

"Fake fire on my rope too," Desirae says. "And footholds, not that you could have seen them while you were gasping for air." She snorts.

Keep her talking.

"You got perfect scores on trial two, so you obviously knew the answers ahead of time."

"Trial two is always fun. Of course, this one didn't end with as much excitement as I was hoping."

It clicks. "Were you the one who sabotaged me?"

"I was pissed they found out before you typed that last answer. But it looks like I'll still get the honor of killing you anyway."

My forehead crinkles. "They didn't tell you to sabotage me?"

"Please." She scoffs. "I did that brilliant work all on my own."

That doesn't make sense. Plants are spies meant to catch the troublemakers, not kill them before they do anything wrong.

"Fine," I say. "You knew the answers for two, probably suffered in silence through three, knowing not to touch the food. How'd you get past the maze?"

She revolves around me like a cobra ready to strike. "I coded the maze myself. Memorized the safe path." Of course she did. That's how she programmed the yellow wall to block me. "Been through the obstacle course two dozen times; I could do it with my eyes closed. I wasn't planning on dying so brutally in it, of course, but it all worked out in the end. The so-called lie detector in trial five was a plain old wristband. A fear tactic."

"But your collar . . ."

Desirae rips the metal off her neck and throws it to the floor. "Fake. Tattoo's courtesy of Sharpie marker. Any more useless questions intended to distract me?" She huffs. "I don't like you, Evelyn. You're a freak, a killer, and a selfish bitch. You've had an ass whooping coming for years."

It stings to realize she's not wrong. "Desirae. Please don't do this. You don't have to hurt us."

"I love how you play the victim, Summers. Seriously, you should get an award for those crocodile tears. You don't really feel guilty for anything you've done. You'd do it all again."

Her words punch me in the gut. "You're wrong."

"Am I, slinger?"

Keep her talking.

"You're calling *me* a slinger?" I force a weak laugh. "When you were working undercover for them?"

If she'd only look the other way, I could grab my pistol.

"Aw, don't be so shocked," she says. "My acting skills must be stellar. You're making me blush." She circles back to my front and stops, the barrel of the gun inches from my face.

"Okay, let's just calm down." Carolyn raises her hands. "Desirae, I don't know what got into you, but I hope—"

"I'm not talking to you, Carolyn. I'm talking to the slinger."

My mind races. We're running out of time. I have to get her on our side. "You're one of us, not one of them. You don't have to be one of them. You can come with us. We'll all get out together."

She laughs. "That's quite funny coming from you."

I don't have time to ruminate. "Please. Just don't do this."

"Don't do this?" Desirae snarls, exposing her discolored and chipped front teeth. "Don't do this?" She presses the mouth of her gun against my skin. "Screw you."

"What did I ever do to you? Why do you hate me so much?"

"Did you not hear what I said?" Her voice returns to sickly sweet, a lioness toying with her prey. "Your rehabilitation has failed. And to think, I didn't even need to sabotage you. It seems you threw a hissy fit and did all the hard work for me. They're probably readying the Green Room now. The real question is, what would be more fun? To call the jacks and watch them kill you? Or pull this trigger and have all the fun my—"

Crash!

The metal chair smashes into Desirae's head. She collapses to the floor.

Carolyn stands behind her, fire burning in her eyes. "Bitches before snitches, asshole." She snatches Desirae's gun and turns to me. "You're telling me if I stay here, they'll make me kill someone?"

"Probably me. If not me, someone else."

"And if I don't?"

"You're the next target."

"Got it. All I need to know." She holds Desirae's pistol between her thumb and forefinger like a dirty sock. "Let's get outta here."

It's a miracle the jacks and directors haven't come for us yet. I grab the pistol from my boot.

Carolyn eyes me suspiciously. "You had one too?"

"Not until fifteen minutes ago."

We sprint out of our quarters.

"Wait!" I stop mid-step. "I gotta get one more person."

A gun blasts somewhere in the distance. I force myself not to jump.

We skid to a stop at the Hole. I rip open the panel and flick the lights.

Two dead jacks lie against the window, terror plastered in their lifeless eyes. Blood leaks from their bodies, dripping into a puddle on the cement floor. A message scrawled in black marker smears across the glass for all to see:

I REMEMBER EVERYTHING. I'M COMING FOR YOU, ALLARD.

The alarm wails. We need to get out of here. If the jacks
aren't on our heels yet, it's only a matter of time.

I race down the hall after Carolyn, through the door at
the end. Miles shuffles back and forth on the balls of his feet.

"Is someone gonna tell me what the hell is going on?"
he snaps.

Tom wrings his hands, kneeling over a lifeless jack. Blood
pools from a smattering of bullet holes in the guard's chest.

"I did it." Tears stream from Tom's eyes. "I killed him. I
didn't even know how to work the thing, I just . . . just . . ."

Only one jack came, this whole time? That feels off.

Miles swears, cut off by the screaming alarm. He cringes,
grimacing at the speaker on the ceiling. "Hey!" He snaps his

fingers. "Someone's going to tell me what's going on right now, or I'm going back inside." He angrily gestures his hands toward Tom. "He's supposed to be dead but comes barreling into our bedroom with a rifle, yanks me out here without stringing so much as two words together, mumbles your name, and shoots a jack! You got something to tell us, Evelyn?"

I whirl toward him. "The trials were never over. If you stay, they're going to make you kill someone. It'll likely be Tom. Or me. Or someone else."

"I thought Tom was already dead! Is this some sort of test? You're not joking . . . are you?"

"Shut up!" Carolyn shoves Miles by the shoulders. "We're wasting time. Take his gun. Let's get out of here."

He clenches his teeth.

"She's right." Tears run down Tom's face, dripping onto the dead jack's uniform. "That's the truth."

Miles sneers. "And why isn't Des here?"

"She's a plant," Carolyn says. "She had a gun and threatened us."

Tom's jaw drops. "No way."

"And all this time I thought Evelyn was the spy."

"And why should I trust Evelyn?" Miles glares at me. "I'd never trust a slinger."

I chew my bottom lip.

"Because I do," Carolyn says.

Tom nods. "Me too."

"Okay. This is getting weird." Miles shakes his head.

"Whatever. What's the plan?"

"We're breaking out." I force myself to sound stronger than I feel. "I know the way."

Maybe we can still survive. Maybe it's not too late.

Miles hoists Tom off the floor. "Come on, man. Pull it together."

I take the loaded gun from the dead jack's holster, replacing it with the one-bullet execution pistol. There could be swarms of jacks waiting for us right outside.

Carolyn points to the blinking security camera in the ceiling. "We need to take those out. They'll see us."

Miles takes the guard's AK-47. With a quick aim, he releases a string of bullets, annihilating the camera. "Let's go."

"Where's Andrew?" I pull back the slide to cock the gun.

"They took him," Miles says, "about twenty minutes ago. Do you think we should—"

"No time. Let's go."

We race down the hall and around a corner.

"There!" A man shouts. Nine jacks stand clustered together, their rifles drawn and aimed at us. I jump back to the wall, shoving Tom behind me out of range. I fire a shot around the corner; it misses.

Thunder erupts as gunshots blaze from the line of jacks, fifty feet away. We press our backs to the wall on the other side.

"Hold your fire!" a jack shouts. "She only had one bullet; they're out of ammo. You know Hugo's orders, we take E.S.-124 alive."

I peek around the corner. A jack tiptoes toward us, his hands braced to thwart an attack.

"What do we do?" Tom whispers. "We can't turn back. We'll be trapped."

Damn it, I'm not dying in here. "We take them out."

"I'm not killing anyone," Miles says.

Tom nods. "We'll debilitate only."

"You guys." I close my eyes, hating what I'm about to say. "It's going to come down to them or us."

"Then you do it," Miles snaps. "You're the murderer."

His words hit me harder than a bullet.

"You're both going to get us killed." Carolyn flings her arm around the corner, tugs her trigger, and it *click, click, clicks,* but nothing happens. Miles rolls his eyes, grabs her pistol, and cocks it before thrusting it back to her.

Tom crouches behind me and fires blindly at the guards, striking a jack in the knee.

"Shit, they're armed." A jack returns fire; his shot ricochets into the wall, sending chips of cement flying into the air.

Miles unloads his automatic weapon around the corner, striking three jacks in their legs. He discards the empty AK-47 on the floor.

"There's too many of them." Carolyn fires a shot around the bend and it strikes the wall, at least twenty feet from her target. "We gotta kill them."

Miles presses his lips together, staring at the ground.

We're screwed. Miles is the only one who knows how to use a gun, and he won't kill the guards. I don't know which is worse: that the others' refusal to kill might get us slaughtered, or that I'm the only monster willing to do it.

I'm a murderer already. It doesn't matter.

Bullets rip from the jacks in a deafening roar. Carolyn presses her hands over her ears, her weapon sandwiched between her knees. Tom drops his empty pistol, pressing his back to the wall. He closes his eyes and inhales a string of shallow breaths.

Carolyn gets in Miles's face. "Can you *please* take them down?"

"I won't aim to kill."

"Well, they won't offer you the same courtesy," she snaps.

"Here." I toss my handgun to Miles. "Tom, you know what to do."

Tom looks skeptically at me. "You can't fight bullets."

Miles points my pistol around the wall and shoots, striking a jack in the foot.

I peer around the corner at the four remaining guards. "Just do it. Wait till I get close."

I take a deep breath, put my hands up, and step into the open.

"Take her alive, no fatalities," a jack commands.

I stride toward the guards in fake surrender. Two cautiously approach me, weapons in hand. Three injured jacks sprawl across the floor, blood oozing from their wounds. The jack Tom nailed in the leg sits against the wall, his face pallid. We've culled their ranks, but it's not over.

An approaching guard raises his weapon. "Don't try anything funny, E.S.-124." They close the gap, and a jack grabs my upper arm. "All right, you're coming with—"

"*Facultas!*"

My mind goes blank. I spin around, knocking the pistol from the closest jack's hands. A bullet grazes my left shoulder, but I don't feel it. I wheel kick the offending jack in the stomach before he can react. He grunts and doubles over, dropping his pistol to the floor.

The second jack throws me down by my shoulders. I slam into the cement, but adrenaline blocks the sting. He moves to kick me, but I roll to the side, dodging the blow, and leap to my feet. I jab him in the trachea with the web of my thumb and forefinger. He falls to the floor in a heap, choking.

Another jack plows his fist at me, but I duck, catch his arm, and twist, breaking the bone with a crack. I grab him by the ears and smash his head into the concrete wall.

The final jack takes a swing. I wipe my hand down to block his fist and swirl back up to jab him in the eye. He yelps, and I sink my knee into his groin.

The whole fight is over in seconds. My hypnotized eyes scan the wounded guards littering the floor.

"*Desine!*"

I suck in a sharp breath, my arms falling limp at my sides. My eyes widen as I survey the destruction left in my wake. Nausea swirls inside me at the sight of the dead and unconscious bodies.

I did this.

It doesn't bother me as much as it should.

"Evelyn!" Miles shouts. "Get down!"

Before I can process, someone shoves earplugs into my ears. A guard wraps his hands around my neck. I gasp for air, kicking and punching but unable to reach him. Tom mouths the trigger word, but the foam blocks the sound. I flail and writhe but can't shake his grip. My vision blurs.

Metal bites my wrists as a second jack handcuffs me. Miles and Tom lunge, tackling him to the ground.

A gunshot blasts behind me, and the strangling subsides. My assailant sinks to the floor, a gaping wound in his back. Carolyn stands behind the dead guard, smoke curling from her pistol.

Miles straddles the second jack, raining punches onto his face. I rip out the earplugs and clutch my throat, barely registering what's happening. When the guard lies unconscious and bloody, Miles relents.

Carolyn is still staring at her weapon and the dead jack. "I killed him."

"Carolyn—" I reach out to comfort her, but recoil at the broken cuffs encircling my wrists like bracelets.

Holy shit.

I broke them.

Like Alex did at his intake.

How did I not see it sooner?

Alex and I are the same.

We're both weapons.

As the adrenaline drains from my body, the pain returns. My shoulder throbs like someone rammed a knife into my arm. I cup my hand over the graze wound, blinking back water that fogs my eyes. The sight of blood oozing from the bullet trail makes my stomach flip.

"You're injured," Tom says. "We gotta wrap it."

He reaches for my arm, but I jerk it away. "I'm fine."

"What the hell were those moves back there?" Carolyn flexes her hands, eying me with suspicion. "Where'd you learn how to fight like that?"

I open my mouth to answer, but Tom cuts me off.

"No time," he says. "Let's go."

"Not even gonna ask." Miles grabs a second pistol off the

nearest jack. He releases the clip and slides in a new magazine, then takes out the three security cameras with perfect aim.

I swipe two pistols from the jacks' lifeless bodies. Miles reloads everyone's guns from the rounds dangling off their utility belts.

"Guess his skill comes from all that armed-robbery practice," Carolyn mumbles.

Miles glowers at her. "I'm saving your ass right now."

"Well, I wouldn't know. I don't know how to use that thing!"

"Oh yeah, that's right. You were shooting up heroin before you—"

"Guys, come on," Tom says.

I click the safety and slip the second pistol into my boot. My wounded arm stings from the movement.

Shouts mingled with stomping footsteps echo down the hall behind us.

"They're coming," Tom whispers.

My blood runs cold. They've sent another troop of jacks. We took down nine; how many are there? The shouts and footsteps grow louder, closer, seconds from closing in.

We race down the hall, away from the oncoming jacks, toward the elevator. Miles trips the silencer on his pistol and takes out the cameras, one by one.

Our boots patter against the cement with more grace than I'd expect from four people trampling like bulls escaping slaughter. The screeching alarm drowns out most other noise; I've grown numb to the sound. The shouts behind us grow louder. We turn right, then left, then right again, in an attempt to lose them. They're gaining on us.

"This way." Tom leads us into the darkened kitchen.

We crouch behind the cabinets with bated breath, just in time. Our pursuers race past, their black boots stomping against the cement, oblivious to our hiding spot ten feet away. My heart thrums so loud, I feel like it might rocket out of my chest. When the guards are out of sight and their shouts fade into nothing, Carolyn leads us back into the hall.

It unnerves me that we've seen dozens of jacks, but no directors. Where are Allard and the others? And where is Alex?

We creep out of the kitchen, back into the deserted corridor. I peek around the corner, where two jacks wait.

"On my count," I whisper. The others nod. "One . . . two . . ."—I jump out and fire a shot—"Three!"

"Over there!" The jack returns fire, but I drop to the floor and his bullet skims the wall. Miles nails a jack in the shoulder. I shoot twice and miss.

A bullet rips into Carolyn's thigh. She groans and sinks to the floor. The guards are trained professionals; they could kill us in half a second if they wanted to.

Tom hits the second jack in the chest—seemingly a lucky and unintended shot. The jack collapses, dead. Tom presses his hand over his mouth in disbelief.

Blood streams from Carolyn's leg, gathering in a crimson puddle on the floor. Her eyes dilate in and out of focus.

"You good?" I ask.

"Yeah." She doesn't look good. Carolyn's dark skin pales. Blood blooms from her wound, staining her white pant leg. I discard the empty pistol and tug the second loaded Glock from my boot.

"Carolyn, come on." I nudge her shoulder. "We can't stay here. We gotta go."

Tom tears the sleeve off his peels, leaving a frayed edge around his shoulder. He drops to his knees and ties it around Carolyn's injury. She winces and grits her teeth but says nothing.

Miles takes out three security cameras while we wait. He's wasting bullets. I teeter back and forth on my feet. This is taking too much time.

"Should we take the bullet out?" Tom asks.

"You're not a doctor!" Carolyn twists away from him. "You're not touching me; you don't know what the hell you're doing."

"I just thought—"

"No time." Carolyn stands, fighting back a grimace. "All right, Evelyn, lead the way."

"You got it."

But an image smashes into my brain, sucking the air from my lungs.

I'm sitting on a cold, sheeted table in the doctor's office. My mom sits on the bench beside me with tearstained cheeks. A doctor strides into the room with a clipboard.

"I've got some bad news. I don't like saying this, but I'm going to be blunt. I'm afraid the tumor is malignant." He shakes his head. *"You have brain cancer. Stage four."*

I clap my hand over my mouth. My mother pelts him with questions, but I feel numb. All I can do is gape.

The knowledge settles inside me like a brick: I'm dying.

The doctor takes a seat on his stool, his gaze hard as he looks into my eyes. "There is one option."

"What's wrong?" Tom asks, urgency in his voice. "Evelyn?"

I snap out of it.

Carolyn and Miles watch me with uncertainty.

I stare at them, then down at my trembling hands. It's fuzzy around the edges.

I was dying.

The headaches. The bad migraines. I had them every day. Because of the tumor.

I was dying.

They did tests. Scans. X-rays. But they caught it too late.

I was dying.

But then . . .

I press the heels of my palms into my eyes and take two heavy, shaky breaths.

They gave me Klaurivex. It was brand-new, barely approved by the FDA—a miracle cure.

And I didn't die.

I ended up here.

Carolyn smacks my cheek with a stinging slap. "Evelyn! Get with it!" She flings back her arm to slap me again, but I duck.

"I'm fine. Let's go." I'm not fine. I'm shaken. I'm confused. I'm sick of these half-assed memories. And I don't know how being sick and taking Klaurivex ended with me being sent to prison—or why the Center erased David's existence and my mom's death. But right now, we need to get out of here. "C'mon."

I need to focus. I wish Alex were here. He'd know. He'd have answers.

I lead the others to the elevator, creating a plan as I go. Even with the Center's security targeting us, they'll never leave the elevator unguarded. I just hope they haven't brought it back up. We'll hold the jack at gunpoint and force him to run the lift from the outside. It's the only way we're all getting out of here.

A million things could go wrong. There could be a fleet of guards watching the lift. The guard could trap us inside. Maybe there's an emergency stop that won't let the elevator move at all. I swallow back the fear and keep going. It's the only plan we've got.

Carolyn limps, grunting each time her right foot hits the cement. The shiny elevator comes into view.

Tom groans. "Seriously, Evelyn? That's your big plan?"

"The escape elevator?" Miles's nostrils flare. "It doesn't even work!"

"It does if you know how to use it," I mutter under my breath.

We charge toward the lift, Carolyn limping several paces behind. I breathe a sigh of relief when only a single guard comes into view. The Center got comfortable thinking they were inescapable. They don't have enough manpower to deal with a revolt, and it makes me smug. They've under-estimated us.

The jack curses and reaches for his weapon. I grab my Glock, mentally preparing myself to hold it to his head and threaten him into operating the elevator.

But someone else beats me to it.

A crack erupts. The jack falls to the floor, blood spurting from the bullet hole between his eyes.

Tom lowers his weapon, his face devoid of all emotion.

"There."

No. No, no, no. We were right there. We were so close. A scream threatens to rip from my mouth. "How?" It comes out a whisper instead. "How could you?"

Carolyn ribs Tom. "Whoa, look who finally showed up to the fight."

"I just want to get out of here," he says in a monotone.

Carolyn limps forward. "Come on, let's get in."

"That's not how it works." I raise my voice. "We needed him to control it. He was our only hope."

"What do you mean?"

My heart races. We don't have much time.

"Someone has to run it from the outside!" I throw my head back. "Fuck!"

Carolyn and Tom break into heated bickering. Miles paces back and forth, mumbling about how they'll find us and kill us in a number of gruesome ways.

They'll be here any moment. Surely they'll know we'll try the elevator.

A growing puddle of blood seeps from the jack's lifeless body, soaking the cement floor. Something emits a series of staticky beeps beneath him. I crouch beside the corpse and fish through his utility belt, uncovering his hand radio.

"Morris . . . do . . . read?" A low static-cut voice crackles from the device. "They . . . swarmed . . . Martinez . . . going . . . kill."

I don't need the missing words to fill in the message.

Alex.

He escaped from the Hole to go after Allard—for some reason. Could his escape have drawn the jacks' and directors' attention away from us? They'd need backup to face him. After all, he broke his handcuffs at intake and killed two jacks in the Hole—why couldn't he snap all their necks just as easily?

Maybe that's the only reason we got this far. Now they're going to capture and kill him. Will Alex be another person who died to save me? Can I live with that?

Sarah, Ariadne, Courtney, Ronnie—they all died, and I could have prevented it. Could have, but didn't. If I leave now, will I be tacking a fifth name on to that list?

Alex and I had something together . . . once. Maybe coworkers. Maybe a friendship. Maybe more.

Can I leave knowing he'll die?

Is that what I want David to think of me? That I'm a killer? That I'm nothing but the selfish bitch everyone here thinks I am?

Miles pounds his fist to the cement wall. "There are no buttons, just this keypad!" He raises his voice to the precipice of screaming himself hoarse. "Tom, what the hell, why'd you have to go and—"

"Quiet!" I swipe the jack's keycard into the credit-card slot, and the doors slide open. "Everybody in. Now."

Without hesitation, Miles, Carolyn, and Tom squeeze into the elevator. Carolyn groans, pressing her hands over her wounded thigh. I scan the keypad, find CLOSE, and ram my finger onto the button. The gate slams shut, sealing the others inside.

"Get in, Evelyn." Tom frantically beckons with his arm. "Come on."

I grab the metal bars. "Keep your voices down. It only works from the outside, and you all know it."

Carolyn's forehead creases. "Evelyn—"

"Shut up. There's no time. We talk about atonement, accountability, and all that shit? Well, this is mine. I killed four hacks, and I'm sorry. Every single day I wish I could go back into Zepp's office two years ago and change what I did, but I can't. Wish I could change my answers to the sixth trial, but I can't. I killed my best friend. That'll haunt me forever." I swallow hard, determined to keep my voice from breaking. "Maybe I never pulled the trigger on any of them, but I still did it."

The others gape at me.

"Helping you guys won't change what I did, but it's the best I can do. The elevator empties into an old garage. Step out, and the sensor will light the place. Stay alert when you get outside."

"But you need someone to say the trigger words," Tom says.

"I'll improvise."

"What about you?" Miles asks. "They'll kill you."

I gulp. Probably.

"I'm not leaving without Alex." I slam my finger on the

second button. The heavy elevator doors slide toward each other.

"Hey, slinger." Carolyn tosses her gun to me through the closing door. "Thanks."

I catch her pistol in one hand as the doors clang shut. The elevator releases an airy moan, carrying the other contenders up to safety.

I close my eyes, instantly regretting my decision. There goes my genius escape plan.

As if triggered by the elevator, the alarm clicks off with one final *beeeeeep.* My ears ring with the sudden silence, as if someone pressed pillows over them and drowned out the noise.

The empty hallway is eerily quiet. I press my hand to my throbbing shoulder and wince. Blood stains my fingers when I pull away.

Come on, Alex. Where are you?

I trudge down the corridor as silently as possible without the alarm covering my footsteps. Pressing my back to the wall, I peer around the corner.

Two dead jacks lie sprawled across the floor in puddles of their own blood. I shiver, forcing myself to look at anything except their dead eyes, open and glassy with eternal fear.

Alex was here.

I hold my pistol at the ready and tiptoe down the corridor, hugging the wall. The jacks' blood on my boots leaves a trail of death behind me, with each wet, red footprint. At every turn, I slide to a crouch and peek around the corner.

Four jacks stand in a circle down the corridor to the right, blocking my path.

"Hugo thinks she's armed," one male jack says, "so stay alert."

I whip back before they see me. The jacks are fifty times more daunting when I'm alone.

"The elevator was activated. Is it possible she escaped?"

"I doubt it, she'd have needed an operator," a female jack says. "Her friends wouldn't have done it and trapped themselves here. She may have other hacks with her. Plus, you heard what Hugo said—she won't leave without Martinez."

My nose wrinkles. Who's Hugo? And how would he know that?

The jack's harsh bark echoes down the hall. "What about Martinez?"

"He's gone after Hugo. How the hell Martinez got his memories back is beyond me, but he's dangerous. I sent Matthews, O'Hare, and Johansson for backup."

"Does . . . does Summers know?"

My ears perk.

"Hugo's been tapping that phone, he wanted to see what they'd do when they met again—"

"Sick bastard's got nothing better to do—"

"I told him, the moment those two started yapping about getting their memories back, to shoot them both, before it's too late. But no, he wouldn't listen. Not ready to let go, and now look what's happened."

I mentally run through my conversations with Alex, praying the directors didn't hear anything too incriminating. Not that it matters; we're already fugitives.

"You watch, he'll get the whole board killed."

"Martinez would do it, no doubt."

"You know Hugo; that freak loves his creepy social experiments. Gonna end up on the wrong side of it one of these days. Get himself killed."

The group shares a hearty laugh.

"Well, if they really have their memories back . . ." He pauses. "God help Hugo Allard."

Curiosity prickles through me, but I need to keep moving. I turn on my heel and race the other direction. No other clues as to where Alex might be, I head to where I think I'll find Allard.

I screech to a halt at the orientation room door. Three dead jacks lie in pools of stagnant blood, riddled with bullet holes like Swiss cheese. Someone unloaded an entire automatic weapon's worth of lead into their bodies.

Bile rockets up my esophagus at the sight. I retch, spewing a load of vomit onto the cement. My body convulses, but I force myself to remain upright. One jack holds his AK-47 in his stiff hands, but the other corpses' hands are empty.

Alex took his rifle.

I wipe my mouth on my sleeve and cradle my injured arm against my chest, giving myself a minute to catch my breath. A camera blinks overhead, but I don't have Miles's aim to take it down, and the last thing I need is to draw more jacks with the gunshot. I cling to the cold wall, trying to steady myself. It'll all be over soon.

I press my ear to the steel. Muffled voices sound from the other side.

"I'm done playing these games." My heart leaps; it's Alex. "This ends now."

"You won't get past the guards, Mr. Martinez," Allard says, his voice smooth as velvet. "They'll kill you on sight."

"You mean the guards I already killed? Or do you wanna send more to try and fight me?"

"Come on, drop the gun. Just calm down, and we can—"

"Calm down? Really?" Alex raises his voice. "After what you did to me—what you did to Eva—" My ears strain, desperate to absorb every word. "You have the balls to tell me to calm down?"

"This is your last warning. Put down the gun."

"Take one more step and I'll blow your head off, you son of a—"

Alex's screams pierce the metal door, accompanying familiar crackling that could only come from the collar. My legs quake, threatening to buckle beneath me.

We're never getting out alive. This was such a bad idea.

I press my fist to my mouth.

I'll never see David again, never see sunlight again . . .

The screams die. I release a heavy gust of air.

"Had enough, Mr. Martinez?" Allard chuckles. "Lauren, take his weapon. Andrew, come here."

Andrew?

"Well, I thought we'd do this differently." Allard sighs. "I never wanted this to happen—especially to you, Mr. Martinez. But given the circumstances, this task will have to do instead. Andrew, to earn your freedom and complete your eighth trial, you must kill prisoner A.M.-624."

I clap my hand to my mouth.

"Deal," Andrew says without hesitation. Something snaps, as if the contender cracked his knuckles.

Plan. I need a plan.

"You won't t-touch me," Alex stammers. "I'll k-kill you if you try."

I can't just run in there; it has to be the right moment.

Allard breaks into a high-pitched laugh. "Still didn't learn your lesson, boy? You can't come barreling in here brandishing a stolen rifle, kill some of our best guards, and expect everything to go your way. There's no circumstance in which this ends well for you. It's over."

Alex doesn't respond.

"Honestly, I'm surprised," Allard says. "I considered you highly intelligent, Mr. Martinez, yet you've shown a reckless disregard for logic by trying this alone."

I burst through the door and raise my pistol. "He's not alone."

Every director's eyes flash to me.

Zepp's AK-47 lowers as quickly as her jaw. "How the hell . . ."

Everyone's attention averted, Alex jumps on Andrew. He grabs his chin and jerks, breaking Andrew's neck with a crack. The former contender falls to the ground, his head bent to the side.

"Alex!" I hurl the spare pistol at him. He catches it midair and points it at Allard's head.

"Drop your weapon," Alex commands. Allard scowls but lets the black remote fall to the floor with a thud.

Alex sneers. "You too, Lauren."

Zepp hesitates, the rifle quivering in her hands.

Fire blazes in Alex's eyes. "I'm gonna count to three before I blow his head off. One . . . two . . ."

Zepp's AK-47 hits the ground with a clang.

"That's better. All of you." Alex cocks the pistol still aimed at Allard. "Hands up, or I blast a hole in this asshole's skull."

The directors glance at one another but comply, slowly lifting their arms over their heads. This is so messed up. All my internal warning bells go off. We're holding the directors hostage. I can't think of any scenario where we survive this. But I force myself not to falter.

I slide my pistol into my boot, grab the discarded AK-47, and point it at the closest director's chest—who happens to be Zane.

Alex's upper lip curls into a snarl. He recoils his fist and plows it into Allard's face with a crack. The man doubles over with a wince.

"That's for shocking me, you sick son of a bitch."

Allard clutches his nose, sputtering blood onto the concrete.

Alex's eyes widen as they coast over me, following the trail of red dripping down my shoulder. "You're bleeding."

I force a smile. "I'm fine."

A grin twitches at the corners of his mouth. "Thanks for coming for me."

"No problem." Our eyes lock, and for a moment, my smile feels sincere.

Something rustles, and my muscles tense.

"Everyone on your knees," I say. "Keep your hands over your heads."

No one moves.

"You heard her!" Alex bellows.

The directors sink to the floor. I scan the line of hostages. While Alex's back is turned, Hannon slowly lowers her hand toward her back pocket.

"Hey!"

She freezes, fumbling another black remote until it falls to the floor. I kick the device across the cement.

Alex scoops it up and shakes his head. "Anyone else have any surprises hiding in their pockets? Cause the next person who tries anything gets a bullet in the head."

His words shoot a chill down my spine—he sounds a lot like an unreformed criminal. But I give a curt nod in solidarity anyway. Alex drops the remote into his back pocket.

Director Hannon sighs. "Expected this from Alex. Didn't expect this from you, Evelyn."

"You directors expect a lot of things from me." I whirl my pistol toward her. "I'm done being your perfect prisoner."

"So you do want to be a murderer, then?" Hannon says.

"Why not? You tried to make me one earlier when you ordered me to kill Tom."

"Executing a dangerous criminal is not the same as murdering an innocent person."

"Innocent? You think you're innocent?" I blink at her, disbelieving. As if the fact that Tom committed a crime somehow means he deserves to be shot in the head. "Tom didn't deserve to die." I raise my voice. "Neither did Sarah, Ariadne, Courtney, Ronnie, Bex, Tiffany, or anyone else you people murdered—yes, it's still murder."

Hannon clicks her tongue. "Now, Ms. Summers, if you'll calm down—"

"No." I press the pistol's mouth to young Director Agarwal's temple. "I'm done with the lies. I want my memory back, and I want my brother back."

"It's not a lie, Evelyn. You almost earned your freedom, only to throw it away—"

"Stop. I don't believe you."

My finger quivers against the trigger. Should I pull it to prove a point? Could I do it?

Agarwal chuckles, but his hollow laughter parades his

fear to the room. "You wouldn't dare."

"You wanna try me?" I almost don't believe what's flying out of my mouth. Maybe if I feign enough bravery, it'll start to feel real. "I'll do it. I swear I will." Will I? Maybe we should kill them, before they can kill us. I try to wrap my brain around point-blank killing, but my muscles freeze. I close my eyes, willing myself to do it. To kill him. But I can't. I don't want to be a murderer anymore. I just want to be free.

Doctor Allard laughs. "This is interesting. Very interesting."

"What's interesting?"

"Science, Evelyn. It always wins in the end. That'll teach me for trying to play God, I suppose."

"We don't have time for this." Alex hooks his arm around Director Levine's neck, holding his gun to her head. "Everybody back away from the door. You all might doubt what Eva will do, but I know none of you doubt me." He yanks Levine to her feet. "Now back off, or I pull the trigger."

I shudder at his harsh tone but force a stony exterior. "Get moving!"

Zane and Hannon scooch back on their knees, clearing a path to the exit. Allard clenches his teeth but also complies. Director Levine closes her eyes as Alex drags her from the clump of directors.

I examine my rifle, seeking a safety lock. I don't even know what I'm supposed to be looking for. Some sort of button?

Agarwal raises his brows. "Never held anything bigger than a pistol, I'd wager—"

"Shut up." I yank open the door. "Alex, you ready?"

"Yep." He withdraws his arm from Levine's neck but keeps the pistol at her temple. "Move." I'm struck with a stab of pity for the director, but I don't let it show.

Alex directs a whimpering Levine out of the room, trailing a step behind her with the loaded weapon. I point my rifle at each remaining director in turn.

"No one follows," I command, with as much authority as I can muster. I join the others in the hall. The heavy door clanks shut behind us. "We should block the door."

"We don't have time."

But before I can move, a stream of memories floods through me like a tidal wave.

I meander through the mall with David while Mom shops for linens.

A scream pierces the air. Suddenly, everyone's running. Before I can make sense of it, gunshots rip through the mall. A group of men and women with rifles plow between stores, indiscriminately firing.

I duck behind a jewelery stall, clamping my hand over David's mouth. One of the shooters prowls on the other side of the stall. My heart pounds like a bass drum. I chance a glance at her, almost giving away our position when I see her face.

Red rings encircle her pupils. There's something terrifying about her. She's not an ordinary person.

Alex gently shakes my arm. "Eva. Eva. Are you okay?"

I can't breathe. All I can think about is what I see next:

my mother, lying dead on the dirty mall floor, a gaping bullet wound in her chest.

They wiped way more than an hour.

Tears well in my eyes, and I can't help it: I sink to the ground and sob. It all comes back to me—sitting with David in family court; the judge appointing Lily our legal guardian despite her being barely old enough to take care of herself; David crying in my arms. It happened. It really happened.

Alex hesitates, looking from Levine to me, as if wanting to come to my side but not daring to abandon our prisoner.

"She was murdered." A hard lump sticks in my throat. "There was . . . there was something wrong with the killers. They were . . . monstrous." Another word spirals through my mind on repeat—epidemic. "I was . . . I was sick. I was on Klaurivex."

"Eva . . ." His face softens. "We all were."

What?

"You still don't remember?" he whispers.

I try to talk, but it feels like cotton balls are lodged in my throat.

"You were sick. So was I—advanced leukemia. Klaurivex saved us, Eva. Hugo invented it. Doctor Allard. He invented Klaurivex."

"A-Allard?"

"It cured us with no issues, but for most people . . . there were side effects. Especially adults. They got . . . aggressive. Violent. 'Belligerent tendencies' is the official term."

The more he talks, the more I fill in the blanks. Memories materialize. The mall killers were enhanced—under the influence of a dangerous drug.

"People abused it," he continues. "It gave their cells the strength to beat their illnesses—and then made them even stronger. Stronger than they should've been."

Levine shakes, her guilt-laced gaze glued to the cement floor. "It's true. It became a street drug. Illegally trafficked everywhere, not just to the terminally ill."

The drug that saved my life made people into criminals. Allard made the drug, and then imprisoned its users. The system has always been rigged against us. He rules the Center with an iron fist, lording over the result of his creation.

It doesn't explain why I'm here. What I did. Whom I killed.

"But if I didn't get the side effects, how did I become a criminal?"

Levine and Alex look at each other but don't reply.

I recall the one scene I never forgot: standing at the music-wing bulletin board, staring at a flyer. The edges sharpen, and I realize it wasn't the music wing at all. It was a different hallway with a similar corkboard for announcements.

The children's hospital.

The writing on the flyer is as clear as if it's written on a sign two inches away:

TEENS WANTED FOR SUMMER JOB. AGES 14–17. HIGH COMPEN-SATION. MUST PASS ENTRY EXAMINATION AND MEET SPECIFIC QUALI-

FICATIONS. KLAURIVEX PATIENTS ONLY. HIGHLY SELECTIVE.

I'd seen the ad on the bulletin board in the hospital the day I took the Klaurivex. I'd kept the phone number on a whim. When Mom died, I'd vowed to earn enough money to get custody of David when I turned eighteen. I'd applied for the job. They only wanted people who met certain qualifications—people who took Klaurivex and got the drug's strength without the violent side effects. People who didn't have red rings around their pupils.

Wind blows through the curtains, wafting a cool draft into David's bedroom.

"Don't leave me, Eva," he says in a quivery voice.

"Don't be afraid." I blink back a sheet of tears. "It's just a summer job."

I feel like I'm one soft breeze from crumpling to the ground. Something happened at that job. It led me to killing someone and being sentenced to the Center—Alex too.

"We worked together," I whisper to Alex. "Where did we work?"

A guilty look washes over his face.

"Where was our job?" I ask again, more frantically. "What did we do?"

His eyebrows draw together. "Eva . . ."

I'm sitting at a long table, my anxious leg bumping against the chair. It's the first day of my new job. A boy with long black hair and light brown skin plops down beside me.

I pluck the name tag off my blazer and sigh.

EVALYN

"Something wrong?" the boy asks.

I shake my head. "They spelled my name wrong."

"Eva-lyn." He grins and holds out his hand. "I'm Alex."

The cement walls around us seem to cave in on me, suffocating me. I soak it all in—this ceiling, this familiar ceiling. The concrete that always stifled me. Director Levine—why do I suddenly want to call her Andrea? I scan the hallway, this building, this place that's been my prison for so long. My hand searches my neck, seeking an ID lanyard long gone. The Stephens' Center. It's familiar. It's all too familiar. It can't be. But it is.

"Here," I whisper. "We worked here."

It all makes sense—the special treatment from Levine, the bizarre warning from Alex at his intake, Director Zane's weird reaction when I showed up for my pre-req.

"How much did you wipe from my memory?" My voice warbles. "How much is gone?"

Levine pinches the bridge of her nose. "Evelyn—"

"How much?"

"A year."

No. I can't believe it. A year of my life, gone. "But what about school?"

"Most schools aren't even open anymore. It's not safe, hasn't been for the past two years. The violence became overwhelming. They couldn't control it. Kids wouldn't be safe in schools, not with all the shootings on every block."

Footsteps clomp in the distance.

"Eva. We gotta go. We can talk about it later." Alex shoves Levine forward. "Take us to the elevator."

"You don't want to go out there," Levine says morosely.

Her words give me pause. "What would we find if we did?"

"Nothing good."

"What, should we stay locked up here forever?" Alex scoffs. "We can survive it. I've done it. Keep walking."

"Wait." I whirl on Levine. "We took the drug and didn't get side effects. Allard recruited us from the hospital, and we ended up working here. Why?"

"Klaurivex users under eighteen weren't as likely to become violent." She wrings her hands. "Hugo felt awful about the drug. He never wanted it to hurt people. We never expected it to go that way."

"Yeah, well, he fucked up," Alex says. "C'mon."

"Why did he need us?" I repeat. "Why hire a couple of kids to work at a juvie prison?"

Levine bites her lip.

"Tell me!"

"The Center's prisoners are Klaurivex addicts. They all committed crimes under the influence. We detox them before intakes to counteract their enhanced strength, but there's no way to permanently remove the drug from a person's body once it's been injected."

"You didn't answer my question. Why did you recruit us?"

She sighs. "You had Klaurivex's strength without the

drug's violence."

"So what?"

"Hugo wanted something good to come of it all. But it . . . backfired."

I remember it all—working as Center guards, forcing slugs into the intake room. Pricking their necks every morning to test their K-levels, making sure the drug's presence was still subdued. Having the strength to easily overpower inmates who misbehaved.

I close my eyes, wishing that wasn't the worst of it.

We consented. We did it for the money. I needed to convince the court I could take care of David without Aunt Lily. That I could be his legal guardian.

I blink.

"Now, allow me to explain," Allard says. *"Imagine regular law-enforcement officers trying to take out Klaurivex criminals. It wouldn't be a fair fight."*

"You need Klaurivex-enhanced people to police other Klaurivex-enhanced people," I say. *"To level the playing field."*

"Precisely. But using the Klaurivex's strength against others with the same abilities is pointless without skill. Which brings me to artificial learning, a sort of muscle memory, if you will. A medical procedure in which skills are inserted into the brain, to give the recipient abilities he or she did not, and could not, previously possess. Years of training within minutes. I can give you the ability to fight, to kill. If I can perfect this process, it could be the only way to protect us all from the violent ones."

"So why not just enhance the older guards?" Alex asks. "Take some adults who are already trained."

"Almost all adults who take the dose become violent. Plus, it's now illegal to administer the Klaurivex, Mr. Martinez. Unfortunately, we need to work with what we have."

Alex folds his arms. "That's a terrible idea. You wanna play God."

"This is a terrible situation," Allard says. "And in terrible situations, sometimes God is what we need. And if the real man in the sky won't swoop in and save us all from destroying ourselves, then maybe it's up to humanity to step up to the role."

I can't believe it. He created the violence then left it up to us to fix his mistake.

"When you were arrested, he didn't detox the Klaurivex from your bodies like the other inmates—it would destroy his theory," Levine says. "You didn't have the side effects. We thought it would be fine. But we had to ingrain you with a trigger word so you couldn't access the strength on your own. Hugo thought it would keep everyone safer."

Alex glowers. "So why don't I have one?"

"We . . . wanted to give you one. The directors, I mean. We couldn't have a prisoner running around the Center who had the implanted fighting skills and could access his strength; we'd never stand a chance. But Hugo insisted we wait. He thought the memory wipe would be enough to ensure you couldn't remember the strength and therefore wouldn't use it."

"That's stupid," I say. "Why would he ever think that would work?"

"I don't know. He tracks everything, writes everything down. I think he believed implanting a trigger word would ruin his hard work. We don't know how to reverse the trigger words once they're implanted. It's an extremely strong level of hypnosis required to activate them. If Alex's strength was blocked by a trigger word, he could never again be the enhanced weapon Hugo intended—not without a chaperone standing behind him, waiting to trigger him at all times. He balked at giving you a trigger word, Evelyn. We only put one in you because . . . we didn't have another choice."

Shouts from guards echo somewhere above us.

I hardly register Alex grabbing my hand and pulling me down the hallway. Our footsteps quicken, pattering against the cement in time with my heart.

He's not threatening Levine anymore, but she follows anyway. "Evelyn, wait. There are things you need to know."

The alarm rings louder in the distance.

"No. I'm done." We round the corner. "You operate the elevator and get us the hell away from here."

"Evelyn, please. Let me explain."

"Shut up!" Alex snarls at her. "Keep moving!"

"Evelyn!"

"Come on!" I shout, racing down the hall.

Levine stops. "Don't you want to know how you went from a guard to a prisoner?" My shoes screech to a halt.

Alex grabs my hand, but I twist out of his grasp. "Don't you want to know who you killed?"

I slowly turn to face the director. "What?"

It shouldn't shock me. I've known I'm a murderer for days now. But still, deep down, part of me hoped it was another trick. That I hadn't actually done it. That maybe Allard locked me up to teach me a lesson or something.

Something happened. I got cured, took the job at the Center, they made me into a weapon, but then . . . it all went wrong.

Alex throws his head back. "There's no time. They're coming."

I remember a phone call.

"Evelyn." Levine's eyes bore into me. "You don't want to be out there without knowing the truth."

"So tell me."

"It's not that simple."

"Tell her, or back off and let us go!"

Outlines and edges form in my memories. "David called me at work." I step toward Andrea as the memories solidify. "He was in trouble. But Allard wouldn't let me leave." My throat feels warm. "He couldn't—I was unstable. I was stronger than I should've been, an untested weapon."

"Your enhanced skills were intended to best those with similar strength—people under the influence of Klaurivex," Levine says. "Not the average person on the street. It was for your own good."

"I snuck out. You—" I turn to Alex. "You helped me. You scanned me into the elevator. You knocked out the guards so I could escape."

Alex nods, his mouth a hard line across his face. There was something there. Something between us. Something that developed over months of working together, training together.

My last thought, as the elevator ascends, is that I hope this isn't the end. And in a moment of half childish wishing and half desperation, I make a promise to myself that I don't know if I can keep: I promise I'll see Alex's face again.

I strain my memory for more, but can't remember a thing after that. It's all blurry. "What happened next?"

Levine's brow creases, but she doesn't reply.

"I murdered someone." I shake her shoulders. "Tell me!"

"Evelyn." Levine tilts her head back and closes her eyes. "Before you know . . . what happened. You have to understand."

"Tell her! Now!"

Levine hangs her head. "None of us are bad people. But sometimes the worst things can come from the best intentions."

"Andrea. I need to know the truth."

Levine presses a gray pill into my hand. "Take this. It'll restore your memories."

"Yeah, right. Like I'd take anything from you."

"You think I'm going to hurt you? You were like a daughter to me, Evelyn. I went to bat for you. Why do you think they agreed to bring you back to the Center? Murderers on Klaurivex get executed—yes, even the minors."

I hesitate.

"I'm not telling you what happened. But you have a right to see it for yourself."

There's no hint of lies in her eyes. For some reason, I trust her.

"Eva—"

Before Alex can drag me away, I close my eyes and knock back the pill.

"I'm sorry, Evelyn." Levine's face is heavy as the dry pill disintegrates on my tongue. "For what it's worth, I'm so sorry."

At first, nothing happens. I flex my hands, bracing myself for the flood of memories. After all this time, I'll finally know.

Alex's eyes flick between Levine and me. For a moment, everything is silent.

A headache prickles behind my forehead, growing into searing pain. I wince, struck with déjà vu of the illness that started this. My feet are swept out from under me, like being tugged by the strong undertow of a wave.

Colors and edges whirl together like watercolor paints. As if putting on glasses for the first time, everything comes into focus, and I see it all. I'm back in the past, two years ago—one year after I took the job at the Center. Like I'm an actor in a play about my own life.

The aroma of freshly fallen rain mixes with the stench of new death in the air. Black, starless sky covers me like a blanket. I'm standing on my old street—but it looks different somehow. More sinister.

Something pulls at me, beckoning me to run; I comply, tearing across the pavement toward my old home.

Dread boils inside me. Whatever happened, I'm moments away from it. But I can't stop. My feet are on autopilot, forcing me to relive my past step by step like I'm in another one of Allard's virtual simulations.

It's changed—everything has. Busted windows and cracked siding adorn every house, but there's not a resident in sight. It looks like a ghost town.

A gunshot echoes from somewhere, mingling with distant shouts. I pray I don't encounter anyone, but I'm ready to defend myself if I do. Klaurivex flows thickly through my veins, mingled with Allard's enhanced training. I am unstoppable. And that frightens me.

I stop short on my mother's crunchy yellow lawn. The place has grown eerily akin to a haunted house since my mom died and I left to work at the Center. Weeds dominate the lawn and creep through cracks in the driveway. Towering pine trees block the moonlight, casting a shadow over the small split-level. The tangled bushes by the door have overgrown. When Mom was here, a halo of warmth covered the house. It wasn't the biggest house on the block, or even the nicest, but that didn't matter. It doesn't look like my home anymore. Aunt Lily has let the place fall to shambles. Hatred for her swirls like poison inside me.

My hand hovers over the doorknob. For a split second, I hesitate. I murdered someone in my own home. The place that was my solace became my crime scene. All to save David from . . . something.

An inkling suddenly horrifies me. Did I kill my aunt Lily?

With one smooth motion, I fling open the door.

I blaze inside, slipping on the tattered rug in the hall and steadying myself against the fading teapot wallpaper.

"David?" I call, as if reading lines off a cue card. "Where are you?"

Despite the pit knotting in my stomach, a veil of calm drifts over me, back in the place that once held so many happy memories. Back home.

"David?" I try again. No answer.

Raised voices echo in the stairwell. I bolt upstairs as fast as my legs can carry, reaching the ominous hallway at the summit. I know it's not real; I'm standing in the Center with Alex and Director Levine. But still, seeing the source of my nightmares for the first time in years makes me jittery.

I burst into David's bedroom. Blue curtains flutter like ghosts, cloaking the cracked-open window.

A male figure stands in the corner with his back to me. There's something familiar about him. David cowers on the floor beneath him, his cheeks gaunt.

"Eva!"

"David!" I spring toward him.

The strange man whirls around. I stop dead. He's not a man at all—he's a nineteen-year-old college freshman with messy brown hair and sharp cheekbones.

My forehead wrinkles. "Matt?"

Matt sways as if caught in a breeze. Recognition doesn't dawn on him—he doesn't even look like he hears me. His red-rimmed pupils stare back at me like lasers.

Klaurivex.

I can't comprehend it. Matt Houston. In my house. High on Klaurivex. Standing over my baby brother. The usual Matt-induced butterflies don't flutter in my chest. He's changed.

"Eva!" My brother plows toward me, but Matt yanks him back by his T-shirt. The fact that he's keeping my brother from me floods me with rage.

Venom sears in my veins. "You lay a hand on my brother, and I'll kill you myself." I shove past him and throw my arms around David. "Oh my God, are you okay? What happened?"

He shakes. "I was scared. They left me."

"Don't worry." I press my hand to his cheek. "I'm here. I won't let them hurt you."

Something shatters, and I whirl around. Aunt Lily stands behind us, her frumpy silhouette framed in the doorway. She's only twenty-two, but her face looks older. Worn.

"I got the stuff," she mutters, not acknowledging

my presence.

David's rocket-ship lamp lies in broken ceramic shards on the floor beside her. She flings a plastic bag filled with white powder onto the dresser and steps into the light. Red rims encircle her black pupils.

I step back, my hand latched around David's wrist. "You too?"

"What're you doing back here?" she slurs, recognition dawning behind her eyes.

Matt slinks over and grabs her ass. It's like I'm looking at my old crush and seeing a different person. I blink a few times, not believing the truth that's sinking slowly into my bones.

"Lily's the older woman you dumped me for." I intend to scream it, but my words come out softer than a whisper. Even as I speak, it seems too bizarre to be true. Matt wouldn't be with her. He's too good for her.

But the more I watch them—the dazed, lustful look in his eyes that he never got when he looked at me—the more real it becomes. The more similar they become.

"You're just another one of her conquests." My voice gets louder, infused with the vitriol pumping through me. "That's gross." I feel my face contorting into a look of pure disgust.

I expected Lily to betray me. But him? This feels like the carpet has been ripped out from under me.

"You could've protected him." I force the words through gritted teeth.

Lily slaps his hand away, giggling. "Stop it, Matt!"

They're not even paying attention to me. They don't care.

I swallow down the hot ball of anger in my throat, fighting back the urge to beat them both senseless. "I won't interrupt. We were just leaving."

Aunt Lily steps in front, blocking our getaway. "You're not going anywhere. You've seen too much."

"You don't want to fight me, Lily." Part of me wants her to try. Wants her to see what happens when she challenges a human weapon with a personal grudge.

A door creaks downstairs.

"Stay here," a woman's voice commands. "I'll get her."

Matt swears. "There are people here." His shaky fingers stuff the bag of powdered Klaurivex into his jeans pocket. My brother's grip tightens like a vice around my hand.

"Lily." I labor to keep my voice even. "Move. We're leaving."

Director Levine rushes into the room brandishing a pistol. The moment she sees me, she visibly relaxes and sheathes her weapon in her holster. A jack follows quickly behind her.

"We've got a situation here," the jack mutters into his radio. "We're gonna need backup. Call the police."

"No cops!" Matt slams his fist onto the dresser. His eyes grow frantic.

Levine ignores them. "Evelyn, you need to come back.

Hugo's on the warpath. You're lucky I found you before he did."

"Don't go," my brother cries.

"I'm not leaving without David." I'm not leaving my brother here with these incompetent assholes.

"David can come with us. He can stay in your room. He'll be safe. I promise."

Lily's nostrils flare. "David's in my custody."

"Screw you." I yank David toward Director Levine. "We're leaving."

Levine's attention turned, Matt grabs the pistol from her holster and aims at the cop-calling jack. I drop David's hand and lunge to stop him, but it's too late.

The gunshot cracks through the cramped room. Trained in combat, the jack drops to the floor to avoid the blow.

The bullet misses Matt's target and nails David instead.

He presses his hands to his chest, framing his fingers around the gaping wound. A red patch spreads like an infection across his green Spider-Man T-shirt. He stumbles backward, falling into my arms. Crimson splotches dapple the carpet beneath him as he collapses.

Someone gasps. Someone else screams.

But I don't pay attention to any of it.

Matt did it. Matt did it. Matt did it.

Everything stops. Mouths open but no sound comes out. My mind goes blank. The Klaurivex inside me takes over. I see nothing but red. Red eyes, red blood, red rage seeping through my skin.

Betrayal. Rage. Kill.

I lay my brother's trembling body gently on the carpet. The gunshot replays in my mind: *bang, bang, bang.*

Maybe it's Allard's training. Maybe it's the Klaurivex. Maybe it's just good old-fashioned revenge. My crosshairs land on everything in sight. The weapon inside me revs to life.

I'm slightly aware of the snap of a bone, the crunch of my fist meeting my aunt's jaw, Lily's pained scream as she crawls from the room.

Matt puts up a fight. Klaurivex flows through him, but he's no match for my enhanced training. It's almost too easy. A spin and twist of his neck, and his body falls to the floor like a ragdoll. Dead.

Something smashes into my skull. Everything goes black.

Little jolts of memory flash through me: waking up strapped to a bed in the Center; Allard insisting he's spent too much time and money to reverse the procedure that made me who I am; Levine tearfully demanding that they don't execute me; the idea to implant a trigger word inside me instead. Overhearing the directors' hushed whispers that Alex escaped the night I left; their frantic plans to find him and bring him back before his weaponized body does the same harm as mine did. The decision to lock me in the Center, have me serve my time alongside the hacks I used to warden over—the hacks whose memories would be altered so they'd forget I ever worked here.

I suck in a sharp breath. I'm back in the Center's hallway, as if the whole memory took place within a single blink.

Grief weighs me down like an anchor. David's gone. He's really gone.

I have no family left. No home to return to. Nothing left to lose. I should collapse here on the floor and let them kill me.

Alex tosses my pistol back to me. In my daze, I nearly miss but snatch the weapon midair. "We gotta get outta here." He starts walking, but I can't move.

"I don't have anywhere to go." I push the words past the growing lump in my throat. "I don't have anyone left."

"Yes, you do." He goes to touch me, but his hand falls softly back to his side. "We had something once. But I left you. They took me to the surface to help find you and I . . . I bolted. I knew if I went back down there, they'd never let me go. I've regretted it every day." He lowers his eyes. "I'm so sorry."

I swallow hard. I know what that's like—to save yourself first, by any means necessary.

"But I'm not doing that again. I promise, Eva."

I don't know what that means. I don't know if his promises are any good, or if I even want them. I don't know what we had—if we could ever have anything again. Right now, all I know is my brother is gone. Tears burn hot in my eyes.

"Evelyn." Levine grabs for my hand, but I recoil. My sadness frosts over. Hatred seeps into my veins. My knuckles grow white around the barrel of the gun.

"You promised me he would be safe." I point the pistol directly between Levine's eyes. "You lied to me."

"I'm so . . . sorry. But it's not—"

"You let him die." I step toward her as she backs away.

"Evelyn, I didn't!"

"Eva, let's go, come on."

"No," I seethe. "Not while she's alive and David's dead."

"But, Evelyn—"

"Shut up!" I cock the pistol. "One more word, and I swear to God—"

"He's not dead!"

I freeze. "What?"

"The bullet missed his heart," Levine says. "He had surgery to remove it; he had the best doctors in the country.

Hugo's paying an arm and a leg to keep that boy safe. We're not bad people, Evelyn."

"I don't believe you. If he's still alive, where is he?"

"At a secure, militarized boarding school about two hours away."

I blink back the tear before it can roll down my cheek and broadcast my relief to the world. "Really?" The word comes out more of a croak.

"Yes."

Alex nods. "We'll find him, Eva."

Levine wrings her hands. "Hugo will never allow it."

"He doesn't get to dictate my life anymore." None of this would have happened without Allard. He has taken everything from me. I will not give him the satisfaction of taking my life. I will escape, and I will live, and every second I'm alive will be a second Hugo Allard failed.

"We're getting out of here." Anger fuels me, forcing my feet forward. "And if I find him before we reach the elevator, I will break him. Let's go."

Alex nods, a smug look on his face. "Walk," he commands, pressing the mouth of his pistol to Levine's back. She whimpers but steps forward. "If we meet any jacks and I trigger Eva, you're not to say that other word to turn her off."

She nods.

I press my back to the wall, glancing up and down the empty hallway. My pulse races as we creep to the end of the corridor. It's too quiet.

Elevator, I mouth, pointing up the next flight of stairs. Alex nods.

We tiptoe upstairs, Alex in front, Levine sandwiched in the middle. Alex opens the door at the top, and we filter out.

"Stop right there." Desirae blocks our path, a pistol quivering in her hands.

Alex presses his weapon to Levine's temple. "You pull the trigger, and I'll kill her."

"You'll still be dead." Desirae cocks her weapon. "I may not be special like the two of you, but I never miss a shot."

"Alex," I mutter. "Don't."

She's too far away; if we make a move, she'll kill us. I can't escape and find David if I'm dead. I drop my weapon and slowly put up my hands.

"You're going straight to Allard," she hisses. "And then I never have to see you again."

"Why are you doing this?" Alex's jaw clenches. "You were on our side once. We were friends."

"We *were* friends." She grimaces, exposing her discolored top tooth. "A long time ago."

I blink, and the memories come creeping back. The three of us worked in the Center together. We were inseparable. I remember long nights laughing in the break room, having sleepovers in our bunks. But Desirae wasn't a Klaurivex patient—her parents paid Allard to keep her safe when the world outside started crumbling. She didn't have our enhanced strength. She wasn't allowed to train with us because she was no match for the people who'd taken the drug.

"We ditched you," I whisper. "I remember it now."

Desirae's gun doesn't falter.

"We were supposed to be on guard duty together." I say. "But I blew you off to see Alex. To train with him." To kiss him, my mind finishes.

Her upper lip curls back. "They left me for dead."

I remember it now. I remember them wheeling her in on a stretcher after the inmates beat her senseless and knocked out her teeth. I remember how she could barely see out of her swollen, blackened eyes. I remember hardly being there for her because I was selfishly thinking about my own shit. All I cared about was seeing Alex and training to be a better weapon. I ditched my friend for a guy—just like I ditched Sherri for that scumbag Matt.

Ronnie wasn't the only friend I sacrificed. Sarah, Ariadne, and Courtney weren't the first people who suffered from my selfishness.

I hate who I was. I hate that I threw the people I loved under the bus. I was selfish, shallow, and thoughtless. I never want to be that girl again.

"I'm sorry, Des," I whisper.

Fury twitches across her face, but she doesn't pull the trigger.

"I should have been there. I shouldn't have been such a shitty friend."

She doesn't respond. She just watches me with icicles in her eyes.

"If I could go back and change what I did—who I became—I'd do it in a heartbeat."

"You're selfish, Evelyn. You always have been."

"I know."

Alex fidgets beside me, not knowing what to do.

"Do you remember what we called ourselves?" Desirae steps closer, her voice smooth as poisoned honey. "Back before you decided you were too good for me?"

I swallow hard. "Yes."

"The Stockyard Trio." Desirae laughs. "It's funny in hindsight. The more I get to know people, the more I realize hatred is a cycle." She steadies her weapon with both hands. "Sometimes I'm shocked at how vicious I've become—yes, I know I can be a bitch. But that's how it works, right? Nice person gets screwed over by a bad person, becomes a bad person themselves, and the cycle continues. If you break a bone, it grows back stronger. We harden. We grow thicker skins so they can't hurt us anymore. We become the thing that does the hurting. That's how it works."

"Maybe you're right . . . about some of it. But not everything. You're not a bad person, Des."

She snorts. "No. Not like you."

I wish she were wrong. Part of me wishes these memories would vanish back into the abyss, so I could go on believing I was innocent. But I was a monster long before they made me one. "I've done so many bad things," I whisper, more to myself.

"Yes, you have." Desirae presses her lips together.

"I remember now. I remember it all. And God, I'm so sorry, Des." I press the heels of my palms into my eyes. "You were my best friend. And I let you down. I left you when you needed me most. I could have stopped it if I'd been there, and I wasn't."

"No, you weren't."

"I fucked up. I did. I can't believe that's who I used to be."

"It's not easy when your mistakes come back to haunt you, is it, Ev? A mirror image you don't want to see." Her gun doesn't falter.

"I know," I say. "Looking back, there's all these . . . these tiny moments. These snapshots in time. Where you make one thoughtless decision, and it ripples and ruins everything." I think about that afternoon in Zepp's office two years ago and that split second before I gave the directors my answer for the sixth trial. I thought they were just words. At the time, I never thought I'd be ending someone's life. That me, a quiet good girl with the best intentions, could have the power to destroy with a few simple, meaningless sentences. I wanted to get out. I wanted to pass my trials, and I couldn't think of anything or anyone beyond myself. I'd say they were all just mistakes, but that word sounds so innocuous—so small—compared to what I've done.

"I made a stupid decision. I thought I was blowing off

guard duty. I never in a million years thought anything bad would happen to you. You were my best friend. Hell, I'd have quit the job on day one if you weren't there."

Des shifts her eyes to the ground.

"If I'd known, even a little bit—" My voice breaks. "I never would've done it. I'm so sorry. I was selfish, and I hurt you. If I could go back to that day—God, I wish I could go back to that day—I'd be different. It should've been me on guard duty. I should've been beside you."

"Yes." Des's voice drops to a whisper. "You should've been."

"I'm sorry for what I did. But I'm ending the cycle now." Taking a deep breath, I reach out and push Alex's hand down, lowering his gun.

Desirae blinks, taken aback.

"Maybe I don't deserve your forgiveness," I say. "But for what it's worth, I'm sorry, Des. I really am."

The ice in her eyes melts, and for a moment, I wonder if she's going to cry.

Footsteps echo in the halls around us. My heart races. "Des. Please."

She stands stoic as a statue, unyielding.

"Check the elevator!" shouts a voice.

I stiffen. "Please."

She closes her eyes for a moment, inhaling deeply.

"Desirae—"

"Screw you." She throws her weapon down and storms

away from us.

"Come with us," I call after her.

She doesn't look back.

"Leave her," Alex says. "We gotta go." He grabs Levine's arm and tugs her around the corner toward the lift.

I pick up Desirae's discarded weapon, and my brows lower at the pistol's light weight. I slide out the bolt expecting a handful of bullets, but it's empty. Guilt washes over me.

"Bring us up," Alex orders.

Levine swipes her card into the slot. "Are you sure you want to do this?"

I step into the elevator, answering her question. Alex follows.

Levine sighs. "Take care of yourselves out there." She presses the button and the gate closes.

"What's the name of David's school?" I ask, as the massive metal doors slowly come together.

"Chesterwood Academy."

The doors close, sealing us inside.

Alex and I are silent as we ascend. He gives me a reassuring nod but can't hide the fear on his face. I keep my pistol ready.

With a ding, the elevator grinds to a halt. I take a deep breath as the doors open. Light floods the room.

Jacks rush at us from either side as if someone stumbled over a hornet's nest and awakened the hive. The five remaining directors surround the elevator; we walked into an ambush.

"Hands up!" A jack slams the butt of his rifle into Alex's face and wrenches the pistol from his hands. I aim my weapon, but another jack disarms me in seconds.

No. It can't end this way. Not before I find my brother. "Move! Get out of my way or I'll kill each and every one of you!" I frantically dodge around the guard.

Five more jacks swarm from the shadows.

"Don't kill them!" Allard shouts.

Allard.

"*Facultas!*" Alex sputters, spitting a mouthful of blood onto the floor.

My foot jabs the nearest jack's kneecap. A fist slams into my ribs, but I break the offender's arm with a crack. I'm half aware of Alex beating the other jack into the ground beside me. Hugo's plan backfired. His own weapons turned against him.

Usually the trigger word sucks the control from my body, turning me into a senseless weapon, but I hold on to a thread of myself this time, channeling every ounce of control I can muster. I let the anger seep into my bloodstream, infusing my body with hatred. They want a monster? I'll give them one.

Alex spin-kicks a jack, and the guard doubles over. I pounce like a tiger and knock another jack to the ground, straddling my knees over his chest.

It's us or them. I'm not letting them stop us. We're getting away.

I dart my eyes up; my gaze lands on a cowering Doctor Allard.

Doctor Allard, who made me into the monster who murdered Matt.

Who is responsible for the drug that led to my mother's death.

Who locked me up for two years because I did what he programed me to do—kill.

Who tortured me in the Freedom Trials and would've put a bullet in my head the second I messed up.

Who tricked me into killing one of my best friends.

I charge toward him and ram the doctor to the ground.

"Evelyn! Please!"

"You son of a bitch." I slam his head into the concrete. "This is all your fault."

A jack grabs me around the middle and yanks me off the doctor. I slither from his grasp and knee him in the balls, smashing the butt of his rifle into his chin. Another jack raises his pistol at me, but I twist his arm behind him, dislocating his shoulder with a snap. I turn his weapon back on him right as he fires it.

These people ruined my life. I'm already a murderer.

I'll kill them all if I have to.

"*Desine!*" Hannon shouts.

"*Facultas!*" counters Alex.

They go back and forth, but I barely hear them.

Allard scurries across the floor backward on his hands

and feet like a crab. I launch myself at him. He grunts as I slam into his chest.

I lay my fingers into Allard's neck and squeeze.

"D-d-d," he sputters, but I don't let him say the trigger word; I press harder.

He flails his arms, slashing and punching me, but I feel nothing as I choke the life from his eyes. Blood leaks from my throbbing shoulder, but I don't stop. I pin his legs to the ground as he thrashes.

Maybe I should feel something. Remorse. Fear. Pain.

But all I feel is numb.

I know I should stop—I know, deep down, that this is wrong. But I can't stop pressing.

I want to watch him die. My body craves it like oxygen.

I'm terrified of my strength, terrified of my will—but I don't stop.

"What do you think, Hugo?" He gags and sputters, but I constrict tighter around his neck. "Have I reformed?"

"*Desine!*" Director Hannon shouts over the grunts and cries.

I don't relent, but the strength flushes from my limbs, draining like liquid from a sieve. Two jacks rip me off of him, my arms dangling weakly at my sides. They pin my hands behind my back. Allard coughs and pulls himself up, clutching his throat.

"*Facultas!*" Alex bellows, between pummeling Agarwal and Marewood.

My arms snap up. I smash the back of my head into the face of the jack holding me. Her hand slices into my wounded shoulder and I yelp, collapsing to the ground. I swing my foot and knock her off her balance. Alex jumps from behind, wild-eyed, and smashes his rifle into her skull; the jack falls to the floor.

"Give up!" I plunge my fist into Hannon's face. "You made us this way." I smash my other fist into a jack's eye. "Just let us go."

Alex thrusts his knee into the last half-conscious jack's face. The guard drops to the ground.

"*Desine!*" Zepp cries.

My shoulders droop as the strength deflates from my body. Director Marewood and the jacks lie still around me in a mass grave. Several directors wince and groan from the floor.

Alex grabs my hand. "Come on, let's get out of here." He shoves past a quaking Director Agarwal.

"Enough!" Allard stands, brushing off his wrinkled suit. "That is enough."

He lunges for the stolen remote in Alex's back pocket. He aims the device at my head and swipes his finger across the buttons.

"No!"

Alex dives in front and the beam hits him head-on.

He screams and falls to the ground, his pistol sliding across the floor. I race toward Allard, but Zane lunges and catches me around the middle. He throws me down, and I crash into the cement.

"Let him go!"

"No."

Alex writhes on the floor, twitching and screaming.

"Stop! Please." I crawl to Alex's side. His collar sparks and cracks. "You're going to kill him."

Allard doesn't falter.

Black smoke billows from Alex's collar, swirling into the air. A putrid stench floods my nostrils.

"Please!" My voice goes hoarse.

"I'll stop," Allard says. "On one condition."

"Name it."

"You both come back to work with me. Complete the project. Finish what you started."

"No chance in hell."

"You and Mr. Martinez come back to work for the Center," Allard says, "or he dies."

I grab an abandoned pistol off a dead jack, cock it, and aim for Allard's head. "Or I could kill you first."

The elevator dings. A team of jacks run out, their rifles raised and pointed at my head. Levine follows with her hands up.

"Fine, kill me," Allard says. "But only if you want to die too. I ordered them to keep you alive, but if I die, you die with me. You're outnumbered, Evelyn." He nods toward the onslaught of jacks. "They'll have sixteen bullets in your chest before I take my last breath, even if you take some of them down with you. You may be powerful, but there are some things even you can't do." His tone is low and venomous. "So go ahead. Kill me. But it will be the last thing you and Alex ever do. You'll never see David again."

Alex's echoing cries shatter the hallway, prickling the hairs on my neck. Jacks surround us in a circle, at least twenty, thirty, or more.

"It's over, Evelyn. Give up."

My jaw tightens, but I don't lower my weapon. "You're a monster."

"I'm a scientist."

"My mom would still be alive if you hadn't pedaled your drug to the world."

"Yes, and you'd be dead." Allard laughs. "You and Mr. Martinez should be groveling at my feet. I saved your lives. Where would you be without my drug? Dying? Or already gone?"

"That doesn't justify all the lives your drug took—all the killers it created."

"It's not that clear cut. I saved lives. Sometimes the ends justify the means."

"Evelyn." Levine's words drip with exasperation. "Do you really want another death on your conscience? Another murder?"

I open my mouth, but don't know what to say. A death. Another death. Taking a life in exchange for a life. Isn't this what it's always been? My mother's dead; my best friends are dead. Can I let Alex die for me too? A martyr for the Center's cause? Blood with blood, fire with fire. An eye for an eye.

If I go down that path, I'm no better than Allard.

Alex's life is worth more to me than that.

"No."

I unclench my sweaty hand. The pistol falls from my grip and hits the cement with a clang.

Allard swipes his finger across the buttons and the remote beeps. Alex twitches on the floor until his limbs grow still. He lets out a long groan. I leap toward him.

But four jacks are already at my side. They rip my arms behind my back, and the familiar, cold metal bites my wrists.

Zane and Zepp whisper together, glaring daggers at me and shaking their heads.

Agarwal winces as he pries his bent leg out from under him. A tear stretches the length of his shirt, and blood seeps through his pant leg. Director Marewood lies motionless on the floor, along with a dozen jacks.

"What do we do with them?" Hannon cradles her injured arm in the corner. She nods toward Alex and me. "Kill them?"

"We're not killing anyone." Allard crosses his arms "Not today, at least."

The jacks strap shackles over Alex's feet and hands. He glowers at them.

"First, we change Ms. Summers's trigger word to something neither will know. Then we ingrain a trigger word in Mr. Martinez's mind as well." The color drains from Alex's face at the doctor's words. "I've put it off for the sake of research and hope for his ability as a future guard, but unfortunately, that cause has proven dangerous to you all. For that, I must offer my most sincere apologies. From now on, no more rampant strength whenever he chooses. It's a sacrifice I must make for the good of everyone in this facility."

Terror pulsates in Alex's gaze as they casually discuss stripping his defenses. Declawing the feral cat so it won't scratch its master.

"Next, we erase their memories. Everything from the past two years. For all they know when they wake up, they still work here and never left. We'll tell them the tattoos were required to be realistic plants. Pretend none of this ever happened."

I gasp. "No. You can't."

"It's the only way. The inmates who knew you as a prisoner will assume you were a plant this whole time. I'll be wiping Ms. Ishida's memory as well, unfortunately. If you're going to be coworkers again, you'll need to get along, and with your current distaste for each other, that's impossible. I liked it better when we were all friends."

I'm struck with a pang of pity for Desirae. Maybe she's not "one of them" the way she once thought. Maybe she's like me—she's never fit in anywhere.

The jacks haul Alex into the elevator by his underarms. His head droops with defeat. It's a sick flashback to his intake—the look of a man who stopped fighting.

"Let's go, Evelyn," a jack says.

I nod.

Because what else can I do?

My eyes burn as the elevator descends, lowering us back into the place with no light.

The jacks dump Alex and me into a small, empty custodial closet and lock the door. It's barely wide enough to stretch our arms without touching both walls. A single fluorescent light flickers down at us from the cement ceiling. The sharp stench of ammonia overpowers me. We sit in silence, not meeting each other's eyes.

Within ten minutes, the door clicks open. Alex and I jump to our feet, but they're not here for us. A guard shoves an angry-looking Desirae into our tiny closet and locks the door behind her.

Des huffs and sinks to the floor, her hair matted. Alex and I cast a glance at each other, then at Desirae. She keeps her eyes on the ceiling. Her face is flushed red, and I can't help wondering if she gave Allard a piece of her mind when he told her the news. I wish I'd been there to hear it.

Ten more minutes pass before the door creaks open again.

Alex, Des, and I snap to our feet, an unspoken layer of tension in the air. But it's not a guard this time—it's Nurse Ellen. I relax when I see her. Of all the people the Center could have sent, she's probably the only one I trust.

"Yes, yes, hello." Ellen pushes into the tiny closet and shuts the door behind her. I can feel the heat emanating off all four bodies, tightly packed in the small room. Desirae's chest bumps into my back, and I quickly pull away, inching closer to Alex.

"What's going on?" I ask. "What are they going to do?"

Nurse Ellen digs in the pocket of her scrubs and pulls out an orange canister. "I'm here to give you some painkillers." She pops the lid off the bottle and a handful of large yellow pills spills into her palm. One by one, she passes them out to us. "The memory wipes can come with some nasty side effects. Headaches, nausea, the whole works."

Desirae's nose wrinkles at the massive pill. "You didn't give us any water."

"They're quick dissolving. Works faster that way. Come now, in they go." Nurse Ellen watches expectantly as we hesitantly take the meds. The lemony pill fizzes on my tongue and disintegrates before I can chew.

"Good." Ellen nods. "I'll get the guards."

Desirae scowls. "Can't wait."

We sit in silence for five more minutes. The next time the door clicks open, six jacks wait beyond it with enough handcuffs to shackle an army. Of course.

The jacks lead me to the intake room, jerking and prodding me like I'm a wild animal ready to be put down. They take Alex somewhere else—our eyes meet one last time before he's around a corner, out of my sight. I don't see where they take Desirae. I never thought I'd miss my nemesis, but the moment she's gone, I wish they'd bring her back. For the first time, it feels like we're on the same side, caught in some gray area between "us" and "them."

I wonder if Allard will try tracking Carolyn, Miles, and Tom, or if they don't matter to the Center anymore. Collateral damage. I hope they're far away anyway.

We step around destruction and debris in the hallway. Level Ones will likely be here soon, sweeping away all evidence that a fight ever happened.

Agarwal and Zane strap me to the table with thick cords around my wrists, ankles, neck, and stomach. They tie me tighter than necessary, forcing the air from my lungs with each tug. I wonder what it was like the first time they wiped my memory. Was I afraid? Did I struggle? Did I cry?

Doctor Wang bustles around, preparing the equipment.

"Two minutes. Let's fire up the machine," Allard says. "We've got three wipes to do, and then, damn it, I want things back to normal around here."

A jack approaches with a slick black remote. I flinch, but the pain doesn't come. Something beeps, then a click, and my collar loosens. It falls off my neck and lies limp on the table. The jack rips it out from under me.

I inhale deeply, relishing the lack of constriction around my throat. I long to touch my bare skin, savor the air flow, but my arms are bound too tight to move. I'm still a prisoner in my own body. Out of the literal collar, into the figurative one.

"Employees don't need collars, Evelyn." Levine walks over and kneels beside the medical bed. She brushes a strand of hair from my eyes. I'd knock her hand away if I wasn't strapped in. The most I can do is glare at her, so I do.

"You'll see your brother again," she whispers. I wish I could believe her.

Something dawns on me. "My prerequisite task had nothing to do with helping the intake process." It's so obvious it practically screams. "It was about Alex. You knew he'd try to talk to me. You wanted to see if I'd react. If I'd want to abandon my rehabilitation and go with him. That was my real pre-req."

She flashes a sheepish grin. "Yes. You're right. But I must say, we didn't think he'd get violent toward the staff. You were both part of our Center family once."

"You got violent toward us first—your so-called family. Why let me talk to Alex at all?"

"It was Hugo's idea. He wanted to test how strong the memory wipes really are. See if you'd start to question everything the moment you reconnected, or if you'd pass each other like strangers and not give each other a second glance. It was foolish of him to think that would work. There are some things we can't erase. Feelings, honest feelings, will always come back to the surface, no matter how hard we try to wipe them away."

"How poetic." I roll my eyes. "Really, how do you people sleep at night?"

"I know you don't believe me, but we really are good people. Even Hugo. We're just trying to undo the mistakes we made, help the teens who fell victim to Klaurivex before they're too far gone."

"You treat us like we're all killers or monsters. It's sick." I don't know why this is all pouring out now, but I can't stop it. "Carolyn's crime was drug trafficking. That hardly seems worth forcing her to go through all this crap."

Levine arches a brow. "Klaurivex trafficking, you mean? You're all lucky the Center found you before the police. Committing any crime under the influence of Klaurivex is punishable by death if they catch you. We saved you."

"Saved us?" I snort. "You execute more prisoners than you save."

"You'd all be executed if you'd remained on the outside, Evelyn—or worse. Extreme, desperate times call for extreme, desperate measures. We can't risk keeping prisoners alive who'd become a risk to us."

"That sounds like a stretch. Why even have the trials at all? If there's nothing to return to, what's the point? Why not just keep us here forever?"

Levine bites her lip.

"You're gonna wipe it all anyway," I snap. "Why not just tell me the truth?"

"For one thing, the trials are an incentive. Why would criminals behave if there was nothing to work toward? They're a beacon of light, so to speak."

"More like a beacon of torture and death meant to scare us."

"You don't get it. The outside world isn't safe to release teenagers into. It hasn't been for several years now—where would they even go? Most have lost their families already. We do release our rehabilitated prisoners, if they truly want to assume that risk and leave. The trials hopefully weed out those who would be tempted to return to their old ways once they're back on the surface, surrounded by crime. But most freed prisoners become guards or soldiers. They're always given the option to stay here and work for us, putting their skills and their prison knowledge to good use. Their enhanced strength helps keep the inmates in line, and the nurses moderate their K-levels every morning just like they do the prisoners. Most of them are very happy working here."

I swallow, thinking of all the jacks barely older than me. Did they win their freedom, only to realize the outside world wasn't the place they remembered?

"That's the other purpose of the trials. Hugo designed them to discover who'd be ideal recruits for prison guards. At least, until it's safe to return to the outside. Some of the older guards were taken from the adult prison, before executing all Klaurivex users became law of the land."

"That's the trials' purpose? To help Hugo?"

"Like I said, that's one purpose," Levine says. "He does keep track of every . . . result. Everything that happens in every trial, in the whole history of the Center. He writes it all down, charts it out. He's a fan of his experiments, that man. If you ask me, he's determined to map out exactly how Klaurivex impacts a person's physical and mental capability to improve the drug and make it safe again. He's a good person, Evelyn. He just wants to make things right."

"Last time I checked, none of us volunteered to be his guinea pigs."

She smiles sadly at me. "I know. It's not an ideal situation."

"To put it lightly."

"Okay, Andrea, we've gotta get started." Nurse Ellen pulls on a pair of latex gloves that snap against her skin. Levine nods and stands to leave.

A sudden wave of dizziness washes over me. I shake it off. "Wait, Andrea." I call after her. "Why'd they erase David and my mom's death?"

She glances at the other directors and the nurse, conversing in the corner, then back at me. "The team—well, some members of the team—considered David a liability. They noticed your most intense and uncontrollable reaction occurred due to your desire to protect him. They erased him to eliminate that risk."

"And my mom? You didn't erase her completely, just her death. Why?"

"That was my idea." She sighs. "When you came to us originally, you had so much going on. So much to deal with between losing your mom, moving in with your aunt, and everything with your brother. I guess I didn't want to see you in pain anymore."

"You erased my pain?" Nothing should surprise me anymore but it's still horrifying. "What is wrong with you people?"

Levine looks away. "I thought you'd be glad to be rid of your painful memories."

"I'll be glad when I have control over my own life." The edges of the room go blurry, fading in and out of focus.

Nurse Ellen shuffles over. "Okay, Andrea, you gotta go." She shoos the director toward the door. "We gotta get started if we're going to finish these procedures this year. Goodness."

Levine nods and strides back into the hall. The door behind her slams shut, leaving me alone, despite the presence of half a dozen people.

Allard rests a hand on my shoulder. I try to shrug it off, but my binds are too tight. My eyelids suddenly grow heavy, like it's taking all my effort to keep them open. What is going on?

"Ellen, when you're ready," he says.

"You got it." Nurse Ellen sets the white helmet on my head, snapping the plastic cage over my face. She crouches beside me to tighten my straps and whispers too low for anyone else to hear. "You'll be okay, Evelyn."

I wish I could believe her. Before I can reply, she's back on her feet, typing into the keypad. "All set, Hugo!"

"While you're out, we'll stitch up that pesky bullet

wound in your arm." Allard winks. "See you soon, Ms. Summers."

Exhaustion descends over me like a shroud. I feel myself fading.

Doctor Wang clicks some buttons.

She pulls the lamp down over my eyes, drowning me in white light.

Searing morning sun pierces my retinas. I groan, wrenching my eyes open. Light peeks through the gap in the tattered green curtains, bathing the room in sunlight. Something soft cushions my head. My dry tongue sticks to the roof of my mouth.

Where am I?

I sit up in bed, pushing the checkered quilt off my body. I'm still wearing my white peels. How long was I asleep?

Wooden walls surround me, each made up of thick logs, like I'm in a cabin from a fairy tale. Picture frames displaying dried flowers adorn the walls. A wooden dresser lit by a dim lamp sits beside the doorway. The whole room smells like pine.

This definitely doesn't look like the Center.

My heart races. I feel around my ankles, waiting for the sharp bite of metal shackles, but nothing's holding me down.

Am I dreaming?

Another bed lies five feet away, the sheets pulled back and empty, tousled from a night's sleep.

Still groggy, I push myself to my wobbly feet and peer out the small, musty window. Overgrown grass and shrubs grow all the way up to the glass. In the distance, a silver Honda is parked on a gravel driveway. Whoever brought me here didn't make it all that difficult to escape.

Soft laughter drifts through the cracked open doorway.

I creep toward the door, wrapping my hand around a steel candlestick holder on the dresser.

The hinges creak as I push the door open. I blink back the haze of sleep, taking in the small wooden table surrounded by chairs. I recognize the blond-haired Level One girl sitting in one of the chairs, but it takes me a second to realize who she is. Probably because the last time I saw her, she wasn't smiling. It's Ashley Preston, the girl I helped intake for my pre-req, sipping a cup of juice in her orange prison uniform.

Across the table, Desirae frantically chats with a man and woman I've never seen before. I can't process the weirdness of this situation. Desirae, Ashley, me, and a couple of random adults, somehow ended up at this . . . cabin?

The tantalizing aroma of sizzling eggs and cheese wafts around the room. I follow the scent to Alex, standing over the stove. My muscles relax. If Alex is here, we must be safe—at least, for now.

"There she is!" He nearly drops his spatula on the floor.

Everyone stops and looks up at me.

I freeze.

"Your drugs wear off yet?" Desirae rubs her forehead. "Mine are still kicking my ass. Remind me to thank Ellen for the migraine later."

My grip loosens on the candlestick. "Where are we? What's going on?" The words feel like sandpaper in my throat. For all I know, I'm wearing a helmet in a room somewhere, and this is trial nine, and the trials are actually intended to torture me forever until I die.

"Hello, Evelyn." The woman pulls out a chair for me. She's wearing camo pants and a black T-shirt. "I'm Doctor Corson. Come chat with us."

Still in a daze, I take a seat beside her. Alex puts a plate of steaming eggs and a cup of orange juice in front of me. "You should eat."

My stomach grumbles like it hasn't seen food in days. I rest my makeshift weapon on the table and shovel a forkful of eggs into my mouth. "Where are we?" I repeat, my mouth bulging with food. I swallow it down and take a swig of lukewarm juice. "Are we still at the Center?"

"We're in the Berkshires," the other adult says. He's a fat, middle-aged man with a gray blazer and pink button-down. "Western Massachusetts. About thirty miles from the Center."

Thirty miles. A million questions churn inside me—whose house is this? How long have we been here? Who brought us here? But all I can muster is a weak, "Why?"

The two adults, Ashley, and Alex toss glances at one another.

"Thank you." Desirae scoffs. "Now maybe someone will answer me. Why'd you bring us here? What is this place?"

The man's brow creases. "What do you mean? We freed you."

"You kidnapped us," Desirae counters.

Alex sighs, pulling up a chair beside me. "You remember everything, right? Ellen's pill worked?"

"What pill?"

"The yellow dissolving pills she gave us in the custodian closet. They blocked the wipe from working and knocked us out. Instead of the recovery room, her team snuck us out."

My mouth falls open. I do remember everything, right up until they lowered that searing lamp over my face. "I think so."

"I was always supposed to set you free. When I broke out two years ago, I found a movement of people against Allard." He gestures at the adults sitting with us. "Ellen's in it too. Lots of people are. We made a plan. I'd come back to the Center, be a prisoner, wait for my memories to return. They'd ship Ellen supplies disguised as medical equipment."

"Our goal is to eventually free all the inmates," Doctor Corson says. "But we started with you, Ashley, and Desirae."

Suddenly, Alex's words at his intake make sense—*I'm going to get us out. They're coming for us.* Maybe Ellen's expired Memoria was never a mistake.

"Why didn't you tell me sooner?" My hoarse voice cracks.

"You should rest that voice." The woman pats my hand. "The drugs will take a few hours to fully leave your system."

I get what she means. This grogginess feels like a warm blanket, enveloping me and dulling my senses.

"It was too risky to tell you sooner, with all the directors swarming around," Alex says. "I almost blew the whole thing at my intake. I lost control when I saw what they'd done to you."

I blink, still comprehending. Alex had this planned for months. "Why the four of us, though? There are hundreds of prisoners there."

Doctor Corson nudges the young inmate. "Ashley's my daughter." I shrink down, struck with guilt for my part in enrolling her to the Center. But neither Ashley nor Doctor Corson seem to care. "As long as her K-levels are under control, she shouldn't be locked in that awful place."

"None of you should," adds the man. "That's why we're working with Ellen on the inside to get you all out."

My heart swells. Soon, they'll all be free. Finally.

"Not that it's much better out here." She solemnly shakes her head. "You'd be hard-pressed to find a safe place out in the world anymore with all those Klaurivex addicts running wild."

"But we're safe here for now," Alex quickly adds.

"For now," Ashley echoes.

"The Center is just as dangerous, at the rate they execute

people," the man says. "Out here, at least you've got your freedom."

Everyone nods in agreement.

"Okay, but why me?" I ask. "Why Des?"

"You're valuable to our team," Doctor Corson says. "With your and Alex's strength and combat abilities, we might be able to close the Center down for good. And Desirae's intel and coding skills are unmatched."

Desirae smiles weakly at the compliment.

"What about my brother?"

"We know where he is," Alex says. "Remember? Levine told us. We can find him. He's not far."

"We're hoping you'll help us get the others out too," the man says. "The movement's huge. We have an untested antidote for Klaurivex that's almost ready, and we have the resources. We just need help disseminating it to the public. We can end this, once and for all."

"What about the directors?" I ask.

"What about them?" says Doctor Corson. "They're still at the center, terrorizing the inmates, no doubt."

I shiver, thinking of all that time I spent working beside them before my sentence.

Ashley swigs back a gulp of juice. "If you ask me, they're the ones who need to learn some accountability."

Alex laughs, holding up his own juice glass. "I'll drink to that."

"So, will you help us?" Doctor Corson asks. She poses

the question to the table, but her eyes are glued to mine.

I don't even have to think about it. "Of course."

Alex grins. "You already knew I was in."

"Me too," says Ashley. "Obviously."

Desirae plays with a loose thread on her uniform. "I need a minute."

No one tries to stop her as she rises from her seat and plows through the screen door, which slams shut behind her.

"Should someone warn her not to travel too far beyond the yard? We're secluded, but we're not that secluded." The man starts to stand, but Doctor Corson rests her hand on his arm.

"This is . . . a lot to process." The woman offers a sad smile to the ground. "After living on the other side of it all, I'm not surprised she needs time."

Alex rolls his eyes. "She better not take too long."

"I don't think she'll go far," I say. "But I'll go talk to her."

//

The moment I'm outside, my body absorbs the sunlight like a sponge.

Outside. I haven't been outside in years. At least, not as a free woman.

Desirae stands twenty feet away with her back to me, gazing into the forest.

My shoes crunch on the gravel as I make my way toward

her. I savor the bee buzzing past, the pine trees towering high over my head, the scent of wildflowers all around me. It feels so normal.

Maybe I'll need to think about this more, after the drug-induced haze wears off. Part of me is weirded out that Ellen drugged me and Alex arranged this behind my back, but I'm too grateful to care. I'm here. I'm alive. My brother is out there, and maybe the Center inmates have hope after all.

I stand beside Desirae, my former best friend turned enemy turned . . . something. It's awkward. Who knows where we even stand anymore.

"I knew they wouldn't kill you." She keeps her eyes focused straight ahead. "In the trials."

"What?"

"The sabotage. I was . . . trying to mess with you. Get revenge, or . . . something. I knew Allard wouldn't let you die."

"Oh." I think back to almost being strangled at trial two, to the bizarre yellow wall in trial four, and the box that almost finally got me at the end. I'm not sure what to believe. I'd rather not believe there's someone working beside me who actually wants me dead, so I'll take her word for it. "Well, that's good. I guess."

She nods, not looking at me. We stand in silence for a few minutes. Birds chirp overhead, and it's such a natural sound, I can't help smiling.

"Beautiful day," I say.

Desirae nods, not meeting my eyes. "It is."

An unspoken understanding passes between us. We can't take back the awful things we've done to each other. But maybe we can move on from them. We're in it together now. Us against this broken, mangled world.

I inhale a deep breath of fresh, sweet air.

I am free.

ACKNOWLEDGMENTS

I am so grateful to everyone who helped *Freedom Trials* get to where it is.

First and foremost, thank you to my wonderful editor, Lauren Knowles, who first saw something in this weird manuscript. I'm so grateful that *Freedom Trials* had such a great, insightful editor who really "got" the story. Your notes made it so much darker and creepier and better!

A big thank you to Will Kiester, the head of Page Street, who helped make *Freedom Trials* into an actual book. I'm so grateful to be a part of the wonderful Page Street family.

Also thank you to editor Ashley Hearn who has been a big supporter of this story.

To everyone at Macmillan and Page Street—this book wouldn't be here without all of you. Thank you for being excited about my story.

A big thanks to copyeditor extraordinaire Rebecca Behrens.

Jamie Howard—I am forever so, so thankful you responded to my #CPMatch tweet back in 2014. You're not only the best critique partner anyone could have, but also one of the best friends in the world. *Freedom Trials* wouldn't be half the book it is if it wasn't for your great notes and insights. Thanks for not letting me give up on this story even when I was up to my eyeballs in rejections and wanted to quit.

Molly Dean Stevens—thank you for all your help on this manuscript and for believing in this story. Evelyn and friends have come a long way since the beginning, and a big part of that is because of your thoughtful and insightful critiques.

Amanda Heger and Marie Meyer—my St. Louis girls! I'm so lucky to have you both in my corner. Thanks for all your support in bringing this book into the world.

To everyone in The Write Pack—despite the miles between us now, I'll always be a lifelong member. *Freedom Trials* began its journey during our Thursday night write-ins, and I couldn't have done it without your support. Miss you all.

Jennifer Stolzer—thank you everything you've done for me and this book. Especially for reading and supporting *Freedom Trials* when it was just a baby draft, for drawing my characters, and for your friendship, support, and awesome critiquing over the years—and of course, all the writing-break Pokémon hunts!

Jamie Krakover—I'm so grateful we connected on Twitter all those years ago. Thanks for all your help, support, and beta reading this (and other) book(s), and most of all, for your friendship. Miss you lots.

A big thank you to Taryn Albright—to this day I'm so grateful you took the time to read and critique this story. There were many days when I wanted to quit, and I'd go back and read your notes and it would empower me to keep going. Your support for *Freedom Trials* has meant so much to me!

Ron Walters—my time zone buddy! Thank you so much for beta reading this book and for all your support, encouragement, and time spent listening to me vent. I'm so grateful for your friendship!

Joanna Ruth Meyer—my first ever friend on #TeamPage-Street! Thanks for all your support!

To everyone who read or critiqued chapters of this book—thank you for all the insight you provided! It was all appreciated and used to improve the story.

To the NAC—Marnee Blake, Diana Gardin, Ara Grigorian, Amanda Heger, Sophia Henry, Jamie Howard, Kate L. Mary, Marie Meyer, Jess Ruddick, Annika Sharma, Laura Steven, and Tegan Wren—Thank you for always believing in me and my dystopian stories.

To the Electric Eighteens—I'm so grateful I got to be a part of this amazing group of 2018 debuts. I can't wait to see what big things you all accomplish over the year and beyond!

Thank you to all the agents and industry professionals who have ever given me feedback on this book. It was all appreciated, taken into consideration, and used to improve the manuscript.

Thank you to everyone in YA Force, Writing Cabal Treehouse, and the St. Louis Writer's Guild for all the support and encouragement you've given me and my book. I'm lucky to have so many wonderful and supportive friends in the writing community!

To my love, Vincent, the best husband in the world—thank you for everything. You've spent many hours reading and rereading countless rough drafts. Words cannot express how much I love you. Thanks for believing in Evelyn and me.

To Paul Tate, the best dad in the world—Thank you for believing in me and supporting me and my stories, and for reading the very first draft of *Freedom Trials* back in the day. I love you.

To all the Servellos, Murrays, and Bombardiers—thanks for being the best in-laws ever and supporting me and my writerly pursuits.

Caitlin Clark—to my beloved trash panda, partner in crime, and one of the best friends anyone could have, I am forever thankful for your friendship and support (and for countless games of UNO at True Brew when I should've been editing).

Kristina Rieger—to one of the best friends anyone could have! Thank you for all your support and encouragement over the years. I'm so grateful to have you in my life.

Kirsten Cowan—you're one of the few people who has read everything I've ever written, and for that I'm extremely grateful. Thanks for beta reading *Freedom Trials*, for being one of the best friends ever, and for entertaining me with inappropriate memes in the wee hours of the morning.

Bekah Mar-Tang—the Stanley to my Kevin. I'm forever grateful for your friendship. Thanks for always being there, supporting my career, and being one of the best friends anyone could have.

Caitlin Stevenson and Sarah Winters—my MSW girls! Thanks for all the support, laughter, and friendship over the years.

Monica Craver—thanks for all your support and for not judging me for all the ugly rough drafts you've read—and thanks for being such a great friend over the years.

Katie Levesque—thanks for taking such great author photos and for being such a great friend!

Caity Bean—thanks for keeping me sane at True Brew all those days I came in with my laptop and ordered weird combinations off the menu—and for being such a great friend.

To Jill Schaffer, Ashley Taylor Ward, Alexis Carr, Audrey Desbiens, Brett Roell, Corey Landsman, Katie Gill, Molly Hyant, Joanna Wolbert, Amy Debevoise, Paige Donaldson, Eric and Amy Lousararian, and everyone else—you know who you are—thanks for being so supportive over the years. I really do have the greatest friends in the world.

Kordas—thanks for being the best high school Latin teacher ever who made me love Latin enough to include it in this book!

Thank you to Barbara, Ed, all the Dizzy Dames, and to Robin and Larry Corson.

All my Twitter friends—your friendship and support mean the world to me.

To everyone at Kaldi's Coffee in Kirkwood—I'm pretty sure 90 percent of this book was written while sitting at your big table in the corner. Thanks for letting me leech off your Wi-Fi and for making such delicious tea and avocado toast.

To my one true love, Dunkin Donuts—your coffee has fueled everything I've ever written! Bring mocha flavoring to Switzerland, please <3.

Sia—you have no idea who I am, but your music inspired this book. Thanks for being such an awesome singer and inspiration.

To all my family and friends, and for anyone I've forgotten to mention who has helped *Freedom Trials* get to where it is—thank you!

Finally, to all the girls and women out there fighting inequality and oppressive systems—you're my inspiration. Keep fighting the good fight!

Meredith Tate grew up in Concord, New Hampshire, where she discovered Harry Potter and subsequently fell in love with the many worlds of science fiction and fantasy. In college, Meredith regularly stayed up late working on her first novel. Pursuing her love of travel, Meredith spent a semester in London and then backpacked in Europe for a month before earning her master's degree in social work from the University of New Hampshire. After graduation, Meredith worked in the field in Boston for a few years before deciding to pursue her true dream of telling stories. Her first book, *Missing Pieces*, came out in 2015. Meredith and her husband spent three wonderful years in St. Louis, Missouri. They recently moved to Zurich, Switzerland, as expats. Meredith spends her days eating cheese and chocolate by the lake and writing stories about characters way braver than she is.